DAWN
OF THE
DEAD

DAWN
OF THE
DEAD

GEORGE A. ROMERO
AND SUSANNA SPARROW

G

GALLERY BOOKS

New York   London   Toronto   Sydney   New Delhi

G

Gallery Books
An Imprint of Simon & Schuster, Inc.
1230 Avenue of the Americas
New York, NY 10020

First Gallery Books trade paperback edition May 2015

GALLERY BOOKS and colophon are registered trademarks of Simon & Schuster, Inc.

For information about special discounts for bulk purchases, please contact Simon & Schuster Special Sales at 1-866-506-1949 or business@simonandschuster.com.

The Simon & Schuster Speakers Bureau can bring authors to your live event. For more information or to book an event, contact the Simon & Schuster Speakers Bureau at 1-866-248-3049 or visit our website at www.simonspeakers.com.

Manufactured in the United States of America

10 9 8 7 6 5 4 3 2

ISBN 978-1-4767-9183-8
ISBN 978-1-4767-9184-5 (ebook)

INTRODUCTION
BY SIMON PEGG

I became aware of George A. Romero's seminal zombie classic, *Dawn of the Dead*, long before I saw it on the small screen. It became the stuff of legend during my childhood, after it was banned in the early '80s in a moral panic that followed the arrival of VHS. Video snuck up on the British Government like a couple of zombie children in an abandoned gas station and frightened the life out of it. To the panicky moral guardians of the UK's impressionable youth, it threatened a sudden unchecked influx of filth and degradation and needed to be figuratively shot in the head before it could do any lasting damage. Truth is, few people truly understood the implications of this new medium, aside from those canny chaps in the pornography industry, who saw its potential from the start. Apathy from studio executives, who grossly underestimated the huge financial potential home video presented, meant that newer films were held back from video distribution, leaving the door wide open for an extensive array of archival cinema to become available to the public for home viewing. With no statutory laws in place to regulate classification, a flood of gory low budget horror flicks found their way onto the video rental shop shelves, unfettered by the censorship laws that previously consigned them to theatrical obscurity.

The ensuing panic was feverish. Terrified that the populace would be subjected to an avalanche of filth, a blanket ban was enforced on what became known as "Video Nasties." As a result of this witch hunt, a number of smart, innovative, well-written and soon-to-be-classic horror films got caught in the crossfire. One of them was *Dawn of the Dead*.

Of course, *Dawn of the Dead* didn't disappear completely; copies already in circulation were pirated and distributed among gore-hounds, beneath school desks and pub tables. I never came into possession of one of these elusive delights myself, but I knew people that did. I heard snippets of dialogue and detail from various sources and always lapped up the accounts with relish: the helicopter decapitation, the screwdriver in the ear, the machete in the head, the brilliant use of jaunty counter-scoring as the credits roll and the audience try to digest the grim climax. Even as a child I was thrilled by these ideas and by their apparent masterful execution; the idea that one of these so-called "Video Nasties" could be good and not simply exploitation. This film—this fabled cinematic spectacle—was without doubt the best film I had never seen.

I pored over a number of stills from the movie, featured in my *Encyclopaedia of Horror*, and marveled at the synopsis describing a suburban American shopping mall becoming "awash with blood." I couldn't grasp why the book praised the film so highly and yet I was somehow not allowed to watch it. The arrival of video had seemingly surmounted the problem of sneaking into cinemas to see films deemed unsuitable for my age. You only needed an older brother or a kindly/ irresponsible video shop clerk to gain access to forbidden fruit. I watched John Landis's *An American Werewolf in London* and John Carpenter's *The Thing* way before I officially should have and yet Romero's vaunted masterpiece eluded me. My growing love of horror only made my desire to view this grail-like offering more fervent. It was a full fourteen years after its theatrical release before I finally witnessed the film that would change my life.

When I finally saw the film as a university student in 1992, I was almost glad to have not had the experience as an impressionable young child. Not because it would have upset or disturbed me, but because I don't think I would have been able to appreciate what a truly superb piece of cinema it is. The version I saw still suffered at the hands of artless censors, who had cut out some of the more outrageous moments of gore with all the artistic precision of zombie teeth, totally missing the humor in Romero's crayon-red Grand Guignol. For my part, I was profoundly impressed by the film on the deepest level, in ways I find hard to describe, even now.

Firstly it is a testament to Romero's skill and vision as a filmmaker that *Dawn of the Dead* is rarely considered a sequel to his landmark 1968 zombie film *Night of the Living Dead*; rather it is seen as a separate chapter in the same story. It acknowledges its forbear, not least in subject matter, but can exist as a self-contained story, gaining dramatic weight and effect from the lack of set-up and back-story. The story commences several weeks, or even months, after the events of the first film and in a completely different location. There are nods to its predecessor for those faithful enough to pay attention. As Peter, Roger, Fran and Stephen make their escape from Pittsburgh, toward their retail paradise, they fly over an area of agricultural land and a farmhouse that could well be the location of the first film. The narrative pauses for a brief intermission as we witness events on the ground. The sequence feels almost like a news report as we witness a posse of good old boys relishing the apocalypse as an opportunity for beer and target practice. The same sense of grim enjoyment that suffused the close of Romero's first zombie film pervades here, part callback, part social commentary. The moment lingers in the memory and demonstrates a sensitivity key to Romero's success.

This second instalment of his opus is deliciously dark and ironic, embracing the absurdity of a species on the brink of extinction, unable to relinquish the small comforts that once distracted from life's hardships—the irony being that in this world, life has become the greatest hardship of all. Even the zombies themselves cannot let go of the behavior that shaped them in life. They spend the movie staggering aimlessly about the mall, only stopping to inflict violence on unsuspecting humans if distracted from their bizarre automated window-shopping.

Herein lies one of the key fascinations of *Dawn of the Dead* and another of Romero's masterstrokes. In most horror movies the threat to the human protagonists is a malevolent force, motivated by spite or evil or an egotistical desire to commit acts of moral transgression. Romero's zombies are victims themselves, tragic figures who have prematurely succumbed to that destiny that awaits us all: death. They cannot be blamed for their actions, nor can they be held accountable; it is simply not their fault. We can no more blame them for the atrocities they commit than we can a cat for catching a mouse. They have no compass, moral or otherwise; they are the walking manifestation of inevitability and, as such, no more wicked than death itself. We yearn to catch and punish the murderer that steals our loved ones away but bear no grudge against death, not really. We dream of eradicating cancer but our anger toward it is misdirected—it can't help it, it's cancer.

I found the original novelization of *Dawn of the Dead* online, in a small second hand bookstore in the US. I felt keen to experience the story in a different way, to let it play out in my head rather than before my eyes—after all, there is no greater projector than the imagination. A book is arguably a more challenging medium than film. Cinema is wonderful, inspiring and essential, but does more work for us, so perhaps we work a little less. It is delivered to us more comprehensively in sights, sounds and prescriptions, whereas a book is all about personal perception: we build worlds inspired by words and those realizations are only limited by the boundaries of our imagination. Unbound by conventional running times, books can linger on ideas and expand them into joyful digressions or character-swelling diversions to bolster the emotional content of the story. This is what I hoped the novelization of *Dawn of the Dead* would provide for me and I was not disappointed.

As a companion to the film, this book is a wonderful opportunity to get lost in a familiar story. As a piece of literature, it is a chance to play out a chilling and thoughtful story in your own head, to create or add your own visuals to Romero's dark ideas, to put yourself behind that fake wall at the top north corner of the Monroeville Mall and know in your heart that the comfort and security you build there, like life itself, is fleeting. Death will find you no matter where you hide. This is a story to savor and enjoy, to inspire debate, speculation and reflection. What would you do, were you faced with an army of the walking dead and a fully stocked, empty shopping mall? The possibilities are endless and terrifying.

Happy shopping.

Simon Pegg

1

Sleep did not come easily to Francine Parker. It was a struggle every night to block out the events of the day and the memories of the past that kept up their pounding conflict within her head. Now, as she slept, the expression of anguish on her face belied any sweet dreams.

At twenty-three, she was slender, and very attractive. After her divorce, she had traded in her glasses for contacts, her brown hair for silver blonde, and her extra twenty-five pounds of pasta, chocolate cake and domesticity for a knockout figure.

It was a comic dream she was having now, really. If she were awake, she would have laughed at its inherent symbolism—she was tied to the kitchen sink, her arms elbow deep in soap suds, and her ex-husband Charlie was kissing her neck.

Finally, the buzzing sounds of voices, electronic hums and general bustle of a frantic television studio in the throes of a national disaster impinged upon the ludicrous plight of the housewife, and Francine started to wake up. In her confusion, she couldn't place where she was—and then she remembered: she was Ms. Francine Parker, assistant station manager, WGON-TV. She was no longer Mrs. Charles Parker, III, housewife at nineteen, bored at twenty-one. In the two years since her divorce, she had really made strides, but now was not the time for self-congratulation, not with a national emergency on their hands.

Suddenly, Fran lurched forward into strong waiting arms. Her long hair hung in greasy strands about her sweaty face. Her jeans and blouse, which she had been wearing for days, were creased and molded to her body and gave off a distinct odor of perspiration. She had been sitting against the wall, covered by an old overcoat.

"You OK?" a voice entered her fog.

Fran stared at the young man, and for a minute she couldn't place him. She was shaking and speechless.

"The shit's really hitting the fan," said the young man, whom she finally recognized as the copy boy, Tony. His dark hair was tousled, and his olive complexion was streaked with grime and perspiration. Yet, he calmly moved on to the other sleeping forms on the floor, shaking them awake just as gently as he had Fran.

The whine of the voices grew louder and took on definition. Fran realized that the sounds were being broadcast, over a monitor. Still unable to shake herself out of the foolish dream, she looked about. At the far end of the room around the monitor there was a commotion. Small electronic shapes, moving with the awkwardness of stick figures, argued emotionally. All around, people were exhausted and disheveled; however, they managed to buzz frantically about.

"What's making it happen? What the hell difference does it make what's making it happen," said Sidney Berman defiantly, his frizzy black-haired head bobbing up and down rhythmically. His face was flushed—this wasn't the type of problem, such as how to stop losing your hair, that was often discussed on his well-known morning talk show. This was a matter of life and death. Boy, he marveled, almost every set in the nation tuned to this channel. He wondered what his ratings were now.

"Yes, but that's..." Dr. James Foster said calmly, his bespectacled eyes glistening under the hot studio lights. His thinning sandy hair was moist with perspiration.

"That's a whole other study," Berman cut in. "They're trying—"

"But if we knew that, we could..." Dr. Foster moved toward the edge of his chair and gestured with the middle finger of his right hand.

Berman immediately reacted to the gesture and then realized that it was unconscious on the good doctor's part.

"We don't know that," Berman countered. "We don't know that. We've gotta operate on what we *do* know."

Francine's eyes shifted from the electronic argument to the pandemonium in the room. Copy people ran wildly with teletype sheets; secretaries organized the stacks of bulletins as they arrived into the different reporters' boxes. Yet besides the seemingly organized reactions there were others: people frantically scrambled all over the room, tripping over cables and generally getting into each other's way.

"I'm still dreaming," said a voice, and for a moment, in her drowsiness, Fran thought she had said it. Then she realized it was a man's voice. She turned toward him. It was a young man she had never seen before, someone that Tony had awakened on his rounds.

"No, you're not," Fran said gently.

"My turn with the coat," said a young woman whom Fran recognized as the style and arts editor. The woman held out a cup of coffee as an exchange for the heavy overcoat that had served as Fran's blanket. Fran accepted the coffee gratefully and thought to herself: what a story, "what the well-dressed woman wears to a national disaster—a mangy old overcoat!"

"The guys on the crew are getting crazy," she told Fran confidentially. "A bunch of 'em flew the coop already. I don't know how much longer we'll be able to stay on the air."

The woman wrapped the overcoat around her and settled down for a nap. Fran staggered over to the control consoles. The technicians seemed to be cracking under the pressure of confusion and chaos.

"Watch camera two... Who the hell's on camera two, a blind man?" one screamed.

"Watch the frame... watch the frame..." another mumbled, as if to himself. "Roll the rescue stations again."

"We got a report that half those rescue stations have been knocked out," said the first one, "so get me a new list."

"Sure," said his partner belligerently, "I'll pull it outa my ass."

As if she were a sleepwalker, Fran stood transfixed in the middle of the newsroom, mesmerized by the madness surrounding her. A sudden feeling of helplessness overwhelmed her as she realized the hopelessness of the situation. Her attention was drawn again to the conversation over the monitor.

Sidney Berman loosened his tie with a chubby hand and thrust his chest out.

"I don't believe that, Doctor, and I don't believe..."

"Do you believe the dead are returning to life?" Dr. Foster asked pointedly. The power of his words, which were being sent over the airwaves, sent a shock wave throughout the entire newsroom. They had been reading those words all day—but to hear them—it gave them a new solidarity, a new reality.

"I'm not so..." said Berman, a bit more subdued. He half sensed the finality of the doctor's words, too.

"Do you believe the dead are returning to life and attacking the living?" Foster repeated.

"I'm not so sure what to believe, Doctor!"

At the studio, a few doors down from the newsroom, a sense of panic was overtaking the crew. Disgruntled murmurings were heard. This wasn't a television series—this was real life!

"All we get is what you people tell us," Berman was bellowing. "And it's hard enough to believe...It's hard enough to believe without you coming in here and telling us we have to forget all human dignity and..." Berman wiped a sweaty brow with the back of his hand.

"Human dig...you can't..." the doctor sputtered.

"Forget all human dignity," Berman repeated as if pleased with the solemnity of the phrase.

"You're not running a talk show here, Mr. Berman," Foster said indignantly. "You can forget pitching an audience the moral bullshit they want to hear." The doctor's calm exterior suddenly seemed to shatter.

"You're talking about abandoning every human code of behavior, and there's a lot of us who aren't ready for that, Doc Foster..."

The furor of the crowd of stagehands and cameramen grew to a fever pitch. A great cry of assent went up from the studio floor. The doctor's glasses were now sliding halfway down his nose, and he was frustrated at the abominable pomposity of the talk show host and also flustered by the apparent agreement of the audience and crew. Stagehands and cameramen left their posts and came at him with clenched fists, swearing and calling him names. Police guards tried to control the mêlée inside the studio and to prevent people from storming in from the hallway.

Fran stared dumbly at the control panel and the uproar on the screen.

"Frannie," a man called, "get on the new list of rescue stations. Charlie's receiving on the emergencies."

Fran managed to pull herself away from the ludicrous scene on the console screen. She fought her way through the heavy traffic of panicking people and reached Charlie—a harassed typist who held the receiver of an emergency radio unit under his chin.

"Say again...can't hear you," Charlie was saying into the receiver.

"Rescue stations?" Fran asked, leafing through the sheets of paper on Charlie's desk.

"Half those aren't operative any more," he told her as he tried to take notes from the speaker on the other end. "I'm trying to find out at least about the immediate area. We've had old information on the air for the last twelve hours."

"These are rescue stations," Fran said with concern. "We can't send people to inoperative—"

"Say again, New Hope..." Charlie repeated as he took down the information.

He handed the notes to Fran. Still listening to the receiver he said, "I'm doin' what I can. These are definite as of now. Skip and Dusty are on the radio, too. Good luck."

He patted her on the backside as she gathered up the sheets from his messy desk and moved across the room.

At the console, she stopped and said to the technician at the controls: "I'm gonna knock off the old rescue stations. I'll have the new ones ready as soon as I can."

"Givens wants 'em on," said the gruff technician with a big beer-belly and graying hair.

Fran always had trouble with this one. He resented a pretty young thing's giving him orders. She had spoken with Mr. Givens before about this man's chauvinistic attitude. Apparently, he had ignored any warning—if there had been one. But now was not the time to raise his consciousness.

8

"We're sending people to places that have closed down," she said firmly. "I'm gonna kill the old list."

As she moved toward the other control room, an armed officer stopped her. For a moment, she tried to get by, thinking he had brushed her by mistake.

"Hey, she's all right," Tony said as he rushed by with copy.

"Where's your badge?" the young officer asked insistently.

Fran reached for the lapel of her blouse instinctively. To her surprise, she found the badge was missing, and she was sure she had pinned it on securely this morning—or was it yesterday morning? The days, hours and minutes were all jumbled in one terrifying moment of confusion. If she stopped to think about it, she knew she would panic. The only thing to do was to keep busy, trying not to rationalize the horror going on outside the studio.

"Jesus," she shouted.

"She's all right," one of the reporters said as he passed by.

"I had it," Fran tried to convince the officer. "I was asleep over there..."

She pointed toward the mound of sleeping bodies across the room.

"Somebody stole it," the reporter told them both. "There's a lot of 'em missing."

He turned to the officer. "She's all right. Let her through."

Reluctantly, the officer stepped aside, giving both Fran and the reporter a deadly look.

The two of them moved down the crowded hallway and into a small camera room. It was as though they were in the subway at rush hour. The hallway was wall-to-wall people.

"I don't believe it," Fran told him as they tried to make their way down the hall.

"One of those little badges can open a lot of doors. You avoid a lot of hassles if you got a badge... any kind of badge."

"It's really going crazy," she said, more to herself than to the young man, as they reached a small camera installation. The camera was aimed at a machine that was rolling out a list of rescue stations. The list was superimposed over the live broadcast as it went out.

A red-haired cameraman turned to Fran as she entered. "You got new ones?"

"I gotta type 'em up. Kill the old ones."

"Givens wants 'em—"

"Kill 'em, Dick. Tell Givens to see me!" she said with finality. Now was not the time to let these guys get away with murder. When it came to making decisions, she was the boss.

The man clicked off the camera and picked up his cigarettes, clearing away from the controls. Fran moved toward the studio. As the list of rescue stations blinked off the monitor, she noticed the debate was still going on between Berman and Foster.

Fran walked down the center aisle and found an empty seat at the end of the fifth row from the stage. She practically collapsed into the seat, feeling for the first time how physically weak she really was. The doctor had told her she would start to feel tired, but she hadn't given it much thought in the past few days. The only reminder she had was her constant nausea.

Berman was holding court: "Well, I don't believe in ghosts, Doctor."

"These are not ghosts. Nor are these humans! These are dead corpses. Any unburied human corpse with its brain intact will in fact reactivate. And it's precisely because of incitement by irresponsible public figures like yourself that this situation is being dealt with irresponsibly by the public at large!"

As if on command, another outraged cry went up from the stagehands and observers.

"You have not listened," Dr. Foster tried to outscream the cries. "You have not listened . . . for the last three weeks . . . What does it take . . . what does it take to make people see?"

Fran took a deep breath and pushed herself out of the comfortable seat and moved into the large studio area, surrounded by the wires and mikes and cables of the live presentation. The uproar was deafening. She stared at the two speakers as if they were puppets.

"This situation is controllable," Dr. Foster said in a pleading tone, holding his glasses before him as if he were making a peace offering. "People must come to grips with this concept. It's extremely difficult...with friends...with family...but a dead body must be deactivated by either destroying the brain or severing the brain from the rest of the body."

Another outburst shattered the studio. Over the outcry Dr. Foster tried to be heard.

"The situation must be controlled...before it's too late...They are multiplying too rapidly..."

Fran could take no more of the aggravation, watching the poor helpless man try to convince a bunch of yelling and pushing lunatics, urged on by the frenetic Berman, that what he was saying was for their own good, for the country's good.

She moved off through the crowded room to another emergency radio installation. Skip and Dusty were there, trying to listen to their receivers. They jotted down notes hurriedly.

Fran came up to the two young men quietly, not wanting to disturb their intense concentration.

"Operative rescue stations?"

"They're dropping like flies," said Dusty, who looked more like a cowboy off the range than a TV reporter. "Here's a few. You know, I think Foster's right. I think we're losing the war."

"Yeah, but not to the enemy," Fran said philosophically. "We're blowin' it ourselves."

In a gesture of friendship, she offered what was left of her lukewarm coffee to the two dedicated men.

"Not much left, but have a ball."

Both Dusty and Skip were grateful for a sip of coffee. Fran rushed off toward a large TelePrompTer typing machine.

Over the din of the station, the broadcaster's argument could still be heard. "People aren't willing to accept your solutions, Doctor," Berman argued emotionally. "And I, for one, don't blame them."

"Every dead body that is not exterminated becomes one of them! It gets up and kills! The people it kills get up and kill!"

The doctor's hair was disheveled. His eyes were wild as he tried to get his point across. But, it was a hopeless battle. The audience and Berman just didn't want to understand. They wanted to be pampered, to believe that by magic their government would chase "the bad people" away and the next morning on the news everything would be happiness and light and football scores and sunny weather. But, it just wouldn't be like that again, at least not for a very long time.

Fran handed the list of active rescue stations to the TelePrompTer typist, and then she rushed back toward the control room.

There was havoc around the monitor consoles, and the commotion was made even more lunatic by the angered Dan Givens, the station manager.

"Nobody has the authority to do that. I want..." he was bellowing angrily. As Fran came around the corner, he spotted her, but continued his tirade:

"Garrett, who told you to kill the rescue station supers?"

"Nobody," Fran intervened. "I killed 'em. They're out of date," she said simply, trying to steady her nerves.

"I want those supers on the air all the time," Givens roared, his already red face turning a deeper shade of crimson.

"Are you willing to murder people by sending them out to stations that have closed down?" Fran demanded.

"Without those rescue stations on screen every minute, people won't watch us. They'll tune out!"

Fran stared at the tall, dark-haired, red-faced man in disbelief. At a time like this he was thinking about a stupid thing like ratings. She just wanted to get out of this alive—not win any awards.

"I want that list up on the screen every minute that we're on the air," Givens repeated. But before Fran was able to retort angrily, one of the technicians, having overheard Givens, got up from the control panel and started to walk away. The station manager was livid.

"Lucas...Lucas, what the hell are you doing? Get on that console. Lucas...we're on the air!"

The squat, middle-aged man merely looked over his shoulder and shouted into the commotion, "Anybody need a ride?"

Two men from the other side of the control panel picked up their briefcases and followed the technician toward the door.

The door was guarded by the same officer who had stopped Fran before. But the pressure had gotten to him, and he eyed the three departing men nervously.

"Officer, Officer," Givens called out, "you stop them. Stop those men, Lucas, get back on this console..."

A frenzied rumble began over the lack of console control. People started to rush in and out, and over the hubbub, the floor director's voice could be heard barking out orders over a talkback system:

"What the hell's goin' on in there. Switch... switch...there's no switcher...We're losing the picture."

Over the turmoil, Givens cried to no avail: "Officer... stop those men..."

15

The young officer faced the men as they reached his post. Then, as if he had made a decision, he took a grip on his rifle, opened the door and let the group through. Without a backward glance to the now screaming Givens, he ran out the door himself, deserting the losing cause and the crazed pandemonium.

"Get somebody in here that knows how to run this thing," Givens shouted as he jumped toward the console. He frantically tried to work the complex dials. "Come on, I'll triple the money for the man that can run this thing...triple the money. We're staying on the air!" He said the last part as if it were a threat. Fran just shook her head in disbelief and moved off slowly toward the studio.

In the big room the tension was thicker than ever. Newspeople went about their business earnestly, trying to perform their various functions, but they wore faces of stone. It was as though any mention of crisis would crack their seemingly calm exteriors. But, the burden of staying calm was even greater with the sound of the agitated discussion that was being played over the airways in counterpoint to the newspeople's desperate actions.

"They kill for one reason," Dr. Foster said, as if in a trance. He had his suit jacket off and was mopping his brow with a handkerchief. "They kill for food. They eat their victims, do you understand that,

Mr. Berman?" he asked carefully, as though speaking to a child. "That's what keeps them going."

A wave of nausea overcame Fran, and she had to lean against the hallway wall, in the shadows. People frantically rushed past her as though running to catch a train. She tried to calm herself and listened to the argument. TV station employees were filing past her, some leaving the studio in disgust.

"If we'd listened. If we'd dealt with the phenomenon properly...without emotion...without...emotion. It wouldn't have come to this!" Dr. Foster pleaded with the thinning crowd.

Foster wiped his sweat-drenched brow with the now soaking dirty handkerchief. He pulled his tie away from his tight collar and popped the shirt button open. The once calm, collected doctor was now a bundle of nerves, desperate, shivering with anger and frustration. Fran had never seen so radical a change come over a person. She herself was shivering now, and clutched at her shoulders in the thin blouse. She felt so tired, so worn out, she just wanted to lie down and forget the whole mess.

But the rasping, hoarse voice of Dr. Foster droned on, begging the people to heed his cry.

"There is a state of martial law in effect in Philadelphia, as in all other major cities in the country. Citizens must understand the dire...dire consequences of this phenomenon. Should we be unable to check the spread...because of the emotional attitudes of the citizenry...toward...these issues of...morality." The man's frail shoulders seemed to crumble inward. He stood now, clutching the back of his chair with one hand and raising the other in a gesture of defiance:

"By command of the federal government, the president of the United States...citizens may no longer occupy private residences. No matter how safely protected or well stocked..."

The murmur in the studio began to build to an emotional crescendo. One woman gave a bloodcurdling scream and fell to the floor in a heap, another man cried out over and over again, "Air, air, I can't breathe..." Foster tried to talk over the furor, but his voice cracked, and he could barely be heard.

"Citizens will be moved into central areas of the city..." Foster cried to the technicians abandoning their posts, the cameramen dropping their headsets on the floor and breaking for the door. One cameraman's instrument spun on its liquid head, and on the monitors a whirling blur was seen as Foster continued to speak. Fran moved quickly toward the unmanned spinning camera. She tried to remember what Givens had told her to do in case of an emergency, but her mind was a blank. She aimed the camera at Foster and managed to stare through the viewfinder, not believing what she was seeing.

Foster was on the table, his shirt hanging out of his pants, his eyes like those of a wild man. His voice screeched out. He seemed like a prophet of old, foretelling of doom to an unbelieving population of barbarians:

"The bodies of the dead will be delivered over to specially equipped squads of the National Guard for organized disposition..."

Suddenly, a man darted out of the charging crowd and came running quickly up to Fran. She jumped as the figure flashed into her view.

"Frannie," the man, whom she recognized as Steve, cried, "at nine o'clock meet me on the roof. We're getting out." The force of his words caused Fran to let the camera slip slightly. "Stephen... I don't believe this... What—"

"We're getting out. In the chopper."

Another technician stepped over to take the camera from Fran. Steve pulled her over, away from the man's hearing, and spoke more quietly.

"Nine p.m. All right?"

"Steve, we can't... we've got to—" she protested.

But Steve was forceful. "We've got to nothing, Fran. We've got to survive."

She looked into the soft brown eyes of the man she now loved. His dark hair was a mess, his clothes in disarray. His slight body, barely taller than hers, shook with a combination of nerves, fatigue and astonishment at what he was about to do.

"Somebody's got to survive," he tried to convince her. "Now you be up there at nine. Don't make me come lookin' for ya."

Just as swiftly as he had surprised her, he was gone. Fran looked nervously back at the cameraman, feeling guilty that he might have heard their plotting. As the room emptied, the sound of Foster and Berman's senseless argument grew louder and louder.

"Go ahead," the cameraman said to Fran, without taking his eye from the viewfinder, speaking quietly and slowly. "We'll be off the air by midnight anyway. Emergency networks are taking over. Our responsibility . . . is finished, I'm afraid."

Trancelike once again, Fran walked to the corner of the room where she had left her pocketbook and coat. All she had to do now was wait the forty minutes until nine o'clock. And what then? What next? The thought made her shudder.

Compared to the frenzied excitement of the newsroom, the rest of the dusk-laden city of Philadelphia was calm. The buildings of the sprawling low-income housing project, interconnected by walkways and playground areas, stood like tombstones as the first stars tried valiantly to appear in the murky, pollution-filled, dark blue sky.

Suddenly, the glint of a grappling hook was noticeable against the lip surrounding the roof. Silent figures, as graceful as ballet dancers, climbed to the top of the building. Men in the armored vests of the S.W.A.T. police, clutching the latest in special weapons to their breasts, took position on the roofs and in the dark corners of the development.

In the shadows, squatting alongside the entrance to one of the building's fire stairs, Roger DeMarco felt a sharp shooting pain in his thigh. Still in a squatting position, he tried to stretch out the aching leg to relieve the charley horse. Three other team members were poised silently beside him.

The stillness was deceptive: it didn't seem that this was the national disaster that the politicians had been crying about for months. The population really felt that the government was putting one over on them. No one, particularly the uneducated, the superstitious and the very religious, really believed the government's explanations of why the dead were returning to life. No one wanted to believe that the husband, the wife, the child or the parent that they had just lost would return to terrorize and devour human flesh. Even Roger, who wasn't particularly politically astute, realized that the administration in power didn't have the faith and confidence of the people. The stock market had plummeted way below the lowest point of the Carter administration; unemployment had soared, and inflation was rampant. With a presidential election coming up, most citizens felt this was just another ploy to get the country behind the administration's candidate.

Roger looked at his watch. The figures next to him checked their weapons. The sweep hand on his watch reached twelve.

"Lights," Roger mumbled to himself.

As if on cue, large searchlights bathed the side of the building in a soft amber glow.

"Martinez," came the sound of a disembodied voice from behind a large truck. It was the troop commander, shouting through an electronic bullhorn. "You've been watching," he continued to the Puerto Rican leader of the tenants' uprising. They had refused to evacuate the building and were creating their own cemetery in the basement of their building. "You know we have the building surrounded . . ."

At the sound of the electronically amplified voice, any lights inside the project that had remained on blinked out one at a time.

"Little bastard's got 'em all moved into one building . . . dumb little bastard," the commander said to the sergeant on his left.

"Looks like they're gonna try to fight us," the sergeant responded.

The commander took up the bullhorn again.

"Martinez . . . the people in this project are your responsibility. We don't want any of them hurt, and neither do you!"

Roger cocked his ear for the reply but was met with silence. The great concrete slab was mute to the commander's demands. The four S.W.A.T. team members crouched in readiness.

"I'm giving you three minutes, Martinez . . ." Roger mouthed as the commander bellowed the familiar refrain through the bullhorn.

"Turn over your weapons and surrender..." the commander, a brisk, wiry, gray-haired man in his fifties, continued.

"There are no charges against you..." Roger mouthed.

The commander repeated, "There are no charges against you or any of your people..."

"Yet," Roger said aloud, to no one in particular. The men beside him were struggling with their own feelings of nervousness and excitement toward the impending battle.

"Three minutes, Martinez," the amplified voice of the commander boomed out across the inanimate fortresses, the deserted playgrounds, the parking lots filled with rusting second-hand cars, a few pimps' Cadillacs sprinkled throughout.

Roger lifted the luminous dial of his watch to his face.

"And counting..."

The project was like a still-life photograph.

"Come on, Martinez!" Roger rooted out loud.

One of the silent squatting figures suddenly lurched toward Roger.

"Yeah, come on, Martinez," Wooley lashed out viciously. "Show your greasy little Puerto Rican ass... so I can blow it off," spat the seasoned veteran, a redneck of the first order, who had come up North like a mercenary.

Distressed, Roger looked over at the big man, who was so caught up in his violence that he jumped up from under cover and was a perfect moving target for the snipers.

"I'll blow all their asses off," he rambled on. "Low-life bastards. Blow all their little low-life Puerto Rican and nigger asses right off..."

Roger could see that the Alabama man was starting to crack. He was also concerned about the smooth-faced rookie sitting on Wooley's other side. The boy's eyes flickered nervously from Wooley to the ground below.

"Keep cool," Roger cautioned quietly. "Just don't pop off in there when we go in."

The boy nodded gratefully. Roger was pleased that in this confusion and terror he was able to add a word or two of human kindness.

Wouldn't Louise be surprised at him now. She was always screaming at him that he didn't have an ounce of human kindness or consideration in his five-foot-ten, one-hundred-and-seventy-five-pound muscular body. She claimed he loved his guns and his Vietnam medals of commendation more than her, and sometimes he wondered if he did, too. He often wondered if her attraction to him was only physical—he was often told by women that his sandy hair, well-chiseled face and good build really turned them on. But for all her screaming and hollering at him, he would give anything to be with her now, curled up on the sofa watching Johnny Carson. Even though they'd been divorced for almost two years, he would marry her all over again just to be away from this mess.

His thoughts were interrupted by Wooley's strident voice:

"Why the hell do we stick these low-lifes in these big-ass fancy hotels anyway? Shit, man. This's better than I got. You ain't gonna talk 'em outa here. You gotta blow 'em out. Blow their asses!"

The boy had listened to this sickening tirade and his face was ashen.

"You gonna be all right?" Roger asked.

The boy managed to nod in the affirmative.

"Let's get on with it," Wooley snarled and started pacing like a caged animal. "This is a waste of *my* time!"

Abruptly, without warning, the metal door to the fire stair burst open, and several figures rushed out of the cavernous darkness. Shots fired from handguns crisscrossed in the night air. A bullet smashed through the skull of the ashen-faced rookie. He died with an expression of confusion on his face, falling against Roger, a pleading look in his eyes. Roger experienced a sinking feeling, but then darkness-cloaked figures charged here and there, distracting him. More gunfire echoed through the night, and other S.W.A.T. men dodged and dove for cover. Wooley stood, unprotected and arrogant, and fired off a round with his automatic weapon.

On the street, the commander, upon hearing the gunfire, ordered through the bullhorn:

"Move in . . . move in. Goddammit!"

"All units, all units," the sergeant screamed into the walkie-talkie. "All units, full operation!"

With a sense of repulsion mixed with sadness, Roger struggled to remove the dead weight of the young rookie. His M16 was wedged between the inside lip of the roof and the boy's torso. Random shots rang out, making it hard for Roger to manipulate the body and stay clear of the bullets.

A small group of black and Puerto Rican youngsters scattered about the rooftop, almost as if in play. Suddenly, another S.W.A.T. patrol, their guns drawn, emerged from behind a large elevator housing. A blast of gunfire, and the retreating young civilians had to step over the bodies of their less lucky comrades who were mowed down in their haste.

Adding insult to injury, another bullet smashed against the dead rookie's back. In another second, as Roger finally managed to free himself, a bullet caught him squarely in the chest, but luckily the armor cushioned the impact. Roger was thrown off balance, and he struggled to catch his wind as his weapon skittered across the roof. Roger dove for it, but before he reached it he was cut off by the looming figure of one of the black youths. The kid brandished a pistol in his hand, and he looked like he knew how to use it. Roger froze like a deer before flight. The young man aimed his gun meticulously, as if in slow motion. Just as he was about to pull the trigger, a sudden barrage of bullets ripped through his back and he fell to the rooftop, a pool of blood forming beneath him. Roger looked around quickly, still not believing his close escape. He felt like crossing himself, something he had not done since he was an eight-year-old altar boy.

"Come on, you dumb bastards...come and get 'em," Wooley cried out, totally unaware that he had just saved Roger's life. Roger shuddered with the thought that Wooley might have just as easily fired the gun at Roger's own darkened shadow.

As if he were a wind-up mechanical soldier gone haywire, Wooley fired again and again, even though the skirmish was winding down.

Roger's weapon tempted him from the middle of the rooftop. He saw that there was an incinerator housing just past where his rifle lay, and in one desperate burst of energy he charged for the weapon, snatched it up and ran for cover. Another figure hid in the shadows. It was a young civilian hiding there, trying to load his gun. The startled boy made a break as Roger skidded into his shelter.

"Hey, hold it..." Roger called out.

The boy froze for a moment, then, making a decision, broke into a run across the roof.

"Hold it, kid...Don't run out there!" Roger tried to warn him. But before the words were out of his mouth, the slight figure was mowed down in a shower of bullets. Roger fell against the wall of the incinerator housing in a heap. Somehow, this was worse than Nam. This was his hometown, his country, and they weren't fighting against funny-looking slant-eyes, but against their own citizens. Nothing in his Marine training had prepared him for this.

"Jesus," he thought. "I'm acting like a real fucking sissy. Must be thinking too much."

He strapped his rifle on his back and filed down the stairway and inside the building with the handful of survivors.

Inside the building, it looked like a raid. S.W.A.T. teams, along with units of the National Guard, were crashing through the hallways and breaking into apartments. People were herded into the hallway like cattle and held at gunpoint.

Some of the civilians, although armed with handguns, rifles, tire irons, switchblades, even a bow and arrow, surrendered willingly, a look of despair in their eyes. Others tried desperately, but to no avail, to retaliate against the invading force. On every floor of the structure, little senseless skirmishes developed.

Untouched by any bullets, just a trace of sweat on his upper lip, the commander barked into the bullhorn:

"Masks..."

"Masks for gas...masks for gas..." the sergeant transmitted through the walkie-talkie.

A rainfall of tear gas cannisters crashed through the windows, and the halls were filled with clouds of gas. Many civilians who were not already in the halls rushed out to join the others, and they all became a mass of choking, coughing refugees. Some even attempted to shoot their way out of the mêlée but were blinded by their tears, and their bullets bounced off walls and doorways aimlessly, wounding some of the innocent victims who were scurrying out of their doorways.

More and more survivors of the battle on the roof charged down to join the units working the hallways.

"Work your way down," one of the S.W.A.T. team commanders ordered. His voice came from behind the gas mask paraphernalia, making him look like some prehistoric mammoth. "A floor at a time. Hold 'em in the halls till we can work 'em down the stairs."

Roger, Wooley and the men in their unit snapped on their equally bizarre-looking masks.

Wooley seemed to have calmed down somewhat. In fact, Roger felt he seemed too calm, almost serene. The big man's face was bright red, and sweat poured off his forehead. But when he snapped on his gas mask, he looked as ludicrous and unhuman as the hundred other S.W.A.T. and National Guard members.

A group of troopers came to a locked door on the top floor. Six of them formed a human wedge and broke the flimsy door down. An old Puerto Rican couple knelt in prayer at a small altar. Their son, a slight man in his early thirties, and his wife and four small children huddled in the corner. The young husband surrendered his gun to a trooper. Roger watched painfully as the family was led into the hallway. The youngest grandchild clutched at a battered stuffed rabbit.

The hallway seemed relatively calm until a sudden movement caught the trooper's eyes. A young black man charged out of one of the apartments, and a woman appeared at the doorway screaming for him to stop. As he broke through the cloud of gas, Wooley snapped to attention and fired his automatic. The black man crashed to the floor, and the now hysterical woman ran to his side. A crazed Wooley kicked in the door of another apartment and fired randomly into the room.

The orderly line of civilian refugees suddenly broke and scattered aimlessly. Panicking, the younger ones tried to escape, while the older people knelt or fell to the floor in prayer. Their prayers were unanswered as Wooley continued his frenzied dance.

"Wooley's gone ape shit, man..." another masked S.W.A.T. team member commented to no one in particular.

"Wooley?" Roger shouted, but the big man just kicked in the door of another apartment. Roger charged at him and grabbed him around the shoulders. Even with his size, Roger felt dwarfed next to the redneck soldier. Wooley tried to twist himself out of Roger's grasp. His gun fired and the bullets exploded wildly. Roger felt as if he were trying to lash down a massive ship in a storm.

"Gimme a hand...somebody," he called out.

Out of the mist of the tear gas, another S.W.A.T. team member stepped out. He was as big as Wooley, and just as broad. A sense of mystery pervaded him as he spoke out in a deep, resonant voice.

"Step away from him."

"Gimme a hand," Roger repeated.

In a sudden movement, Wooley threw his body around and slammed Roger against the wall. Roger was able to grab him just as he was about to level off his gun at the open apartment door.

"Goddammit, help me," Roger called to the mysterious figure. "He's crazy!"

"Step away from him," the voice boomed.

Roger was so taken back by the authority of the voice, that for one split second he loosened his grip on

Wooley, and this gave Wooley a chance to wrench free and push Roger across the hallway. That was all the time that the inscrutable trooper needed. He carefully aimed his weapon and fired one shot point-blank through Wooley's head. The big man fell back and shuddered to the floor with such violence that even the experienced troopers gasped.

Then, the big trooper turned and hurried down the hall. Other S.W.A.T. officers turned to face him threateningly, but none of them made any attempt to stop him from barreling down the narrow passageway. He merely stared at them menacingly. His dark, piercing eyes glared at them through the mask. The group parted for him and let him pass. He disappeared through the smoke as other officers began to restore order among the civilians.

Roger was still too stunned to move. There was something about the mysterious trooper that fascinated him. Maybe it was his cool, cold-blooded manner. Maybe it was the way he sized up the situation objectively and then, matter-of-factly, pulled the trigger on a trooper who was obviously out of his mind and threatening to destroy the morale of the others.

A shrill, piercing scream drew Roger out of his moment of luxurious reverie. A hand reached out of the tear gas fog and helped Roger to his feet. His eyes wide and staring through the insect-like lenses of his mask,

Roger perceived what it was that had finally pushed Wooley over the edge. The other trooper who had given Roger a hand followed his gaze and his eyes were transfixed, too, on the sight visible through the door that Wooley had kicked open.

In the darkened apartment, lying in a pool of blood, were the partial remains of what had been a human body. It had been ripped to shreds and looked like a piece of meat that had been attacked by a pack of ravenous dogs!

Roger felt as if the wind were knocked out of him. He staggered to the door and leaned against the frame. The other trooper, a tall, thin blond man in his late twenties, moved inside. To the left of the remains was another corpse, also mutilated, one leg missing, one arm badly mangled. *It was trying to move—to reach the troopers!*

Again, the shrill, piercing scream. As Roger turned around, startled, he saw that a woman in the hall had seen the grisly sight. Maybe it was a relative, a neighbor of hers, but now it was nothing but a mass of bloodied flesh and shattered bones.

The woman ran screaming down the hall, causing a commotion and more confusion as civilians pushed through the troopers who tried to hold them back.

"Jesus, holy Jesus," the trooper in the apartment with Roger moaned, totally repulsed.

A third officer entered the apartment. The blond trooper motioned toward the writhing corpse on the floor.

"Shoot it," the recently arrived trooper hissed. "Shoot it through the head."

The young officer was frozen to the spot. Never in all his training was he prepared for a moment like this. The third officer pulled out his pistol. Before he was able to fire, however, from out of the shadows a specter-like figure lunged at him. It was a wild-haired woman who flailed at him and tried to bite his arms. The officer tried to calm her down and then noticed that there were bleeding wounds all over her body. *She was one of the walking dead!*

The trooper's gun rolled to the floor. He struggled to free himself from the viselike grip that the weak-looking woman had on him. Roger darted into the room and ran to the trooper's assistance. Another creature suddenly appeared in the bedroom doorway. It was unobserved by the young trooper, who had finally come to his senses and was trying to pull the gun from his holster. Without warning, he felt something cold and sticky holding onto his leg. He looked down and to his extreme horror realized that the dismembered corpse was clutching at his ankle, pulling itself closer, its mouth open. The young man tried to pull away, but fell onto the floor, crashing over a table and a lamp. He tried to crawl away, but the weight of the clutching corpse made it impossible. He dragged the corpse along as he tried to wrestle his gun from the holster.

Roger and the third officer, a balding, middle-aged trooper with a dark five o'clock shadow, flung their weight against the woman zombie. As if she were on an elastic string, she flew against the wall and then bounced back immediately, with the same ferocious force. The dark officer fired his gun, aiming directly at the woman's chest. The bullet hit its mark, but it still didn't stop her. He fired another shot to her neck, but she still barreled toward him, blood dripping from the wound in her neck onto her housedress and apron.

The blond young officer finally managed to loosen his pistol from the holster and leveled a shot at the ghoulish creature that was drawing closer and closer, trying to bite the young man's leg. The shot, fired at such a close range, splattered the monster's head all over the wall and on his trousers. But the kid, who was shaking violently, was so relieved that the zombie had at last released its grip that he didn't notice the globs of brain and tissue collected on his leg. He was in such a state of shock that he raised his arm and kept firing his gun into the ceiling again, and again, and again, until the older trooper knocked it from his hand and slapped him hard across the face.

"It's one of them...My God. It's one of them," another S.W.A.T. officer cried when the male zombie appeared in the hall. The other troopers tried to calm the panicking crowd.

"Shoot for the head," still another S.W.A.T. man directed.

A young, dark-haired woman rushed toward them, pushing toward the crowd as the zombie advanced.

"No! No!" she cried as she threw her arms around the creature, immune to the trooper's attempts to stop her. "Miguel...Dios mio...Miguelito..."

The zombie stared at her with vacant eyes. She tightened her grip.

"Miguel...mi vida...Miguelito..."

"Grab her, get her out of there," cried the S.W.A.T. officer who had first noticed the male zombie. He leveled his gun at the creature, but the clutching woman was directly in his line of fire.

By now, the zombie was grabbing at her, trying to bite her neck and her arm. The woman's face contorted with the horrible realization that this was no longer her husband, but a terrifying monster locked within his body. She gave out a blood-curdling shriek as he bit at her again, and she tried to pull away. But the zombie only tightened his grip. A trooper tried to attack from behind the creature and wrestle him away as another trooper attempted to pry the woman out of the demon's grasp. The zombie managed to pull another piece of flesh off the woman's arm, and she screamed hysterically, her eyes rolling to the top of her head in terror.

"Stand clear . . . for Christ's sake, stand clear!" the officer bellowed as he tried to get off the shot.

Roger watched in horror as the young officer snapped out of his frenzy and tried to extricate himself from the remains of the splattered zombie. Suddenly, the female zombie lunged at the darker trooper, and the two tumbled to the floor. Roger attacked her with a violent burst of energy and wrestled her away from the trooper. Then, with all his might, he threw her against the wall. Again, she bounced back and advanced toward him. This time Roger raised his gun, and just as she was about to reach him, he fired at her forehead. The bullet finally halted her.

Out in the hallway, a trooper brought his gun butt against the male ghoul's head. The creature loosened his grip on the out-of-control, insanely screaming woman. The trooper who had been holding her pulled her free across the floor. The S.W.A.T. officer who had been aiming his pistol at the male zombie was finally able to fire. The first bullet tore through the zombie's shoulder. The second ripped through his neck, and the third passed neatly through his skull. With an anguished moan, the zombie fell to the floor.

For a second, there was silence as each human present breathed a sigh of relief. Then, a few citizens mumbled a brief prayer of thanks. Soon, a rustle of movement was heard as troopers and confused elderly people alike drifted through the clouds of gas in a totally dazed state.

Roger and the older trooper signalled each other with glazed eyes and drifted into the hallway. Roger stepped aside as the dark trooper walked into the streaming crowd of almost hypnotized people. Leaning against the door-jamb, a sudden, loud gunshot made Roger duck and spin around. In the apartment, he was met with a distressing sight: the young trooper, still covered with the ghastly remains of the ghoul, had shot himself through the head. He lay entangled with the female zombie—a coupling possible only in death.

Roger found himself reeling headlong, against the flow of human traffic, toward the dark sanctuary of the fire stairs. He burst through the metal door from the hallway and fell retching against the stair railing. Since he hadn't eaten in over twelve hours, he had the dry heaves. In the silent stairway, his heavy breathing was amplified. He tried to calm himself with deep gasps of air, which he exhaled slowly. Removing the gas mask, he coughed slightly in the lingering mist.

A rumbling sounded through the quiet, dark landing. "You're not alone, brother."

On impulse, Roger tightened and reached for his gun. In the shadows, however, he wasn't able to pinpoint the location of the speaker, but he sensed that it was in close proximity. Looking up, Roger was stunned to see the trooper who had shot Wooley, recognizable in spite of the gas mask, sitting on the stair above him, aiming his rifle at Roger's head.

"You was in Wooley's unit," the voice threatened.

"I didn't see nothin'," Roger stammered, slinging his rifle to show that he was no longer the aggressor.

The trooper relaxed and lowered his gun. As he removed his gas mask, Roger noticed that he was black.

Roger didn't know why he was so surprised at this fact; but the stranger had such a sense of mystery around him that he had eluded classification.

"You runnin'?" Roger asked, trying to sound friendly.

The big burly man shrugged his shoulders and shook his head indecisively.

"I don't mean 'cause of Wooley," Roger went on to explain. For all of Roger's courage, this man really made him feel uneasy. "I just mean 'cause of..." he stammered, feeling as if he were a kid brought before the principal.

"Yeah, I know," the deep voice cut him off.

In his nervousness, Roger ran off at the mouth, "There's a lot of people runnin'. I could run."

Roger stared long and hard at the grim-faced man, who didn't seem to react to any of Roger's heartfelt sentiments.

"I could run right tonight," Roger repeated almost to himself.

The trooper stared straight into Roger's eyes, his level gaze never once flinching. That's the gaze of a coldblooded killer, thought Roger. But it's also the gaze of a man who's seen everything, done everything, and just doesn't have the patience or the time to be afraid.

Contritely, Roger went on: "Friend of mine got a helicopter. He does traffic for WGON. Got a helicopter and he's runnin' out with it. Asked me to come."

Roger's heart was pounding with this admission of weakness, but the trooper only smiled.

Roger took the smile as an encouragement of his position. "You think it's right to run?" he asked, but just as soon as the words were out of his mouth he felt foolish for asking. Jesus, he thought, it's like asking this dude for permission to piss.

The smile disappeared, as if he had told himself a private joke but now had to return to the stone-faced gaze. The broad shoulders shrugged in answer. Then, standing to his full six-foot, five-inch height, the man walked down the stairs. He turned past Roger on the landing and continued down into the lingering gas haze. As if he were a faithful hound, Roger followed.

Roger was drawn to the big man's magnetism, to the strength that seemed to radiate from his hulking frame. As they padded down the stairs, trying not to disturb the peaceful silence with the clomp of their heavy boots, they heard a slight noise a few landings down. The two troopers froze in their steps. From the dark stairwell the noise grew louder. The two men shouldered their weapons, assuming the ready-for-fire position.

As the sounds drew closer, they became more distinct. The little scraping thumps were like the weary footfalls of someone, or something, trying to negotiate the stair. Roger hoped that it was not one of the walking dead. He didn't have the strength to do battle with another of those creatures. But not for a moment did he think he would hesitate to do what duty called for. And he knew that the trooper would not give a second thought to shooting whatever came up those stairs right between the eyes.

A low, wheezing sound of labored breathing now accompanied the shuffling steps.

Roger stared into the darkness, and as his eyes became more accustomed to the absence of light, he noticed a figure appearing out of the shadows. It fell against the wall below, and both troopers took it for a sign that the creature was readying for the attack. They raised their weapons, fingers poised on the trigger. The figure pulled away from the wall. As it came through the mist a shape was beginning to form: a ghostly shape, robed in black.

"Señores," a meek voice cried out. "Please to let me

pass?" it inquired weakly, breaking into a low wheezing cough. The figure slumped to the step, collapsing from the agony of the long climb. A frail, gnarled hand hung on to the railing for support.

Roger recognized him as the old priest from the local parish. His flock was made up mostly of Puerto Ricans who had lived in the housing project. Roger stooped next to the weary old man, who was struggling to catch his breath. His pale face and watery hazel eyes made Roger think that he was closer to death's door than he had anticipated.

The old priest clutched at his chest, crushing the crucifix around his neck to the pasty white skin.

"Let's get him to the medics," Roger whispered to the trooper.

"No ... no ... no, please just ... let me pass," the old man uttered with what breath he could muster. "My sister ... I go up to seven floor ... to find my sister ..."

"They're takin' everyone down," Roger tried to explain. "They probably brought her down. Come on," he urged the frail bag of bones.

"My sister," the priest protested. "She is dead ... they tell me. The dead they do not bring down."

Roger and the trooper shot a glance at each other.

The priest struggled to his feet, grabbing the railing.

"Just let me pass. Martinez is dead. The people of one-oh-seven will do what you wish now. These are simple people. But strong. They have little, but they do not give it up easily. And," he said with renewed strength in his shaking voice, "they give up their dead to no one!"

The last outburst was more than his fragile constitution could take, and the old priest crumpled into a coughing fit. The two big troopers looked on: one passively, the other helplessly.

Roger took a tentative step toward the old man, but he held up his hand and continued.

"Many have died on these streets in the last weeks. In the basement of this building, you find them..."

The two men looked at each other in shock. Their greatest fear was being realized.

"I have given them the last rites," the priest said as he staggered to his feet. "Now, you do what you will..."

As the old man started up the stairs, Roger moved to help him, but the trooper held up a huge hand.

"You are stronger than us," the priest called back to them as he weaved his way up the stairs and through the mist. "But soon, I think, they be stronger than you." The sound of the old man's coughing trailed off as he disappeared up the stairwell in the darkening haze.

"The dead walk, señores," he called from the mist. "We must stop killing...or we lose the war..."

Roger looked at his companion and without further word they both shouldered their rifles and began the long climb down to the basement of the large building. The old priest's footsteps were now barely audible.

When the two men arrived in the basement, S.W.A.T. team members were already engaged in prying off the boards that had been haphazardly nailed over the entrance to the storage area. The tenants had been ingenious in their haste—old chair seats, a basketball hoop backing and some pieces of plywood served to keep the door inaccessible from the outside and impenetrable from the inside.

The remainder of the riot troops stood at the ready, high-powered rifles raised high, flamethrowers poised. But the eyes of the troops were vacant; they had experienced more in the past twenty-four hours than in all their years on the force.

There was silence except for the creaking of the nails as they were pulled free. There was a certain expectancy running through the minds of the men as they watched the third to the last, the second to last, and finally as they watched the last board removed. A great tearing sound snapped them all into action. The boards flew off as if a tremendous gust of wind had ravaged through the storage area. Practically ripping the door off its hinges, a flood-water of zombies charged into the hall.

The mostly black and Puerto Rican people were now wide-eyed and terrifying zombies. All ages, sizes and shapes, they moved in one mesmerized, stupefied mass toward the stunned troopers. The men couldn't react quickly enough, and the steady stream of zombies prevented them from having any room to shoot in the tight quarters.

Valiantly, they tried to fight back and wrestle to the ground the oncoming creatures. In the front lines, the zombies bit and clawed at anything in their way. Clamping jaws closed on arms and hands. Some of the troops were trampled in the crush.

The mesmerized commander tore his eyes away from the marauding ghouls and called to his men, "Back off... back off... spread out..."

The rear lines managed to retreat into the wider vestibule, and as the struggling bodies were able to spread out in the open space, many troopers were able to raise their weapons and fire off the desperately needed shots.

The ones not lucky enough to get off some well-placed shots were crushed by the oncoming ghouls, who lunged at them, clutching and clawing at anything in their path.

Roger and the trooper arrived just as the onslaught began, and they were fighting side by side in the middle of the seething battle. Several creatures tried to attack at once, and as Roger slammed them with the butt of his rifle, the trooper picked the stunned creatures off one by one with his rifle shots.

In the dark hallway, little skirmishes took place. The once highly organized troopers were scattered and confused by the mindless onslaught of these creatures. The commander, who had seen action in Korea and Vietnam, was totally at a loss at how to command his troops and had retreated to a corner in hysterics, a ghoul clawing at his once precisely creased trousers.

As the majority of the ghouls moved into the wider area of the hallways, away from the entrance to the storage room, the braver souls among the troopers moved into the room.

There, in the dank and gray storage room, among baby carriages, bicycles chained to pipes, large trunks, cartons of every size and shape, old beds and other furniture, lay remains of dripping, mutilated corpses. Even though many of them had been eaten away, they were still moving, their heads uninjured.

Two of the troopers retreated, retching with revulsion. The sounds of gunfire and screaming from the outside hallways reverberated off the dingy, mildewed walls.

Roger watched in complete astonishment as the big trooper walked calmly into the room. With deliberation, he walked up to each of the writhing creatures and fired neatly and accurately into their heads with his handgun. Roger had to look twice before he realized that tears glistened on the big trooper's cheeks.

Heavy footsteps fell in the room as the man continued his mercy killing: some of the creatures were without arms and legs, some had been gnawed away at the neck and the shoulder. They moaned with a gurgling, guttural sound, as they tried to move.

A young black zombie pulled itself along the floor with one arm. It drew closer to the trooper. The big man aimed his pistol, and Roger heard the click that indicated empty. Roger panicked and started toward the trooper, who quickly and efficiently reached for more ammunition and began to reload. Roger watched, horrified, as the zombie pulled itself closer, his mouth a huge gaping hole. Not once did the trooper flinch or call out for help even though Roger was no more than a few yards away. Shaken out of his stupor, Roger stepped up behind the trooper and fired into the creature's head with his automatic rifle. The creature writhed in agony, yet the man only brushed the tears away from his eyes and continued to load his pistol. He didn't even look up to acknowledge that Roger had just saved his life. But Roger had little time for rationalizing his companion's behavior. He ran to the other side of the room and started systematically disposing of several other creatures. In a corner, several were piled together. Some were still, others writhed and wiggled about. Two on the heap were eating at parts of other bodies. With a shudder of revulsion, Roger shot them. But the creatures never looked up, never noticed him at all.

A loud creaking noise drew Roger's attention to the ceiling above. A double set of loading doors had been opened, and several other troopers looked down into the storage area.

"Jesus Christ," one of them uttered in disbelief.

He shone his light beam toward Roger.

"You OK down there?"

An exhausted, disgusted Roger nodded his head.

"This must be where they dumped 'em in," the trooper with the flashlight observed.

Roger looked down at the pile of corpses beneath the opening. He was just too stunned to register what had been happening for the last half hour.

"You need more men?" the trooper asked and Roger shook his head no.

"Jesus Christ," the trooper repeated.

The opening was filled with two more troopers as soon as the first one had left, muttering and shaking his head. Still in their gas masks, the two troopers just stared at the atrocity below through the weird, round lenses of their masks.

As if someone had turned up the volume, the distant sounds of the battle in the hall flared up again, reminding the men in the storage room that all was not over.

The trooper, who had snapped his loaded clip into his pistol, took a few steps forward. He noticed a corpse wrapped in a bed sheet and tied securely with a clothesline. It looked like a mummy. Writhing and struggling, it worked to free itself. With the same calm, deliberate movement he had been using all day, the trooper shot the mummy through the head.

Nearby, a small corpse, that of a very young child, was also writhing. But, at the end of the shroud, where the child's feet should have been, there was bloodied and shredded flesh. A stump kicked around where the foot was once attached. This time, with a slight shudder of revulsion, the man shot the thing's head off.

"They attack . . . each other," Roger said slowly as he reached the trooper's side.

"Just the fresh corpses . . . before they revive," the man told him softly.

"Why did these people keep them here?" Roger asked. "Why don't they turn them over . . . or . . . or destroy them themselves? It's insane . . . Why do they do it?"

"'Cause they still believe there's respect in dying," the man said as he fired into the head of another squirming zombie.

The two men, connected now by a powerful link, walked into the hallway where their comrades were still falling and being pounced on by the seemingly endless stream of walking dead. Others, the lucky ones, were able to fire their automatics through the heads of attacking zombies. The riot troops were trying to stay organized, even without the help of their retreating commander, but the onslaught was so mindless and random that all reason, tactics and coordination were meaningless.

3

Philadelphia, the city of Brotherly Love, was littered with the bodies of its citizens. Moonlight loomed over the embattled city, illuminating the destruction. In the early morning hours, the few lights remaining on were reflected in the waters of the Delaware. The quiet was interrupted only by the sounds of the lapping water and the occasional creak of wooden floating docks as they strained against one another.

The sign that read "CITY OF PHILADELPHIA—POLICE—NO ADMITTANCE," which usually restrained unwelcome visitors to the marina, was dangling and clanging against metal posts. Its chain had been broken. The few big police launches that were still docked there bobbed about silently.

Off in the distance, the low murmur of automatic weapons and loudspeakers could be heard. A few areas of the city were lit by the bright flames of fires set by irate mobs and looters.

Halfway down the long dock, the corpse of a uniformed guard sat at a radio transmitter.

Stephen Andrews, his eyes straining for the separate floating dock that was painted with a large square landing pattern, sat at the controls of the WGON helicopter. It was a jet turbine helicopter with an engine of about 420 horses. He knew it was powerful enough to carry a maximum of four passengers, including the pilot, although it would be pretty tight. The machine could cruise at about 130 m.p.h., and the jet-fuel-filled tank would last them about three hours between fill-ups. With the ability to fly day or night, with a hydraulically boosted flight control system and facilities for radio communication, Steve felt fairly secure and confident in the chopper. He knew it would get them to a safe place.

Francine Parker, his girlfriend, sat in a dazed stupor beside him. Their silence was conspicuous, but it told more than they could verbalize. They just looked out in utter horror at what had become of their city. Steve now maneuvered the helicopter and landed squarely in the middle of the pattern on the machine's skids. Alongside the dock, afloat separately but securely chained, was a small fuel barge, with pumps and hoses for refueling the police choppers and launches that were used in the area.

While the blades of the chopper still spun loudly from the gear-down, Steve jumped out of the cockpit. Two other bodies, bleeding on the bobbing decks, appeared to him as shadows in the distance. A bell buoy rang out, but no ships or launches had approached since the early evening, when all manpower had been needed to quell the disturbances in the inner city.

"Come on," Steve called to Fran inside the cockpit. "I need you."

Francine unbuckled her safety belt and jumped out of her side of the machine. Steve ran around to the other side, ducking under the whirring blades, grabbed her hand and pulled her toward the fuel pump.

Her head was still clouded from the events of the past few hours, and Francine felt as though she were in a bad dream, a never-ending nightmare. She was so disoriented that she allowed Steve to pull her around as if she were a rag doll.

"I don't see Roger," Steve said, scanning the area. "We'll give him ten minutes," he said, looking at his watch.

"Oh my God!" Fran screamed. She had frozen in mid-stride, her eyes staring at two mangled bodies that lay near the fuel pumps.

Steve followed her gaze. "You haven't been out in it at all," he said sympathetically. "It's tough to get used to."

He said it like an old veteran, but he had only a few hours before been just as frightened and horrified. He marveled at the façade of calm that he exhibited to Fran. What a phony!

He pulled at the woman's arm, but the civilian corpse was in the way and Fran froze again. An ingrained fear prevented her from walking over the dead body. Steve dropped her hand and sprinted over to the fuel pumps. Then, he activated the lever mechanism, checked the tank gauge and trotted back to Fran. He dragged the long, heavy hose over the civilian victim's head, which had been blown out by a powerful bullet. It almost made Steve retch, but he remembered that he had to serve as an example to Fran, and controlled himself. He jumped over the body, still running blood, and moved to the helicopter with Fran following, unaware of what he had just witnessed.

With the blades still spinning overhead, Steve jammed the hose nozzle into the fuel tank receptacle. Fran was still glued to the spot. Her eyes wandered over the deserted area, but she still felt a sense of danger. A sudden jerking movement startled her out of her daze. It was Steve grabbing her hand and wrapping it around the nozzle mechanism of the fuel hose.

"Just like this," he instructed calmly. "Like on a car."

Fran's fingers wrapped themselves around the mechanism, getting the feel of the nozzle trigger.

"That's it. Just hold her there till she spits out at ya."

As Fran took over, Steve ran back to the guard shed. The spinning propeller blades made an eerie, whispering sound as they passed over Fran's head. As her eyes got accustomed to the darkness and her ears to the silence, she was able to pick up other sounds and sights. She heard the gentle, rhythmic sound of the water lapping against the docks and the creaking moans of the shifting old wooden structures. But it was too calm, too peaceful, and she sensed an underlying danger. With the look of a frightened animal, she glanced this way and that, primed for the unknown.

Steve ran into the cluttered guardhouse. The contents had been overturned, and it looked as though a struggle had taken place. The radio operator was slumped over the desk. Steve heard the clicking of a signal coming over the receiver in Morse code. His training in communications in college had included learning Morse code, and now that talent came in handy. The send key was covered by the dead man's body, and Steve had to pull the body away from the key and into an upright position in the chair. He noticed that the cause of death was the small gunshot wound in the back of the operator's head. But as Steve pulled the corpse away from the desk, he saw that the exit of the bullet had all but obliterated the man's face. As he stared in horror at the sight, Steve realized that the wound was still bleeding and that bits of flesh and blood were splattered about the desk and radio unit.

A wave of nausea overcame him, but he soon recovered and clicked on the send switch, tapping out a message in Morse code:

"OPERATOR DEAD . . . POST ABANDONED."

Then he sat down in an empty chair and held his head in his hands. Now was not the time to freak out. Not with Francine barely able to keep it together. Steve thought it ironic that after all his years of praying that something exciting would happen that would turn him into a star reporter, the most exciting thing was now happening to him but there was no one to broadcast to. And to think, after all the complaining he did about riding around in the helicopter—now it would save his life.

On the fuel dock, Fran's arm was getting tired from holding onto the heavy hose. She was really getting jumpy and wished that Steve would hurry back from wherever he'd run off to.

A shadow, one that did not belong to Steve or Fran, moved across the corpse on the bobbing dock. Over the whooshing sound of the helicopter blades, Fran could make out the sound of another engine. She glanced toward the mainland and noticed the headlights of an approaching vehicle.

In the guardhouse, Steve was shaken from his thoughts by the sound of the car. He stepped into the doorway and looked up the dock.

"I hope it's Roger," he called to Fran, more to reassure himself that she was still there than to pass along any information.

"What are you doing?" she asked with an edge of panic to her voice.

"I'll be right there."

Ducking back into the house, he snatched up a first aid kit and threw it into a khaki knapsack that he had brought along for "borrowing" what had been left by the dead men. If he didn't take it, someone else would. Rummaging in the darkened shack, he found a toolbox and grabbed that, too.

Standing up, he backed out of the shack, making sure that he didn't leave anything worth taking. Suddenly, he felt something sharp and hard against his back. He recoiled and spinning around faced a shadowy tall figure in the corner of the shack. Steve didn't know how long he had been there watching him.

The figure stepped forward, and the light from the dockside lamps illuminated the uniform of a police officer. Steve's eye moved from the man's grimly determined face to the rifle that the cop had leveled at his belly. From out of the darkness, another officer emerged. This one had a handgun cocked and aimed at

Steve's head. He knew he was trapped. A caged animal with nowhere to run. But he wasn't guilty of anything but wanting to survive. He wondered if there were others and if they had gotten to Fran. He cringed with the thought of what they would do to her out in the dark night on the isolated dockside.

Fran's attention was no longer on the nozzle, it was slowly dripping its precious supply of gasoline into the water, since she was not holding it securely into the opening. She strained her eyes to see the approaching vehicle. She hoped it was Roger so that they could get going. She really didn't know him—just a few things that Steve had told her. They had been drinking buddies at the neighborhood bar and had become close friends. They vowed one night, after a few drinks, to stay together if things got heavy, and now, in a more than sober state, had remembered their mutual pledge.

Suddenly, through the open sides of the helicopter bubble, Fran noticed something out of the corner of her eye. It was a police van, and she didn't know whether it had been there all along. She hadn't heard it come up. The doors had been flung wide open, as though it had been abandoned hurriedly, and now one of the rear doors was moving. Or at least Fran thought it was moving. For a moment she thought she could be hallucinating. Staring into the blackness for the last few minutes might have caused her to see things that weren't there. She wished Steve would come back. She hadn't heard or seen him for at least fifteen minutes, and she was getting worried, really worried.

But then Fran realized she wasn't hallucinating. She could make out a figure carrying a large packing carton. The figure, she noticed with relief, was in the uniform of the police and was carrying two rifles strapped to his back as he rushed toward the launch dock.

Abruptly, a sound jarred Fran's concentration.

"Just stay cool," a voice muttered out of the darkness.

Fran, already uptight because of the running figure, was shocked to hear the voice coming from behind her. Spinning around, she dropped the fuel nozzle in her surprise, and it clattered to the wooden dock boards. She was looking directly at the nose of a rifle pointed right at her head.

"If you die," the policeman said menacingly, "it'll be your own fault."

Fran stood in stunned disbelief, but the moment was short-lived, because the officer who had been running with the carton shouted toward the guardhouse.

"Come on, Skipper. They got friends comin'."

In the guardhouse, Steve was held at bay by the officer with the rifle while the one with the pistol went to check the progress of the approaching vehicle. The headlights were coming closer every second.

"Who are you?" the officer with the rifle asked.

"We're with WGON. We—"

The other man cut him off. "About a minute and a half," he reported on the vehicle's approach.

The one referred to as Skipper pushed Steve with his gun barrel. The impact caused the slight young man to spin out through the open doorway. Looking up, he noticed that the vehicle was now turning onto the long, narrow pier.

The two officers led Steve over to the helicopter, where Fran stood, shivering with fear. The first officer reached inside the helicopter bubble and pulled out Steve's rifle.

"Now wait a minute," Steve shouted over the whirring of the helicopter blades. "We're just here to refuel. These men were already dead. You were here. You know that. It looks like somebody was after the launches. We had nothing to do with—"

One of the officers who had been in the guardhouse with Steve noticed the insignia on the machine.

"Hey, WGON traffic watch ... Steve Andrews," he said with amusement.

"Right, that's me," Steve perked up, hoping that whatever celebrity or notoriety that gave him would help them out of this mess.

"No shit," the officer answered.

"We'd get a lot further in this bird, Skipper," said the officer who had cornered Fran. He was now happily ensconced in the pilot's seat of the helicopter.

All at once, a terrible feeling overcame Steve. He began to put the pieces together: the wholly unprofessional way that the men conducted themselves; their nervousness over the approaching car; their scurrying around for extra supplies. They were on the run, scavengers like Steve himself. Now he began to worry. These were not men to reason with. He prayed that Roger would be in the approaching vehicle.

The man who was carrying the carton rushed back up the dock, having deposited his load in one of the motor launches.

"Can't all fit," he commented.

"How many will that thing hold?" the imposter who had inquired after Steve's identity asked.

"Hey, man, I ain't goin' nowhere in nothin' I can't drive myself," the man who had held the gun to Steve in the shack announced belligerently.

"That's true," said the man who had returned to the van and was carrying out another carton to the launch. "Somethin' happens to him and 'stuck. Stay with the launch!"

"Get a lot further in this bird!" said the first imposter.

Suddenly, above the two white headlights of the approaching vehicle, a third red light was visible.

"Hey, that's a black and white," said the belligerent one, noticing the spinning bubble-gum top and hearing the blast of the car's siren.

The officer in the helicopter, still holding his gun to Fran's head, said, "They've seen us!"

"It's all right," said the skipper calmly. "We're police."

The man who was loading the launch dumped his carton at the edge of the dock and pulled one rifle from his back. "So what!" he yelled at his three accomplices. "Let's get to the boat!"

The skipper stared hard at Steve. Then, with deliberation, he moved his eyes toward the squad car. Then, back at the young pilot.

"You're runnin', ain't you, Flyboy?"

Steve remained mute. He was more afraid than he'd ever been before. He was glad Fran was there. He had to keep up a good front for her. If he'd been alone, he would have crumbled and begged for mercy.

"You and your friend is runnin' off in the WGON traffic bird..." the skipper taunted him. He started to grin in understanding, feeling more in control of a situation that had been getting out of his reach.

"Sit tight, boys," he said to the others. "They're runnin' too."

Finally, after what seemed an eternity to Fran and Steve, the police car pulled down the dock. Steve took a few tentative steps toward it, squinting and hoping against hope that he would see Roger inside, but the skipper pushed him back to his former position with the barrel of his gun.

The car screeched to a stop, and two armed S.W.A.T. troopers immediately popped out of the front seat from either door. To Steve's relief he saw that it was Roger, but he didn't recognize the big trooper who ran up alongside his friend.

"What's the problem, officer," Roger inquired rather innocently. He didn't make so much as a blink of recognition in Steve's direction.

"Caught your friends here stealin' company gasoline," the skipper told him.

"What do you mean friends?" Roger faked.

"They know, Rog..." Steve cut in, afraid that the skipper would play this game to the limit, making Roger look like a fool in the long run. "They're tryin' to get out, too."

"It'd be crazy to start shootin' at one another, now wouldn't it?" the skipper asked Roger.

"Sure would," he answered, relieved that he wouldn't have to continue with the charade. He was anxious to leave, to get out of this city that held so many bad memories for him.

"All right," said the man who had been sitting in the helicopter. "Let's load up."

He slung his rifle and tossed the other gun back to Fran. Startled, she tried to catch the rifle, but it fell out of her hands and skittered across the dock.

The man looked at her angrily.

"You better learn how to use that thing, woman. Times is tense!"

The bogus policeman turned from the group of the four united friends and started to unload crates and cartons from their van. The big trooper pulled a few supplies from the squad car and carried them toward the helicopter. He hadn't said a word of greeting to either Fran or Steve, or made any attempt to explain his presence.

Fran ran over to Stephen as he emerged from the guardhouse, carrying the toolbox and the knapsack full of supplies. Relieved, she fell into his arms. Roger saw them and trotted over.

"You OK?" he asked, concerned and puzzled.

"Yeah," Steve said, nodding. "Who's he?" he indicated the big trooper.

"His name's Peter Washington. He's all right," Roger said tersely and started moving along toward the helicopter.

"Let's hustle," he said, as Fran and Steve followed.

Meticulously and efficiently, Peter had stowed the supplies in the rear of the cockpit. He was distracted by the strong odor of gasoline and noticed the fuel hose lying on the dock. He tried the nozzle in the receptacle on the chopper and held it in until the tank filled.

Down the dock, the other men were swiftly moving cartons of all their supplies from their van into the launch.

"You guys better move off," Roger shouted to them. "There's a radio report about the dock bein' knocked out."

Fran, Steve and Roger reached the cockpit, which had been filled to the brink with supplies by Peter.

"You sure this'll carry us all?" Fran asked as she climbed in and crouched on the floor in the rear of the bubble.

"Little harder on the fuel, but we'll be OK," Steve reassured her.

As Peter managed just barely to fit his bulk into the helicopter, one of the other men approached Roger.

"Hey," he asked, putting down the last carton, "you got any cigarettes?"

Roger looked at the others one at a time with a strange expression on his face. Fran shook her head no.

"Sorry," he said shortly, trotting around to the passenger seat.

"Where ya headed?" Steve asked from the pilot's seat.

"Down river. Got an idea maybe we can make it to the islands."

"What islands?"

"Any island. What about you? Where you headed?"

"Straight up," Steve said with a smile as the propellers lifted the chopper off the ground.

The imposter rushed off with his two partners. As they untied one of the launches from the dock, the WGON helicopter whined loudly overhead, completing a perfect lift-off.

Then, the police launch started without a hitch and pulled out onto the dark river, leaving just the corpses and the strong smell of gasoline on the creaking pier.

Steve, at last, felt in control again. The last hour had really been hairy. He didn't know if he or Fran would have made it out alive if Roger and Peter hadn't come along. But, now, as the lights on the helicopter blinked over the city of Philadelphia, Steve felt safe and secure in his metal womb.

He took the bird over his favorite sights, almost a farewell salute. He didn't know when, or if, they would be coming back.

First they swooped over the art museum, the floodlights illuminating a path up the stone steps. The Rodin museum was a few hundred yards away. Steve wondered if the walking dead would soon make the city unfit for any kind of habitation. Maybe thousands of years from now archaeologists would uncover this city with all its art and treasures and wonder what disaster caused all its inhabitants to flee.

It was an hour or two before dawn, and the city was now empty. Independence Hall, Betsy Ross's house with the original American flag—all the monuments to a great civilization lay in the grips of an impending disaster. The oldest American heritage stood coldly in the night, awaiting its fate.

For a second, Steve thought of his parents. He hadn't even tried to contact them and wondered where they were, if they were still alive. They had instilled this love of history in him. As teachers, they were always reading, discussing. They were sorely disappointed when he decided to forsake his college education and try for the glamorous job of a reporter. They had hoped he would go for his doctorate at the University of Pennsylvania. They didn't care what he studied, as long as he had a PhD after his name.

In the cockpit, Fran surreptitiously lit a cigarette. Roger did, too. The only comment was Peter's smirk.

The big man leaned back, but was still uncomfortable. He didn't have room to stretch out his legs. He looked down at the city. A wave of sadness overcame him and he spoke to the group for the first time.

"Any of you leavin' people behind?"

"An ex-husband," Fran said without a trace of regret in her voice.

"An ex-wife," Roger said thoughtfully.

"You, Peter?" Steve asked, his eyes straight ahead.

The trooper was quiet for a moment, his gaze still on the city disappearing below.

"Some brothers." And the tone of his voice told them that he didn't want to discuss it any further.

As the copter moved west, the lights on the ground below grew few and far between. It was still dark, even though dawn was approaching. Roger was asleep in the passenger seat, crumpled up like a child on a long journey in a car. Fran and Peter sat very close to each other, cramped in the rear of the cockpit.

Peter was still staring out the window, but Fran could see that his eyes weren't really focused on anything in particular.

"Real brothers?" she asked, picking up the conversation where they had left it almost an hour before.

He turned to look at her, and she noticed what fine strong features he had.

"Real brothers or street brothers?" she asked tentatively.

"Both."

"How many real ones?"

"Two."

"Two," she repeated.

"One's in jail. The other's a pro ballplayer. But we catch up to each other once in a while."

He turned his head, and Fran didn't know quite how to respond. It seemed as if he wanted to cut off any communication and human contact.

But Peter Washington turned his head so that the woman couldn't see the tears that were welling up in his eyes. How could he go off and leave them now? But there wasn't anything he could do. Sammy was locked away in that prison. For what?—for stealing a few bucks from that rip-off liquor store in the ghetto. The guy deserved it. He'd been charging the poor people two, sometimes three, dollars over the standard price for years.

And Tommy? He was a big superjock now. On the road somewhere. Hopefully in the Midwest. At least both of them would be relatively safe.

Peter was really all the family they had left. Their father had deserted them when Peter was still in his teens. And as the eldest brother, he was responsible now. And Mama. Thank God she wasn't alive. Even though she had probably worked herself to death trying to make ends meet, this night would have killed her for sure. But, at least she would have been proud of her eldest boy—he had realized long ago that the only way to make it was on his strength and guts, and he had certainly proved it tonight. All of them in this whirlybird had one thing in common, he thought to himself. They all had the will to survive.

Peter turned toward the slender, blonde-haired, shivering woman beside him. Nodding toward Steve, who wouldn't be able to hear the conversation over the roar of the engine, he asked, "He your man now?"

Fran was taken off guard by Peter's sudden return to conversation. She smiled slightly.

"Most of the time, yeah," she whispered, shaking the hair out of her eyes.

"Just like to know who everybody is," Peter said, a genuine smile coming over his face for the first time in a long time.

"Yeah, me too," she agreed, snuggling down in the seat.

As the light finally dawned on the horizon, the little helicopter chugged through the varying shades of blue and pink, toward an unknown destiny.

4

The morning light now streamed into the helicopter bubble. The brightness caused Peter to shade his eyes with his hand. He hadn't slept at all. His eyes were bloodshot, and they still itched from the tear gas. Fran was still asleep, crushed against the side of the rear cockpit. She seemed so peaceful. And Roger snored happily. Peter didn't know how he could do it.

As far as he could tell, they were somewhere beyond Harrisburg, and had been flying due west since they'd left Philadelphia. He had recognized the Piedmont Plateau of Lancaster. He wondered what the Amish people thought of this disaster, if they realized what was happening. Maybe they believed, as many did, that it was a punishment for the sins of modern living.

They had flown over the lush Lebanon and Cumberland Valleys, which the mighty Susquehanna

River nourished and which surrounded the state capital of Harrisburg. Now, as far as Peter could tell from his high school geography, they were passing into the Appalachian Mountains, which would lead them to the Allegheny Mountains and finally on to Johnstown and Pittsburgh.

A sudden twitching of Steve's head made Peter notice that the pilot was falling asleep. With a swift movement, Peter kicked him gently in the shoulder. Startled, Steve looked behind him, surprised that the big trooper was still awake. Steve smiled slightly, but Peter only stared back coldly.

He's a weird one, thought Steve. Wonder why Roger ever thought to take him along.

"Any more water?" Steve asked, rubbing his face violently and pulling at the skin below his eyes to stay awake.

Peter reached behind him to the supplies and pulled out a plastic container of water. Steve took a deep slug, and then felt guilty for taking so much. More cautiously, he splashed some on his face to revitalize himself. He didn't know how long he had been awake, but it had to be at least twenty-four hours. He knew he had been at the TV station the day before at 4 a.m., and now it was way past that.

He passed the plastic container back to Peter, who also took a hit.

Suddenly, Fran stiffened and woke up with a start, as if from a bad dream. Peter's expression softened when he looked at her. For a moment, she didn't know where she was or who this man was, or even why her bones ached so and her head spun. Then she remembered and the thought made her cringe.

"You know where we are?" Peter asked Stephen.

"I know exactly where we are," Steve said aggressively. He didn't like Peter's attitude toward him, and also he had noticed Peter's change of attitude whenever he spoke to Fran.

"Harrisburg?" Peter asked, trying to trick Steve. He resented the pilot's haughty posture.

"Passed it about an hour ago."

Both men were talking loudly over the drone of the engine and were also trying to talk one another down. Their strident voices woke Roger up. He turned just as Steve told the others, "We're pretty low on fuel. I'm just waitin' for full light so we can see what we're landin' in."

The three other passengers looked down on the ground and could make out several large fires, probably warehouses and factories. The pea-green trucks of a National Guard convoy were also visible as they chugged up a winding country road.

As the sun rose higher, more and more activity was visible on the ground. Search and destroy units made up of police, guardsmen and civilian volunteers moved across the countryside. Occasionally, a lone zombie could be seen wandering or staggering through the trees or over a field. Frequently, the creature was met by the staccato beat of gunfire as it was cut down.

"Jesus," Roger said, rubbing the sleep from his eyes as he watched the horror show below. "It's everywhere."

"We're getting pretty close to Johnstown," Steve told him. "We're better off away from the big cities. This map says there's a little country airfield in Beaverdale. I'm goin' to try and land there to refuel."

As they approached the airfield, quiet in the morning sun, there was no sign of life. A few private planes dotted the area, but the familiar crackle of the air traffic control tower radio was conspicuously absent. The WGON chopper buzzed very low, just outside the tower windows.

As the whirlybird slowly set down near the fuel pumps, its blades created a wind blast that raised great clouds of dust from the dry earth. Sheets of old newspaper and other light debris were sent flying through the air in all directions. The place was as deserted as if an atomic bomb had blasted the area.

One piece of torn newsprint blew flat against a window in one of the little sheds that housed snowplows and other maintenance machinery. The scrap stuck against the glass for a moment, as though glued there, and then it fluttered to the ground. Watching the journey of the scrap through glazed eyes was a zombie with a badly scarred face.

The chopper landed by the fuel pumps, and the passengers, thankful for the opportunity to stretch their legs, scrambled out. Steve immediately ran over to check the pumps.

"Shit, man. Damn near empty."

"Lotta private planes in farm country like this," Roger said as he raised his arms high above his head and started to do a few jumping jacks to get his circulation going again. "Guess they all hit the pumps and took off."

"To where?" Steve asked as he dragged the hose over and started filling the chopper's tank with what was left. "Where the hell can they go?"

"Where *we* goin'?" Peter asked abruptly.

Instead of answering him, Steve moved to the second pump and checked its gauge and then the hose itself. It spurted with more force.

"There's a good bit left in this pump," he said as he stretched the hose toward the chopper. "Damn," he uttered when it didn't reach, "I gotta get it closer."

He jumped back into the cockpit, and the machine lifted off the ground.

Fran, who had been standing around observing the whole encounter, had noticed the hostility between

Steve and Peter. Men, she thought. Always needed their egos massaged. Now wasn't the time to prove who was boss. They had to work together.

She walked slowly backward toward a small rickety hangar area while she watched them interacting. Then she turned and looked down toward the private hangars. Most of them had been left wide open, and the planes they had housed were long gone. Obviously, their owners had been in a great rush, not expecting to ever have to return. It was frightening: where would they go? If the living dead had already caused havoc in this little out-of-the-way town, was anywhere safe?

She noticed that one or two of the old wooden double-doors were still closed and locked with chains and padlocks. Maybe in there were the planes of those who hadn't been fortunate enough to get away. Maybe those planes belonged to the ones who'd chosen to stay and fight the losing battle against the zombies. Or maybe those owners were now zombies themselves!

The wind from the chopper blades blew Fran's hair, and a swirl of debris and dust flew up around her shoulders. She tried to shield her eyes and nose from the dust.

On the other side of the field, Peter kicked open the door to the chart house. The room was filled with dust from the partially opened windows, and it was totally dilapidated. A few small chairs surrounded an old wood table. Several half-finished cups of coffee sat on top of wrinkled flight charts, leaving brown rings soaked into the paper. A half-eaten sandwich was now the home of dozens of flies, which swarmed around and buzzed loudly. An old, cracked and filthy window shade clicked against its window from the gusting wind, which came in through the cracks in the wall. Peter flinched at the sounds and the stench of the room. Somehow he found this kind of situation more threatening out in the middle of nowhere than in the middle of the inner city. He guessed it was just what you were accustomed to that made the difference.

He readied his weapon and walked over to the shade. Then he pulled it down and let it roll up on itself. It made a loud flapping noise, but there was nothing behind it. Peter heaved a sigh of relief.

Outside, Steve was just setting the chopper down as Roger ran over with the hose nozzle. Ducking under the blades, Roger inserted the device into the tank receptacle even before Steve had idled the engine. There was something about this deserted airstrip that gave him the creeps too.

Maybe all those hours in the copter had given him too much time to think, Roger pondered. When there was action, he was always ready. But when there was time to think, sometimes it gave him second thoughts about what he was doing. That had always been his problem with Louise. As soon as he'd had any time off just to sit around the house, he'd grown restless. Idleness made him uneasy.

Steve hopped out of the cockpit and shouted over the engine noise to Roger.

"I'm gonna see what's left in the hangars."

He turned before Roger replied and trotted off after Fran. Frankly, he was a little worried about her exploring around here alone, but he didn't want to alarm her.

Meanwhile, in the chart house, Peter idly kicked an old coffee machine at one end of the room. The machine clicked loudly and, much to Peter's surprise, spat out a cup. It didn't look too appetizing, but the hot brown liquid would be all the warm nourishment he would be getting for a while.

Peter's eyes scanned the bulletin board while he waited for the cup to fill. Notes spilled out off the bulletin board to the coffee machine and even onto the walls. They had all been written hurriedly, in all sorts of handwriting styles and in various inks and colors.

Some of the notes read:

"LUCY—GONE TO JOHNSTOWN."

"Charles—I have the kids; Left with Ben. Mom's dead."

"Couldn't wait. Gone to Erie—Jack Foster."

The wall was plastered with such messages, some frantic, some matter-of-fact. Peter wondered how many of these had even been read by the right people.

He sipped his coffee thoughtfully. A sudden movement from the closet door just across the room attracted his attention. It appeared locked but it rattled against the lock, once, twice, more regularly than if it were caused by wind drafts.

Peter moved toward it cautiously. The door banged violently with a loud crash, and then it stopped. That was no wind, Peter thought, as he set his coffee on the chart table and took his rifle in both hands.

Again, the door banged hard, and the skeleton key that had secured it was knocked out of the keyhole and fell to the floor with a metallic clang. Peter's eyes were drawn to the caked bloodstain where blood had recently run out under the closet door and onto the linoleum floor.

Another bang sounded, and then there was the unmistakable gurgling moan of a zombie. It was trying to break out of the closet!

With remarkable calm, Peter raised his M16 and aimed it at the door about head height. The M16 roared in the little room, shaking the shack to its foundation. Splintery holes appeared in the old wooden door.

At the sharp crack of the gunshots, Fran and Steve snapped to attention. Fran had been standing at the entrance to one of the little wooden hangars, while Steve was inside checking out the cockpit of an old

Cessna. Upon hearing the shot, Steve immediately ran out and grabbed Fran's hand. As they turned the corner to run up the grade toward the helicopter, they were confronted by two zombies. The zombies staggered slowly toward them, appearing in the dust cloud brought up by the blade of the chopper.

Panic seized Fran. They were weaponless, vulnerable. She let out a scream.

Steve gripped her arm more tightly.

"Roger, Roger," he cried, but the trooper couldn't hear him under the whirling blades. He continued to fill the fuel tank, unaware that his friends had no protection and that he was in danger of being surprised from behind by one of the zombies.

A third zombie was now lumbering toward the helicopter and Roger was still totally immersed in filling the tank.

Inside the chart house, Peter stared at the closet door. There was silence for a moment and then another moan, and the door shook again with another bang.

Taking careful aim, Peter fired two shots, lower right and lower left of the first, forming a neat triangle. Then, in a fit of violence, he fired a volley of shots just where the creature's head should be. There was no way that the bullets could have missed their target this time.

For a moment there was quiet. But, as a highly trained soldier, Peter still held his gun high.

All of a sudden, a great crash sounded, and even the calm, collected Peter flinched at the noise. The closet door flew open and two small children, a girl and boy, burst out into the room. They were a ghastly sight, even to Peter's cynical eyes: the little girl had no left arm, the boy had been bleeding from a great wound in his side. Peter felt a touch of sympathy for the pathetic creatures, but then he reminded himself—they were dead!

The two young zombies walked directly toward Peter. He noted that their heads were at least a foot shorter than the bullet holes in the closet door. He had wasted all those bullets for nothing!

Almost as if he were paralyzed, Peter stared down at the creatures. He felt a great repugnance for the two seemingly innocent children. As if by instinct, they ambled toward him. He was so startled by their actions that he did not react quickly. Before he knew it their clammy grasp was upon him. But his survival instincts were just as strong, and he regained his composure. He could not effectively aim his rifle, since they were too close; so he kicked and thrashed at them. The young girl, not more than eight, flew against a wall. The boy, probably about ten, was clinging onto Peter's arm, trying to bite it. The big trooper grabbed the small zombie and flung it back. Just then, the female zombie pounced on his back. He threw it over his shoulders and it crashed against the boy.

The children were dressed in overalls and were fair-haired and blue-eyed. Probably the children of a farmer, Peter thought, as he raised his gun. Maybe they were brother and sister. As the children tried to scramble to their feet, Peter fired several shots in rapid succession. First the little girl fell; then the boy.

Peter continued to fire long after the children stopped twitching. His eyes were dry—but wide with desperation and disgust. Finally the click of the weapon signalled that it was out of ammunition. Peter was sweating profusely now, his breath coming in deep, dry gasps.

Meanwhile, the two creatures continued their advance toward Fran and Steve.

"Just run," Steve shouted at Fran, who stood mesmerized by the monsters and totally petrified. She turned and looked behind them, but they were boxed in by the hangars.

"Run right past 'em," Steve advised her. "Right around 'em. They can't catch you."

She hesitated, and her eyes grew wider with terror as the zombies drew closer.

Steve was screaming now, jumping up and down.

"Run, Frannie. Goddammit, I'm right behind you. We can handle them!"

With one decisive action, Fran started up the little grade. She ran to the right of the creatures, and they moved in her direction, arms outstretched. As their clawing hands drew closer to her, she recoiled in fright. One of them was practically on top of her now.

"Run, Frannie. Move!" Steve yelled, almost in hysterics himself.

Fran stared into the vacant, dazed eyes of the lead zombie. She was almost hypnotized by the creature's steady gaze. At the last instant, she regained her composure and ran just past the creatures. A little way up the grade, she turned and looked back, stopping again.

Fran's heart was pounding and she was shaking with fear. She felt as if there were nowhere to run and that she was merely taunting the zombies. She didn't realize that they didn't think as humans any more, or even react like swift animals, but merely staggered around, bumping into things and people without differentiation.

One of the zombies had now turned up the grade and was after her. The other creature continued to advance on Steve.

Steve ducked into the open hangar. The thin beams of sunlight that cut through the wooden boards of the structure made a striped pattern on the dirt floor. In the corner of the hangar, Steve noticed a pile of greasy tools. He rooted through them until he found an enormous sledgehammer. Grabbing it he ran out of the shed, dodging around the lead zombie. The zombie tottered like a wind-up toy and staggered on even after

Steve had changed direction. Grasping the handle of the giant hammer firmly, Steve charged up the grade toward the zombie. As he reached the creature's back, he brought the twenty-pound steel head of the sledge slamming against the ghoul's skull with all the strength his 138-pound body could muster.

The creature staggered on for a few more steps, its head a bloody pulp, and then it fell to its knees and finally flopped face down in the dust. Blood gushed out around the ghoul and mixed with the dust-laden ground covering.

Without pausing, or breaking stride, Steve grabbed Fran's hand, and the two of them rushed toward the helicopter. The other zombie at the hangar finally realized that its prey had changed direction, and it turned around and was walking up the grade. Its hands clawed at the air, and its bulging eyes glared straight ahead.

Roger, who had been totally unaware of all the excitement, pumped the last drops out of the fuel hose. As he turned around, he was shocked to see the frantic expressions on the faces of the couple as they made their life-or-death dash to the helicopter.

While Steve charged up the grade, he saw the zombie approaching Roger from behind. He shouted and waved his free arm, and Roger spun around. The stumbling creature was almost upon him. It raised its arms, and its hands clutched the air in a bizarre salute. Roger let the fuel nozzle drop to the ground, and he started to run but realized that he was trapped at the side of the machine. He didn't have his rifle and had to fumble with the snap on his handgun holster before he was properly armed.

Suddenly, the blank face of the zombie turned red as the top of its head seemed to disintegrate into a bloody pulp. Roger realized with alarm that the mindless creature had walked directly into the spinning chopper blade. He watched with a mixture of disgust and relief as the body staggered forward another step or two and then collapsed into a bloody heap.

While Roger was watching the repulsive death of the zombie, Steve and Fran had reached the chopper. Steve let go of Fran's hand and dropped his bloody sledge to the ground. He lunged into the cockpit and grabbed his rifle.

The zombie that was stumbling up the grade from the hangars almost lost its footing. Some natural sense of equilibrium caused it to regain its balance, and it advanced steadily toward the helicopter.

Suddenly, Fran was gripped by violent loathing and a physical weakening, and she fell to her knees on the ground, retching and clutching at her stomach. She was directly in line of the zombie's trajectory. Steve raised his gun and, fumbling, aimed at the approaching creature. He fired again, and this time the bullet only grazed the creature's face. It wobbled from the impact but did not fall.

Roger, meanwhile, had retrieved his high-powered rifle from the copter, and he ran to Steve's aid. Steve had fired two more rounds, another miss and a graze on the arm. The creature didn't react at all. It could have been a fly landing on his arm.

Just as Steve was about to shoot once more, Roger stopped him with a hand on the shoulder and stepped up alongside him. Calmly, Roger aimed and fired one shot cleanly through the creature's brain. The zombie fell, and a newspaper blew over him like a shroud.

During all the action outside on the airstrip, Peter had been staring at the small corpses, now dotted with bullet holes. Finally he roused himself and instinctively started to load his weapon without looking at the action, and backing wearily out toward the door of the chart house. Behind him, silhouetted against the brightly sunlit doorway, was another zombie. The creature lumbered forward just as Peter turned. Startled, he reached for more shells and backed away a few steps as he tried to load the bullets into his gun. The creature reached out and took another step into the room.

Peter stared directly at the creature's eyes. Then, suddenly, out in the glaring light, a few hundred feet behind the zombie, Steve appeared with his rifle. He was barely visible behind the zombie's broad back.

Peter could just about see him over the creature's shoulder.

Then, without warning, Steve shouldered the rifle and aimed directly at the zombie. But to Peter's trained eye, it seemed that the barrel was on a straight line, pointing directly at him.

With agility and foresight, Peter ducked quickly to the floor. Steve's gun fired a split second later. The bullet missed the creature and went crashing into the room. It ricocheted off the coffee machine. Another shot crashed through the glass in the front room.

Peter didn't know where to run first—away from the stalking zombie or away from Steve's wild shots. While he crouched, Peter filled his gun with shells. A third of Steve's bullets tore through the creature's shoulder, but it still stood. Slowly, it turned toward the crouching man. Peter crawled under the table as another shot splattered into the coffee cups.

Unless that dude is blind, Peter thought, he's got to see me in here. The bastard's trying to blow my head off too!

Just in time, Roger once again stepped up beside Steve. And once again he took careful aim and fired one super-clean shot, sighting through the telescopic range finder. As Peter finished loading his weapon, the zombie crashed into the room, falling over the table and onto the floor.

With the wind whipping dust and debris in her face, Fran was still doubled over and trying to keep herself from vomiting. She knew it was caused by the excitement, but she also knew the other cause; and she shuddered to think what would become of her now that there was utter chaos and confusion terrorizing the countryside.

A sudden movement and Fran flinched, only to be relieved when she saw Steve rushing to her side.

"Peter," shouted Roger toward the chart house, his rifle poised.

The big man appeared in the doorway, a grim look on his face, snapping the safety on his rifle.

Fran's retching caused her to choke and cough. Steve grasped her shoulders and tried to help her, but he didn't know what to say and had a hard enough time trying to keep himself from shaking.

With long, purposeful strides, Peter advanced upon the couple.

Stephen felt his presence when the trooper was still a dozen steps away.

Immediately, Steve recognized the anger in the man's eyes. He felt a sinking feeling in his stomach, and in the back of his mind he knew why the man was standing there, his rifle aimed directly at Stephen.

Steve tried to stand, but his shaking was so intense now that he tripped and fell on his back in the dust. In an instant, Peter loomed over him with the barrel of his rifle aimed at point-blank range at the convulsing man's forehead.

"No...my God! Don't...what are you doing?" Fran screamed through her choking.

"You never aim a gun at anyone, mister," Peter said to him calmly, in a low tone, barely audible over the whipping propellers. "It's scary, isn't it? *Isn't it?*" he said, poking Stephen in the ribs with the nose of the rifle.

Stephen looked at the big man meekly. He felt himself flush with humiliation. He had thought he had seen something else in the shack, but he hadn't been sure. He was so intent on killing the zombie that the thought that had crossed his mind—where was Peter?—had lodged in his brain.

Peter lowered his weapon and extended his hand, helping Steve up onto his feet.

A subdued Roger cleared the fuel hose from around the runners of the chopper. Peter climbed into the cockpit and sat in the rear of the copter without saying a word. The image of the two children kept playing through his head. And, the glint in Steve's eye as he aimed the rifle directly at his head. Peter was sure he could see that glint even through the barrel of the gun.

Roger helped a shaking Fran climb aboard. She was weakened from the vomiting and felt numbed by what she had just witnessed. The enormity of the situation dawned on her. This wasn't kid stuff, she realized with horror.

Steve walked around to the front of the cockpit bubble and climbed into the pilot's seat with almost studied calmness. Roger climbed in after Fran as she squeezed into her familiar uncomfortable spot by Peter. The man offered her a sip of water as if to say, My beef's with Steve, not with you. She accepted it gratefully and then let her head flop wearily against the rear bulkhead.

"We gotta find fuel," Steve announced with urgency in his voice. He surveyed his flight charts, shuffling the papers and trying to seem very busy after the embarrassment of the incident.

"No, we've gotta stay away from the big cities," Roger told him, hoping that the incident would be forgotten and they could get on their way. "If it's anything like Philly, we might never get out alive."

"We might not get out of *anyplace* alive," Peter broke in, his voice oozing with hostility and double meaning. "We almost didn't get out of here."

"We're getting outa here fine," said Roger, trying to cool him down and keep the peace. He felt responsible for bringing the two together. He hadn't realized it would be like mixing water and oil. "As long as there's not too many of those things we can handle 'em easy."

"Yeah," Peter insisted, "well, it wasn't one of 'those things' that nearly blew me away!"

Steve felt the bile rising in his throat. So what if the guy was bigger than he was. No one was getting nowhere unless he flew this thing, and it was about time they appreciated it. He turned to say something in retort, but Roger stopped him.

"We gotta stay in the sticks," he said seriously. "There's bound to be more little private airports upstate."

"There's the locks along the Allegheny," Steve said somberly, reluctantly returning to his charts. He had hoped a direct confrontation would clear the air. "Fuel stations there, private and state."

"Prob'ly still manned," Roger countered. "We don't need those hassles either."

"They're just after scavengers...looters..." Steve said sanctimoniously.

"Oh," Peter cut in, "you got the papers for this limousine?"

"I got WGON ID," Steve shouted angrily, "and so does Fran."

"Right," Peter said venomously, "and we're out here doin' traffic reports? Wake up, sucker. We're thieves and bad guys is what we are. And we gotta find our own way!"

Peter's words hit them all in the pit of the stomach. He was right. They weren't any better than the looters and the scavengers who roamed the countryside. But what choice did they have? The engine droned on, but the helicopter didn't leave the ground. The men looked at each other silently, steadily. Peter was the first to move as he took a long slug of water from the plastic container.

Finally, Fran spoke. Her voice had an edge of anxiety to it. "Jesus Christ. We don't even know where we're going. We don't have a radio. We're running out of water. We need food..." She looked at each one of the men, their faces haggard and drawn. Steve looked particularly devastated.

"Stephen," she said tenderly, "you need to sleep."

He looked at her earnestly for a second and then turned to the controls of the copter. Without another word he set it in motion. Its props started to spin, and then with a surge of power it lifted off and flew away. The dry earth swirled up into a cloud and blew more bits of paper over the wide-eyed corpses that lay in the morning sunlight.

Peter glanced backward toward the chart house and wiped his hand across his sweating brow. He'd try to get some sleep now. God knew how much he needed it, but he didn't think that he could ever sleep again.

5

The little helicopter chugged off toward the northwest. As it flew across the deserted landscape, it seemed as if its lonely survivors were like Noah in his Ark. About sixty miles north of Pittsburgh, their view was assaulted by the sprawling tentacles of an enormous structure. Half a dozen roads converged on a parking lot the size of six football fields, veined with yellow lines and arrows. It was a huge shopping mall—"Shoppers Paradise," the sign said—created out of the mountainous rocky terrain of the coal mining territory. It had been designed to bring a more suburban influence into the area. Fortresslike, the outer walls were all concrete, and they stretched upward for more than two stories. Entrance to the structure was through four doorways, situated north, south, east and west. Inside was a self-sufficient environment of shops that catered to all the needs of the community: food, clothing, shelter and leisure. A sophisticated system of air ducts and heating apparatus precluded the need for outside windows and focused the shoppers' attention on the flashy consumer products inside.

As the helicopter drew closer, the passengers noted that what few cars remained in the lot were parked haphazardly, some with their doors wide open.

The little machine eased itself down onto the roof of the building. The engine sputtered and coughed, and the blades slowed down so that their whirring noise was only a buzz.

Fran, who was now very uncomfortable, with an uneasy feeling in her stomach, and a pounding headache from lack of food and sleep, looked around in horror. In the parking lot, walking among the abandoned vehicles almost like shoppers on a typical Saturday, were hordes of the living dead. If she hadn't known better, she would have mistaken them for normal people, but their lumbering walk was unfortunately extremely recognizable.

At the north mall entrance, the all-glass revolving door, flanked by two ground-to-ceiling picture windows and several regularly hinged doors, was surrounded by a number of zombies. A few of them had managed to negotiate the hinged doors and enter the building. Others bounced off windows and clawed at the transparent glass in confusion. One creature was trapped in the revolving door and circled endlessly.

The creatures, as was their nature, wandered around aimlessly, with no apparent purpose. Even the whirring sound of the helicopter caused them no alarm.

"Oh, my God!" Fran cried in terror as she watched the loathsome parade from the ledge of the roof.

Stephen ran over to her side. He stared at the creatures moving steadily toward the building.

"No chance," he declared, starting back toward the copter. "Forget it. Let's get out of here."

Roger walked out to the couple and took a glance around the parking lot.

"Wait a minute, wait a minute. They can't get up here."

"Yeah," Steve said, a frantic note in his voice. "And we can't go down there!"

"Let's check it out," Roger said calmly but with authority.

He turned and noticed that Peter had already done so. He was the type who didn't wait for a consensus of opinion but made an affirmative move. Roger trotted over to him.

"Most of the gates are down," Peter said, staring through one of the giant grids of transparent Plexiglas bubbles that faced down into the building. Roger peered through another of the bubbles.

"I don't think they can get into the stores," Peter told him.

From their vantage point, the two troopers were only able to see a small segment of the interior. It was a square plaza with a garden beneath the sunroof of transparent bubbles. The space was open all the way down to the garden, which was only two stories below. Pathways to the entrances of the shops generated from the garden like spokes from the hub of a wheel. All but one of the heavy metal cage gates that protected the stores were down and locked into position.

Roger could see only three or four zombies tottering about. They bounced off the locked gates and would probably wander into the unlocked one eventually.

Peering around the bubble, Roger could see that halfway up the wall a balcony railing surrounded the entire place. There was a second level of stores with the same cagelike gates sealing off the entrances. As far as Roger could tell, none of the ghouls had made it up to the balcony—yet.

Fran and Stephen noticed the two troopers' fascination with the bubbles and jogged over to see what all the interest was about.

"I haven't seen any of them up on the second floor," Roger told Peter.

"The big department stores usually use both floors. You probably have to take an escalator up to those floors from inside the store."

"If we can get in up top—" Roger replied, but Peter was already off, looking across the rest of the expansive rooftop.

Suddenly, he ran toward a series of other housings that jutted up out of the otherwise flat surface. Curious, Roger followed.

Fran was still mesmerized by the scene below the plastic bubble. "What are they doing here?" she asked Steve. "Why do they come here?"

"Some kind of instinct," Steve answered. The profundity of his next statement was almost a parody. "Memory...of what they used to do. This was an important place in their lives."

With morbid fascination, they watched the zombies, who wandered aimlessly over the plaza. Some tried the gates but could not budge them. One, a woman, wandered out of the single opened shop, an appliance store. As the female creature left, she dragged a toaster idly behind her, pulling it by its power cable as it scraped loudly on the floor.

Peter and Roger reached an installation of large reflectors mounted in an intricate metal skeleton that stretched across a large area of the roof's surface. Behind the structures, a large power generator could be seen.

"Solar screens," Peter said quietly. A scheme seemed to be forming in his mind.

"Can't be enough to power this place," Roger stated.

"Emergency system, maybe."

"It's pretty lit up in there," Roger recalled.

"Guess the power's not off in this area," Peter said to Roger's back as the big white man trotted off to another protruding structure on the rooftop. "A lot of Philly's still lit," Peter continued to no one in particular. "Could be nuclear."

But Roger wasn't listening. He had found something very exciting. "Hey, look at this," he called to his three companions. He was peering down through a wire-hatched skylight. There were several of these skylights laid out over this particular area of the roof. He moved to another one, almost as if he were a voyeur in a porno house looking through the peepholes. Peter moved to the first. Fran and Steve ran over to see what *this* excitement was about.

"These don't go down into the mall," Roger exclaimed. "What the hell is this?"

Fran and Steve peered down into the darkness, wondering what the attraction was that this roof had for the two men. All Fran and Steve wanted was to get back on the helicopter and fly off in the opposite direction to this place. It gave them the creeps. Any moment now they expected the zombies to charge up the roof and attack them. Each moment they lingered was precious. They wanted to exploit as many hours of daylight as they could and possibly make it to Canada, where they hoped the situation was different or at least improved.

Peter, in his steadfast, fastidious manner, pulled a flashlight from his utility belt. He had stayed in full uniform all the while. Roger, in the meantime, had stripped off all the police paraphernalia except for his ammunition belt and pistol holster.

Peter shone his light beam down into the space. The floor appeared to be only about seven feet below the window.

"Damn," Peter emitted as he saw that there was absolutely nothing in sight: clear light gray floor, clear light gray walls.

"Hey, over here," Roger called out as he moved to another window. "There's something here."

Peter ran over and shone his beam down again. They could see a vast array of cardboard cartons...hundreds of them.

"Storage?" Roger asked.

"Civil defense," Peter surmised as he moved the light beam. It illuminated a collection of large drums, stacked floor-to-ceiling and running deep past the line of vision. On the face of each drum was the familiar symbol of a triangle within a circle, and the letters "C.D."

"And boxes of canned food!" Roger cried out happily, like a kid finding a toy.

"How do we get down there?" said Stephen. He just wanted to get off the rooftop, either back into the copter or inside the building. He felt vulnerable and exposed on the open rooftop.

For the first time since they'd disembarked from the helicopter, Peter acknowledged Steve's presence. With a sneer on his face, he destroyed Steve with one glance. Then he brought his rifle butt down against the glass and stared directly into Steve's eyes as the shattered pane crashed to the floor below.

They all peered with awe into the vast space. In places, the darkness was interrupted by shafts of sunlight that drifted in from the various skylights. The barren space was very quiet.

Peter shouldered his rifle, replaced his flashlight and dropped, feet first, into the room. He stood for a moment, silhouetted in a sun ray, waiting, watching, as if he were a hunting dog scenting the prey. Then he readied his rifle, looking this way and that across the large room.

"OK," he called quietly, and Roger dropped catlike to the floor.

The two men instantly slung their rifles and moved to the food cartons. They had prearranged that they would carry the big boxes to the spot directly under the open skylight to facilitate Steve and Fran's entrance into the semi-darkened room.

In a few moments, moving quickly and without speaking, they had constructed a pyramid out of the cartons. It seemed as if they had designed a kind of stairway to heaven—except that this stairway could only lead to a greater hell with the monotonously circling zombies waiting below. The creatures had nothing but time on their side.

Fran was shaking as she watched the two troopers piling box upon box. Unsure of herself, she clutched Stephen's arm as he helped her get her footing on the cartons. Then she reached for Roger's outstretched hand and he guided her down the rest of the way. An anxious Steve followed, but whether his anxiety was for Fran or himself, it was hard to tell.

Peter had not waited for the two "civilians" to enter. He was already off, as if on some dangerous mission in an exotic faraway land. He had no patience for the two neophytes. He had already written Steve off as a weakling who, although he could pilot the helicopter, was of no use on the ground. And Fran, while she was certainly spunky, was a woman, and according to Peter, subject to overemotionalism.

In the enormous room, Peter noted only two doors, one at either end. The big trooper moved up to one of them as Roger came up behind him. Roger's gun was readied.

Peter turned the doorknob. A click told him that it was unlocked, and he gave Roger a familiar nod. Roger stood several feet back, his rifle aimed directly at the door and ready to fire. Then, with a sudden, commando-like motion, Peter threw the door open and ducked away flat against the wall. Roger stiffened, his finger all but pulling his rifle trigger, but there was no apparent danger.

Roger shivered slightly and took in a sharp breath. He hadn't realized that he had been holding his breath the whole time Peter was turning the doorknob. The blond trooper was determined not to let the other man see his fear. Roger realized that in order to gain Peter's respect, he had to be as coldhearted and precise as the big trooper. And, even at a time like this, respect was very important to Roger.

It was quite obvious to Roger that Peter had become impatient with Fran and Steve. And, since they were Roger's friends, he felt that he had to become even fiercer and more courageous to make up for his friends' lack. It was so ingrained in him that he had to please the authority figure, that even while his very life was in danger, he could only think about gaining Peter's approval and acceptance.

The door opened into another vast room, which seemed to be about the same dimensions as the first room and also contained stacks of C.D. supplies.

The troopers moved cautiously through the door into the area. The room was also empty, and the sun's rays pierced through the darkness from the skylights in this room as well. The room was dead quiet, and there was a door at the other end of it.

"Double damn," Roger cried out. "Looks like a free lunch, buddy."

In the first room, Stephen had started to open one of the cartons.

"Spam!" Fran said with disgust.

"You bring a can opener?" Roger asked as he walked back into the room.

"Oh." Fran looked disheartened.

"Then don't knock Spam," Roger explained lightly. "It's got its own key."

Fran flipped the can over in her hand and found the little key.

Meanwhile, Peter had walked right past the group, as if they didn't exist. He had a fierce, concentrated look on his face, as though he were alone on a terrible mission. He walked with such a single-minded purpose that Fran mused that he had lapsed into a trance.

Peter strode toward the still-unknown door at the other end of the room. Roger, giving Fran a quick shrug of the shoulders as if he could read her mind, followed obediently.

At the door, the two troopers went through the same stylized S.W.A.T. tactics they'd used at the first door. The door swung open into a very small space. Again, to Roger's relief, there was no immediate danger.

As they entered, the men realized that they were on the top landing of a concrete and metal fire stair. Roger recalled his meeting with Peter, which had taken place in a similar location. Although it was now only twenty-four hours later, it seemed a lifetime.

The space was stifling: no windows; musty, stale air. A lone bare light bulb dangled from the ceiling, but down the stair at the next landing it was quite dark, and further down the stairs the blackness was so thick that Roger felt as if he had been swallowed by a great monster.

"Whatda ya think?" he asked Peter, trepidatiously.

Peter just stared into the darkness and then back into the storage area.

"This is the only way up here," Roger continued, his voice bouncing off the concrete walls, echoing in his ears. "Whatda ya think?"

Peter merely continued staring at the empty space. Then, as if he were alone, he turned and entered the main room, where Steve and Fran waited on pins and needles.

Roger stood for a moment on the landing, and then followed Peter into the main room. He couldn't figure him out, but at least he could rely on him for making the right decision.

Roger walked into the center of the room. As soon as he cleared the door, Peter appeared and slammed the stairway door closed, turning the flimsy lock. Then, without speaking to the other three, who stood by mutely waiting for orders, Peter started stacking the cartons against the door; a barricade against the unknown.

The group of refugees sat on the floor near the pyramid under the open skylight. They had attacked their cans of Spam with relish, and the empty tins littered the area. Stephen slept fitfully, his head in Fran's lap. Her hand was in his hair, and occasionally she patted him as one would a feverish child. This was the first real sleep he was able to have since they'd left Philadelphia.

Roger leaned against the pyramid watching Peter, who sat in the lotus position, his gun across his legs. For the past hour, Peter had not taken his eyes off the doorway to the suspicious stairwell. Infrequently, he and Roger still picked at the cans. Roger swilled water from an empty can that he had filled from one of the C.D. drums.

"You better get some sleep, too, buddy," Roger cautioned, nodding toward Stephen.

"There's an awful lot of stuff down there that we could use, brother," Peter said softly, allowing Roger into his thoughts for the first time that day.

"I know it."

Fran's deceptive tranquillity at having her stomach filled and being out of immediate danger was shattered by the men's talk. Instantly, she realized that this wasn't a rest and recovery stop, but a mercenary raid.

"They're pretty spread out down there," Peter continued. "It's a big place. I think we could outrun 'em."

"Hit and run," Roger agreed, unaware that Fran was now listening and getting increasingly angered.

"Hit and run ... maybe grab us off a radio."

Fran could stand it no longer. What was happening to them? Didn't they realize they would be no better than common criminals?

"You're crazy!" she blurted out. She extricated herself from the sleeping Steve and walked over to the two troopers.

"This place could be a gold mine," Roger said, checking his weaponry and moving quickly toward the door, where he began to remove the carton barricade. "We gotta at least check it out."

"This is exactly what we're trying to get away from," Fran said to the still-seated Peter, who was checking his own guns. "Look what happened at the airport ..."

"The only problem at the airport was stray bullets!" Peter told her belligerently. "We could outfight those dummies blindfolded."

Fran ran over to Stephen and shook him, but the exhausted pilot was dead to the world.

"Leave him be," Peter said, standing to his full height. "We're going ourselves."

He bent over and snatched up Steve's rifle. He snapped off the safety and slammed a shell into the chamber and handed it to the woman.

"That's ready to shoot," he said in a surprisingly gentle tone of voice. "Be careful."

Fran held the gun as if it were about to explode.

"The trigger squeezes real easy, but the weapon'll kick you good when it fires," Peter explained. "Be ready for that."

"Wait a minute, I—"

"Anyone but us comes up them stairs, you guys take off in the machine. We'll try to make it out to the parkin' lot. You can pick us up there."

Fran was speechless. She just stared at the man in total fright, with desperation in her eyes. She knew that the troopers had made up their minds and that her arguments would be useless.

"If we don't show up after a few minutes...we'll catch up to you some other time. You understand?"

His voice was toneless, and Fran sensed a greater meaning behind the words. She felt frozen to the spot and could only shake her head up and down like a little girl.

Roger and Peter, their faces set in stone, proceeded toward the fire stair. They pulled open the door on the top landing and were greeted by the same dimly lit corridor as before. They moved slowly out onto the landing and looked into the darkness below. Then, without looking back at the trembling figure of Fran poised at the doorway clutching her rifle, they moved slowly and silently down the steps. Suddenly, Peter stopped and turned back to Fran as if he'd forgotten to tell her something.

"You'll prob'ly hear some shooting," he said to the frightened woman. "Just don't panic, OK?"

Fran could barely manage a sigh in return.

"You'll be all right. It's our asses that's in the fire."

Fran stood on the landing until she could no longer see the men. She could still hear their footsteps padding down the narrow metal stairs.

Slowly, she turned around, the gun clutched in her arms as if it were her child. She shut the door behind her and locked it. Then, she struggled with a few of the heavier boxes and barricaded the door once again. She glanced at Stephen. How he was able to sleep throughout all this was beyond her. She just hoped that the two troopers would be back soon and that they all could get out of here for good.

By now, the two big men were two landings below the barricaded door. There was almost no light now from the single bulb two landings above. Roger clicked on his flashlight and shone the beam around. He saw that he was in a very small concrete space. The stairs went down no further and there was only one door. Peter eased down the steps behind him.

"This is the only way up there," Roger told him when they were at the same level.

They opened the door slowly and discovered that they were in another cement-walled space that also seemed small, but was fully lit.

They stepped cautiously into the room and found themselves at the end of a very long, narrow hallway. Directly across from them were two open supply rooms. The rooms had the scent of cleaning solutions and ammonia. Buckets with huge wringers and stringy mops were lined up against a stationary sink and toilet.

Their eyes followed the one wall of the hallway, and they could see a dozen or so doorways, some open, some closed. Along the opposite wall, however, there was nothing.

The far end of the hall, about a hundred yards away, opened out onto the second story of the mall proper.

The two men looked at each other, feeling like intruders in so mundane a situation—the mazelike hallway of an office. They walked down the corridor, trying the first two doors, which were locked, and finally getting lucky with the third, which was wide open.

Roger ducked into the room with his rifle raised. It was a large administration office, with rows of desks that were fully equipped for a staff of secretaries and accountants. Papers were scattered all over and chairs overturned as if people had left in a hurry.

Peter continued to the next door, which was closed but unlocked. He swung open the door and silently jumped into a room that was much more spartan, with two metal desks and a few chairs. Several phones were arranged on a plain metal table. The green-gray furniture and lack of any discriminating features except for a few pinup pictures and a girly calendar suggested a maintenance office. On one wall was a large map of the mall, with pin flags and scribbling over an acetate that covered the drawing. At the other end of the room was a huge electrical panel with circuit breakers and an entire series of master controls all keyed by a number code to another map of the mall showing electrical installations.

On the wall behind Peter was a large blackboard and two metal cabinets. The open one contained all sorts of tools, both manual and electric. There were circuit testers, walkie-talkie units and several enormous rings containing hundreds of keys, which were also colored and number-coded.

"The keys to the kingdom," Roger said in awe as he stepped behind Peter, who had grabbed one of the rings.

They scurried back into the hallway, two kids anxious to try a new toy. Roger picked up the keys and tried several in the doorknob of what looked like the corner office. The door opened onto a beautifully plush hallway, carpeted in deep rust pile with mahogany paneling leading to the executive suites, obviously the headquarters of the gigantic mall.

The labyrinth of interconnecting offices were all decorated in chrome and leather and highly polished wood. Peter and Roger wandered in and out finding themselves in the secretaries' anterooms and then ending up in connecting conference rooms. They would each take a different path and end up meeting each other again. The offices were all designer-decorated with huge paintings and sculptures and massive picture windows looking out to the woods beyond the parking lot.

The troopers finally reached a room that was not approachable through either the locked interior or corridor doors. The brass nameplate bore the inscription "C. J. Porter—President."

Roger moved to the corridor, where he joined Peter. They were very near the end of the hall, and the brightly lit shopping area was visible, although they could only make out a small section.

They realized they were in the seat of power—but they didn't realize how much power. Porter was the president of Amalgamated Industries, and the shopping malls were only a tiny part of their clothing firms, fabric mills and department stores, which were spread across the nation. That he had chosen this gigantic out-of-the-way mall for his headquarters was only one example of the eccentricity of the brilliant, powerful billionaire.

The balcony on which Peter and Roger stood was railed off against the open drop to the first floor. Across the vast atrium below they could see the opposite balcony. On the far side, only two storefronts could be seen, and both were closed off by gates.

Just as if they were about to embark across a minefield in Southeast Asia, the two troopers realized the danger inherent in their actions. They looked at each other steadily and then moved forward, each clinging to the opposite walls in the corridor.

As they reached the mall proper, they slowly and carefully peered around their respective corners.

From their viewpoint, they could see that the upper balcony totally surrounded the vast interior of the building. At several points, bridges spanned from one side to the other. Almost as if they were in a marketplace, little shops of all types ran along the entire length of the balcony. At each end there was a spectacular arched entrance to a large department store, gates to the temples of plenty. Both stores—

Porter's and Stacey's—were part, of course, of Amalgamated's empire.

Most of the stores were gated, but a few seemed open. The gates to Porter's, however, were barred and locked. Here and there tall trees reached up toward the skylights in the second-story ceiling, desperately searching for the natural light.

The living dead were conspicuous by their absence. None of them appeared on the upper balcony, although the men could sense their diabolical presence.

The troopers moved slowly and quietly to the railing and then crouched to peer down through the bars of the rail. Below, the sight was even more spectacular.

It was a wonderland of consumer's delights: stores of every type offered gaudy displays of items. There were clothing, appliances, photography equipment, audio and video outlets, even a sporting goods store with weapons in the window. Besides a modern supermarket, there were gourmet shops and natural organic food stores. A bookstore, record store, real estate agency, bank, novelty shop and gift shop were next. Each was shiny and new looking, begging the passing shopper to stop in and take a look. At each end—as in the upper concourse—like the main altars at the end of a cathedral, stood the mammoth two-story department stores, symbols of a consumer society.

The layout of the mall reminded Peter of the time that

he was in Mexico, except that all the shops were outside rather than inside. Down the center of the polished marble floor were little stalls. This was the trading place of the peasants of the consumer society, those who couldn't afford the walls, but who were just as anxious to peddle their wares. Situated among the gardens and park benches were a tobacco specialist; a jewelry stall with imitation gold necklaces, rings and bracelets; a small photography portrait stall, where in happier times mothers took their scrubbed and crying children for their first picture. There were also restaurants and snack bars to feed the exhausted, tired and hungry shoppers and give them energy to buy more and more.

There was an arcade with coin-operated machines selling everything from children's toys to blood pressure readings. Upon a large turntable, designed to spin, but now still, a late model car was on exhibit. Other turntable displays showed futuristic household appliances, many way out of the range of the typical shopper. But, even though they were unable to purchase those time-saving devices, the people still liked to gawk and fantasize that one day they might be able to.

To Roger and Peter, who weren't usually ponderous thinkers, the familiar images appeared as an archaeological discovery, symbolizing the gods and customs of a civilization now gone.

But like any civilization, there were remnants, fossils

that had been unearthed, and they trod lightly below in the aisles of the great cathedral. As the troopers, so removed now from any normal circumstances that their perspective had been distorted, moved toward their treasures, they were unaware that twenty pairs of vacantly staring eyes were watching them.

6

The two big men, in their military regalia, gazed out across the sprawling mall.

"It's Christmastime down there, buddy," Roger said with wonder.

"Fat city, brother. How we gonna work it?"

"We get into the department stores up here," Roger plotted. "They prob'ly have their own escalators inside."

"Let's check those keys," Peter suggested.

At this point, the two troopers had a narrow-minded objective—get as many supplies as possible. Neither of them stopped to think about what would fit into the small helicopter, which barely held its human passengers. They greedily headed toward the administration corridor and moved quickly down the hall toward the maintenance office.

As they left the balcony, a zombie staggered out of one of the open stores several yards away from where they had been standing. It was followed by a second creature, a female without an arm. Steadily, menacingly, they moved along the balcony toward the open corridor.

In the maintenance office, the troopers compared the keys against the coded map on the wall.

"Seventy-two . . . U and D," Roger called out as he pored over the map. "Here it is . . ."

He and Peter checked the keys and Peter found the corresponding numbers.

"Here," he said, holding it out toward Roger.

"Let's hope it's right."

"Look here," Peter said, pointing to the map. "These numbers must all be locks. Front, side, back outside, must be like loading docks. But what are these?"

He pointed to several numbered spots that seemed to be within the big Porter's department store, which they were studying.

"Washroom?" Roger guessed. "Equipment? . . . I dunno."

While Peter still stared at the map, Roger moved off toward the electrical control panel.

"I guess these gotta be the gates," Peter surmised.

Roger wandered around the room cheerfully. He noted something on the control panel with a smile and turned toward Peter.

"How about a little music?"

"What?" Peter asked, totally taken aback by the frivolity of the statement.

The big trooper moved up behind his blond partner. One of the controls on the panel was marked "Music Tape." The master switch was in the off position. Another switch was marked "Floor Exhibits" and a series of others were marked "ESCALATORS." There were dozens of master switches, which were all in the off mode.

"Power switches," Peter said to himself.

"The music might cover the noise we make," Roger said practically.

"Hit 'em all," Peter said magnanimously. "Might as well have power in everything. We might need it."

With a gleam in his eye, Roger hit all the switches one at a time.

Throughout the mall, the dull, droning sound of Muzak poured out through the loudspeakers.

Upstairs, the curious sound reached a startled Fran. She snapped the rifle into her hands, ready to fire, but she couldn't stop her hands from shaking. She had been standing, one ear cocked to the strange music below, just inside the storage area. Now she stepped into the fire stair and tried to see through the darkness. The sounds of the insipid music drifted up toward her.

"Stephen," she cried, leaning into the storage area again. "Stephen!"

His mind still fuzzy from his long-needed rest, Steve roused himself. At first he thought he had been dreaming about the music (which sounded unbelievably like what he used to hear in his dentist's office) and the frantic call of Fran's. He opened his eyes, and for a moment he couldn't place the big, cold room filled with cartons. Then he remembered and jumped up to find Fran.

He found her just inside the storage area, her eyes straining in the darkness, the rifle held to her breast. She looked so tiny in comparison to the big rifle, and she was shuddering with fear. Steve led her into the larger room and closed the door.

"Where the hell are those guys?" he asked, still half-asleep and rubbing his eyes. "What the hell is going on around here?"

Fran had calmed down sufficiently to try to explain what had transpired while Steve was asleep.

"You mean they're actually going to raid the department store? What do they expect to do with stuff from there?"

"That's just it," she told him, a look of fear in her eyes. "It's as if they've lost all perspective. We just wanted to stop here for some food and rest, or so that's what I thought. But they act like they're on some kind of secret mission. I swear, they're acting like a bunch of kids playing cops and robbers!"

Steve reached over and pulled Fran close to him.

"Don't worry," he told her in a voice that he hoped sounded calm. "They're not *that* crazy."

"Then what are we going to do? They said if they didn't come back to leave without them . . . how long should we wait?" She collapsed in a heap, crying and shaking at the same time.

All Steve could do was hold her to him tightly. He knew that if he tried to explain anything, he would break down as well.

Meanwhile, on the first floor of the mall, it looked as if a giant hand had turned on its own special mechanical toy. Only it wasn't a toy—it was an entire shopping center. The automobile turntable started spinning; the great escalators began to move up and down. Two of the living dead, caught just starting up a stalled escalator, fell and rolled down as the mechanical steps began to move.

As if it were a carnival come alive, lights blinked on in the exhibits, mechanical window displays began their robotlike motions. The zombies, bothered by the Muzak, wandered about the floor in increased confusion. Some of them swatted ineffectually at the moving exhibits.

Disturbed by the movement, the tropical birds housed in the floor-to-ceiling cages woke up, chirping and squawking for their feed.

In a pet shop, puppies and kittens in a window display whined and scrambled over one another in fright at the noise, the motion and the tottering creatures.

All that was missing was the real-life action of human shoppers. On one of the floor exhibits, a rear-projection movie started.

A narrator spoke in a friendly voice: "...and for a price that anyone can afford, you can live in these luxurious new homes by Brandon. Fully electric, central air..."

The newly distracted zombies started strutting around at a quicker pace, bumping into each other and the moving displays. Some tried to return the way they'd come in, but they only bounced off the glass door. The one who had been circling endlessly had fallen to the ground, and his head was wedged between the ground and the door, preventing anyone else from entering or leaving.

In the maintenance office, the troopers readied themselves for their raid. Peter secured the vital key ring to his utility belt, and they moved out.

Roger's mind was a million miles away as he moved through the doorway and into the corridor. He was still lightheaded from the thought of all those wonderful goodies waiting for him downstairs. He was totally unprepared for his head-on meeting with one of the zombies from the balcony. Startled, he ducked back into the room. The zombie, blindly reaching out with clutching hands, rounded the corner and appeared in the doorway. With precision accuracy, Peter raised his gun and fired two shots cleanly through the creature's head.

On the top of the fire stair, Fran jumped as the sound of the shots reverberated through the enormous mall.

"Jesus Christ," Steve screamed, grabbing the rifle from the petrified woman. "They're maniacs."

He looked long and hard at Fran. He was torn between staying here with her and charging downstairs to see what was going on. Fran needed protection, but he also needed to prove to her, to himself, and to those two macho supermen downstairs that he could join the battle.

Fran saw the indecision in his eyes.

"Stephen, don't go down there," she pleaded. "Stephen, please!"

"It's all right," he said calmly, starting to make his way down the stairs.

In the corridor of the administration offices below, Roger and Peter were stepping over the corpse.

"What da ya think?" Roger asked as the second zombie, the armless female, came into his view. He fired his weapon and the creature fell in a heap. As if nothing had happened, he continued his conversation.

"Bag it or try for it?" he asked his comrade.

"You game?" Peter asked.

Roger nodded, and the two men ran down the hall toward the mall. With their rifles poised, they seemed like commandos on an important raid.

All that was missing was the blare of the trumpets as Roger and Peter charged into battle. The enemy wandered around the first floor, attracted by the sound but confused by the sudden intrusion of the noise into their quiet domain. In misguided, staggering strides, they walked this way and that, glazed, vacant eyes passing by the stores and shops with their glittering array of goodies.

Several of the zombies walked toward the escalators, which in their dormant state had been easy to negotiate. But now, the moving escalators tossed the zombies this way and that. Some of them tried going up the down escalators, while those few creatures who moved onto the up escalator fell against each other from the movement. They seemed like tumbling pins in a bowling alley.

One of the zombies that fell on the escalator was carried upward despite its awkward position. Another managed to keep its balance by holding onto the handrail.

And unbeknownst to Roger and Peter, several creatures had begun to move up the steps of a stationary stairway that ran from the first to the second floor and was located at the other end of the mall from the administration offices.

Meanwhile, a sweating, nervous Steve was cautiously making his way down the steps of the fire stair. His rifle ready, his palms dripping, he tried to control his jittery nerves. Fran looked anxiously from the top landing.

Several hundred yards away, Roger and Peter were barreling toward the huge gate that locked off the entrance to Porter's. The two troopers came to a crashing halt. Four or five zombies were staggering their way down a side concourse toward the troopers. They were about three hundred feet away.

Roger kept his rifle leveled off in the direction of the creatures while Peter tried the lock at the middle of the big roll gate.

Beads of perspiration formed on his forehead as he fumbled with the keys and finally found the proper one. When it sank with a click into the receptacle that was right at the floor and the tumbler turned successfully, Peter sighed in relief.

"All right!" he yelled to his friend.

Creeping toward them, however, was the creature that had fallen on the escalator. His ghoulish companion, the one who was able to ride the whole way without falling, was also approaching the two unsuspecting troopers.

Suddenly, to Roger's surprise, the head of the standing zombie became visible from Roger's perspective. He raised his gun and aimed for the creature's forehead.

Peter tried to lift the roll gate but it wouldn't move. It was still locked!

"You bastard," Peter screamed in frustration.

"What?" Roger asked, his attention focused on the approaching ghouls.

"Still locked . . . on the side," Peter said, pointing to another assembly. He moved to the far side of the gate. The same key fit, and Peter repeated the process.

But Roger could not share his joy. His attention was on the creature riding the escalator, almost near the top. Just as Roger was about to shoot, something caught his eye.

The fallen zombies, which up until now could not be seen behind the escalator railwall, suddenly came tumbling out onto the balcony floor.

A shaken Roger took fire, but his aim was inaccurate. The pressures were starting to build, and for one moment he stopped to think about the idiocy of what he was doing. That was his downfall, because it disturbed his concentration. His shot hit the standing zombie in the neck, tearing half the throat away. The creature was thrown off balance enough to lose its footing. It fell back down the escalator, but before it reached the bottom, it stopped rolling. The steps carried it back up toward the second floor again. It was still very much alive.

Two more creatures on the balcony struggled to stand. Roger watched them and then looked back over his shoulder. To his horror he saw that zombies from the side concourse were about a hundred and fifty feet away.

Working against time, Peter turned the key in the lock, but again the gate would not budge. It moved slightly, and Peter could see that it was free from the middle and far right mechanism, but that there was a third lock on the far left. He moved to it quickly.

As if they possessed some kind of primitive antennae, the other creatures on the first floor began to take note of the action upstairs, and they, too, started to move.

Zombies surrounded the troopers on all sides now. Those who had managed to climb the stationary stairway were now beginning to reach the second floor, but they were far down the main balcony. In order to reach the entrance to Porter's they would have to pass the administrative corridor.

Roger steadied his nerves and collected his thoughts. In the back of his mind he was wondering what the hell was taking Peter so damn long.

He fired his rifle again and one of the nearby zombies fell in a heap. His confidence restored, he looked around for more of the enemy to mow down.

"For God's sake, Stephen," Fran called down the stairway upon hearing Roger's shot. "Let's get up on the roof..." she cried out to him desperately.

At the middle landing, Steve stared down into the darkness below. More gunfire could be heard from the mall. He was stuck: part of him wanted to run up to Fran and escape with her in the chopper. The other part wanted to go down and get into the action.

"It's all right," he said, trying to convince himself as well. "Those things don't move fast enough to catch us." The last part of his sentence was practically drowned out by the staccato beat of the gunfire.

With a loud rumble, the large gate finally freed itself from its bonds and rolled up. Peter ducked into the store even as the gate was still rising. The momentum of the heavy metal carried the lip out of Peter's grasp, and it rolled out of his reach. It jerked up into its fully open position and rolled back down slightly, but still Peter could not reach the lip. It was over ten feet to the ceiling. The bottom of the gate rested about three feet above Peter's outstretched fingertips.

Panicking for the first time since the whole horrible situation evolved, Peter turned to see the zombies advancing.

Roger had just dropped another with a clean shot through the head, then he backed into the archway of Porter's entranceway. Desperately, Peter looked around for something to stand on in order to reach the elusive gate.

Steadily, the zombies advanced toward the arch.

Peter grabbed a small counter used to display shoes, but it was deceptively heavy, and he called out to Roger.

"Here...come on..."

Unfortunately, Roger had to abandon his strategic post at the arch in order to help Peter drag over the little counter. They dragged it to a point just at the side of the open arch and Peter immediately jumped up on top of it. At that instant, a zombie rounded the corner and grabbed at Peter's leg.

Startled, Peter started to kick, and the awkward motion caused him to fall off the little counter. Gracefully, he landed on his feet, but he was out on the balcony beyond the arch. Quickly, Roger brought his rifle butt around against the creature's head and the zombie fell backward, but it was still alive.

A few other creatures were only a few feet from Peter, who was now unarmed as his gun sat on the small counter inside the store. Roger leveled off his rifle but couldn't fire, since Peter was in his line of vision. Suddenly, Peter made a move, and like a football player, cut to the left and then to the right. Diving, he threw himself at one of the creatures, carrying it into the store.

Roger, all the while, had been firing on the advancing zombies, dropping one and then another. "Behind you, behind you," Peter cried to Roger as he jumped back up on the counter.

The creature trapped in the store had knocked over a cosmetics display and tubes of lipsticks, compacts, cylinders of eye liner and mascara rolled around under its feet. Finally, the creature leaned against the glass case that displayed false eyelashes and plastic nails and was able to regain its footing.

In an instant, Roger turned and fired. The creature fell. In that time, Peter was able to grab the lip of the roll gate, and he started to bring it down.

During all the commotion, several creatures gathered in the archway. They stood there, clutching at the air with clawlike hands. One stood in the middle of the path of the roll gate, blocking its downward progress.

Roger took careful aim and fired point-blank into the forehead of the zombie who was blocking the gate. It flew backward, crashing into a few of its brothers. As the gate started to lower, the clutching hands of the other zombies seemed to reach out and try to strangle Roger for killing one of their own. Roger dropped his rifle and ran to the gate now to try and help pull it down. Peter, still holding onto the lip, jumped off the counter to get more leverage.

The two troopers were now sweating profusely. Large areas of dark were spreading under the arms and on the back of their uniforms. They were struggling to move the gate steadily down. It was now only four feet from the floor, but the creatures, who seemed to feel no pain, were throwing themselves in the path of the descending gate, making it more difficult. One of them tried to crawl underneath, and its torso just got through as the gate slammed down against its chest. Its arms grabbed for Peter's legs, and its mouth gaped open. Its mutilated body prevented the gate from engaging in the floor mechanisms.

Roger let go of the gate as Peter tried to hold it against the creatures outside. Both men were exhausted now, and barely had enough strength to pull the gate down, let alone battle the zombies. But some inner resource, some extra dose of adrenaline, coursed through their veins. Grabbing his rifle, Roger brought the butt straight down, crushing the pawing zombie's skull. The zombie went limp, and Roger tried to push it clear of the gate, but the pressure was too enormous.

"Let up a little . . . let up a little," he gasped to Peter.

Peter let up the pressure and the gate rose a few inches. But, as more and more zombies appeared outside, they too clutched at the roll gate. The openings in the grid were only big enough for their fingers; their hands could not reach through. However, the force of their pushing in unison caused the gate to go higher and higher...higher than Peter intended it to go to clear the obstructing corpse.

With his rifle butt, Roger managed to push the dead zombie clear except for one of its arms. From outside, a creature's hand suddenly grabbed Roger's weapon.

For a moment, the macabre thought passed through Roger's mind: it was like the tug-o-war game he used to play with his friends when he was younger. Only now the stakes were life or death!

"Come on...come on," Peter cried out. He was having a harder time holding the gate, and it inched upward, out of his reach.

Roger decided to let go of the gun barrel, and the creature flew back into the crowd, brandishing its prize. Roger grabbed for the gate to help Peter, and they tried again to close it.

"The arm...that arm's in the way," Peter told him.

Roger squatted and managed to throw the dead zombie's arm, which was now only held onto the body with a thin strand of muscle, clear.

With a slight shiver of revulsion at what he had just done, Roger grabbed the gate again. Now with both of the men focusing their attention and strength on the gate, it moved down more steadily.

At the last moment, another clutching arm jutted into the store, but when the gate hit it, it withdrew. Finally, and not a minute too soon, the gate clicked solidly into place.

The two troopers stepped back from the gate and collapsed against another glass display case. This one held sunglasses, suntan lotion, and various vacation-time necessities. The men gathered their strength and watched in horror as the creatures still moaned and gurgled, slamming against the gate. Their fingers clutched futilely at the grid, but they were unable to budge it.

"Well ... we're in. Now, how the hell we gonna get back?" Roger asked, scanning the department store. About ten or twelve zombies tried to get in. Several others made their way along the balcony. Roger also noted in disgust that six lay dead along the floor, their heads bleeding profusely from gunshot wounds or smashed skulls.

"Let's go shopping first," Peter said, calm, cool and collected once again. Roger marveled at his cold-hearted approach.

The two big troopers backed into the aisles of the store. The creatures outside still pushed and shoved at the gate. The one with Roger's rifle had the instincts to use it as a bludgeon, but it had no effect.

A trembling Stephen opened the door to the administrative corridor. A stench filled his nostrils, and a feeling of claustrophobia enveloped him. Zombies littered the dark, narrow hallway. He could see to the open end of the hallway and noted that it was inactive. He let his eyes roam along slowly, observing the washrooms and the long row of doors that led into the various offices. The sound of his breathing echoed in the corridor, and he could hear the blood pulsating through his veins. He was primed, ready for any attack.

He moved slowly into the corridor, letting the fire stair door close behind him.

Fran, who had been staring at the beam of Steve's flashlight so hard that her eyes hurt, gave a gasp as she watched the beam narrow, flicker, and finally disappear. She heard the door click shut in the darkness.

"Stephen...Jesus God..." she uttered in fright as she backed into the storage area. She moved quickly to the little pyramid of cartons that led up to the roof and sat on the bottom carton, biting her fingers.

The silence was unbearable. Every sound, the creaking of the building, the wind outside, sounded as if it were amplified tenfold.

Meanwhile, in Porter's, Roger was riding down the escalator. On his back was a backpack, already filled with goods. He could have been a regular shopper except for his uniform and rifle. When he got off the moving stair on the ground floor, the recorded music tape ended. He was struck by the eerie quiet of his surroundings, while the tape machine rewound itself.

He moved through the clothing department, browsing through the racks of the latest fashions. His eye was caught by a leather blazer. While he admired it, he backed into one of the store mannequins and the dead, vacantly staring eyes startled him. He snatched up a lined windbreaker and tied it around his waist by its arms, and then he trotted off down another aisle, looking for Peter.

He found the big trooper with a radio under his arm, involved in snatching up a small television.

"Hey man, we can't carry all this shit..." Roger protested.

Peter ignored him, and turned a corner where he dumped the articles into something that Roger could not see. As Roger trotted over, he saw that Peter had a big gardening cart already heaped with goods.

"Oh," Roger remarked sarcastically, "we're gonna just wheel right by 'em, right!"

"We gonna try, brother," Peter said grimly. "We ain't doin' this for the exercise. We might as well try to get what we can."

"There's no way this is gonna happen..." Roger said, confused. Even though he didn't understand the plan, he began to help Peter throw things into the cart.

They raced down the hardware aisle, tossing in tools and other supplies, such as electrical cables, flashlights and batteries. It was almost as if they were contestants on a game show, like Supermarket Sweep, where they had five minutes in a store to grab whatever they could. They tried to put things in that would help them if they were stranded in a primitive area. Their thoughts were to get as far away from this civilization gone berserk as possible.

Stephen, on the other side of the structure, was busily examining maps and electrical equipment in the maintenance office. He rummaged through one of the desks. He wondered where Peter and Roger were now. He hadn't heard any gunfire for at least fifteen minutes and considered the possibility that they had made a get-away. But where would they go by foot? He had the keys to the copter—and they wouldn't get far without him. At least that made him feel useful—and powerful.

At the open end of the corridor that led out to the second-story balcony, zombies wandered past. They headed for the department store entrance, where many of the creatures still clawed at the roll gate.

The zombies moved randomly. Some were already leaving the gate, as their prey was now out of sight within the store. They began to wander aimlessly.

Three of the creatures turned into the administrative corridor and started toward the offices.

Stephen had, meanwhile, found a large binder in a

desk drawer. It contained all the plans for the mall, duplicating the charts on the walls and including many others. He smiled with pleasure at the thought that here was all the material that he needed: a complete maintenance manual revealing all the workings and the entire layout of the huge shopping mall. Minute by minute, Steve's composure and confidence were building. He didn't have that sinking sensation in his stomach that he felt when he thought all was lost. Maybe it would still be possible for him and Fran to start a new life, a family. There must be some area of the North American continent that was free from this terror. They would try for Canada—if only the two troopers weren't with them. With their extra weight, which was almost twice as much as his and Fran's, they were a drain on the fuel supply. But they were fighters and quick thinkers. On the other hand, Steve wouldn't have stopped here in the first place and they might have arrived up north in safety if they hadn't been wasting their time ransacking a department store and playing soldier with a bunch of ghouls. He slammed the drawer shut in disgust.

The elevator doors slid open with a loud whoosh and the two troopers were revealed in the car. They pushed their cart out into the second-story aisle of the big store. Their attention was drawn to the roll gate and the creatures that clawed at it ineffectually. They rolled the overflowing cart up very close to the gate. When the zombies saw their human prey again on the balcony, their moaning and clutching began anew.

The troopers left the cart and disappeared back among the aisles. They ran onto the interior escalator, bounding down faster than the moving steps. Then, they ran across the first floor until they could see the lower level roll gate. Since there hadn't been much going on at the gate for a while, the creatures had moved away, and a few could be seen wandering the concourse.

"Let's go, brother . . . the old okey-doke!" Peter said with animation.

They moved up to the roll gate.

"Hey, ugly," Roger called out to a zombie who lumbered past.

The creature turned slowly. Its expressionless face registered the sound of a movement, and then it lumbered for the gate with a moaning roar. The gaping blood-dripping mouth and clutching hands dove for the gate, which popped forward from its thrust. The action caused Roger to jump, even though there was no immediate danger of the gate giving in.

"Let's raise some hell . . . hey . . . hey . . ." Peter shouted.

"Over here," Roger called out. "Let's go over here."

The creatures' antennae were up again, and the signals they received were coming from the department store entrance. As one, they lumbered along toward the gate. When they reached it, several pushed at the metal grids. The troopers backed away, but stayed in sight of the creatures.

Roger seemed jumpy.

"Just give it time," Peter said in a soothing tone. "Give it time."

Upstairs, the dozen or so zombies at the upper gate were attracted by the commotion on the first floor. They too began to move away from the gate and lumber along the balcony toward the stairways and escalators.

Stephen opened another drawer in the maintenance office. Rummaging around through old tea bags, unsharpened pencils, ones with broken points, bits of string and rubber bands, old forms and pieces of clean rags, he found a loaded handgun, which he stuffed into his belt. Then he moved to the large cabinets containing the walkie-talkies and the keys.

In the corridor outside, stray zombies, who were not attracted to the commotion generated by Peter and Roger, wandered in and out of the executive offices as they drew nearer to the maintenance room.

Steve picked up the maintenance manual and started to leave the office. He was planning to go upstairs and go over all the exits and entranceways with Fran and try to plot out some kind of plan. He didn't want to wait around all day until Roger and Peter stopped masquerading as commandos and took some decisive action.

As he peered around the corner, he saw the first zombie approaching from the hall. The creature saw him as well and reacted by reaching out its arms. Steve estimated it was about twenty feet away. That was all he had to know—he ducked back into the office and slammed the door. His heart began pounding again and a convulsive trembling overtook him. Unbeknownst to him, a second creature was moving up behind the first, and a third entered the corridor from the accounting office.

Steve noticed that the metal door locked only with a key. He fumbled for a moment with his rifle, then he dove for the key cabinet. Panicking, he realized that there were hundreds of keys on the rings. He looked at the wall map. Suddenly, the room spun before him. In his anxiety, he couldn't focus on either the maps or the hundreds of keys. How would he lock the door? he wondered in alarm.

In the hallway, the first creature slammed against the door. It ran its hands blindly along the door, missing the doorknob entirely. Then, in frustration, it pounded on the door with its open hands.

Behind the door, the pounding only increased Steve's panic. He stared at the map, trying to calm the dizziness so that he could focus on the maze of numbers.

Meanwhile, the second creature had reached the door and it, too, was clawing at it. The third approached slowly.

Rattling among the keys, Steve's fingers were shaking so vigorously that he couldn't hold the key ring still in order to decipher the numbers.

Outside, one of the creatures, through its random clutching, was able to take hold of the knob and pushed in and out, not yet turning it.

Steve's eyes bulged with terror as he saw the moving knob. He threw himself against the door, still trying to read the numbers on the keys. The knob turned slowly, and there was pressure from the other side, even against Steve's weight. He managed to slam the door shut despite the creature's insistent pushing. Frustrated in his attempt to read the small numbers on the key ring, Steve threw it down and grabbed his gun.

During Steve's battle with the zombies in the administrative wing, others were falling over one another as they tried to move down the up escalator. They scrambled to their feet and moved toward the department store entrance.

In the concourse, many of the creatures were moving toward the gate, and already there were a dozen or so clinging and shoving at the metal grid.

"OK," Peter reported. "They're coming..." Through the crowd he could see several other creatures lurching down the stationary steps. He readied his walkie-talkie, pulling the antenna out full.

"Go on up," he told Roger. "Stay outa sight, but lemme know when it's clear enough."

Roger, clutching his walkie-talkie, disappeared among the aisles. As if he were running across a minefield in Nam, he crouched, going deeper into the store. Peter tried to hold the attention of the creatures at the gate.

"Right here, babies," he taunted. "This is where it's at...you dumb-ass suckers. You dumb...you are *dumb*!"

Panting, Roger reached the back elevator, and as the doors closed, he breathed a sigh of relief and pushed the button for the balcony level. The doors glided open, and he moved through the second-floor aisles with the stealth of a panther.

"I think we can move the wagon," he said into his walkie-talkie to Peter.

"Clear?" came the crackling reply.

"Not altogether, but they're spread out pretty good...enough to move the wagon."

Just as Peter was about to reply, a few creatures slammed against the first-floor gate, but it held securely. Peter stared at the ghouls for a moment as he lowered his talk unit. Slowly, a confused and upset look on his face, he backed away into the depth of the store. He was an odd sight: an armed and obviously well-worn soldier walking through aisles of the latest in cosmetics, accessories and jewelry.

Upstairs, Roger peered out from behind a counter and saw that the second-floor gate was clear. On the balcony, he noted, several creatures still wandered around aimlessly, but most of them had already moved down the steps and escalators.

Peter was still visible to the zombies at the first-floor entrance. He clipped his talk unit onto his belt and then ducked and disappeared among the aisles.

He ran, crouching out of sight, until he rounded a far wall and came up into the elevator and entered the car. Breathing heavily, and leaning against a side wall for support, he pushed "2" and watched as the doors glided shut. He felt the gears engage and the car move upward.

The doorknob to the maintenance room rotated again, and the door pushed against Steve's weight. His feet slid on the linoleum floor, and this time he could not get the door closed.

Biting his lip so that he drew blood, he made the sign of the cross and backed suddenly into the room, holding his rifle high. The door flew open with a great slam against the interior wall, and the three zombies advanced into the office.

With a sense of calm that amazed even himself, Stephen took careful aim at the leader and fired.

Just as the elevator doors opened on the balcony level, Peter heard the sound of Steve's shot. For a moment he hesitated, as if to get his bearings, and then he ran toward the entrance arch. Roger was at work at one of the side locks on the gate. The gunfire caused him also to stop as he was unlocking the mechanism. He looked at Peter questioningly, the hand with the key poised in the air.

The zombies on the balcony heard the sound as well, and they walked around in confusion, attracted by the noise.

"What the hell is that?" thundered Peter as he walked up behind Roger.

"Fuzz maybe?"

"Or maybe Flyboy," he said gruffly. "Where's it comin' from?"

"Can't tell," Roger said quietly, returning to his work. He had forgotten about Steve and Fran after he'd left them, and now he felt as if he might have deserted them. They certainly weren't equipped to deal with this horror show, and he felt somewhat responsible for their being here.

"Come on," Peter said impatiently. "Open up."

"Maybe we should see what's happenin'..." Roger said, feeling guilty. Peter ignored his plaintive tone.

"Open up. I can get the wagon over. If it is Flyboy, let's get him on *our* side."

Roger moved toward the second lock, confused by Peter's seemingly disjointed answer. Another shot was heard.

Peter set his weapon on the floor.

"You just cover me good, you hear?" he warned.

Roger moved to the third and final lock as Peter stood and grabbed onto the handle of the cart.

To Steve's extreme surprise, the body of a zombie fell to the floor, dead. Its head had been shot clean through. Nearby lay the corpse of the first creature to break into the office, also a surprise to Steve, who was so petrified he was barely conscious of what he was doing.

As the third staggered into the room, Steve was ready for him. He held the rifle out in front, and as the creature walked toward the gun, Steve held his hands on the trigger.

But the creature was too quick for him. Before Steve knew it, the zombie had lunged suddenly and its hands grabbed the gun barrel. Steve fired, but the blast tore through the creature's chest, not slowing him in the least. Steve struggled to raise the barrel, but the motion of the zombie made it impossible to aim accurately. The gun fired again, this time grazing the zombie's neck. The ghoul was covered with dripping blood and pus. Its appearance was so distasteful to Steve that he had a hard time looking at him so as to take proper aim. With a sudden burst of energy, the creature was able to wrench the gun free. Then, it started its slow deliberate approach toward Steve. It had tossed the rifle across the room, where it slammed to the floor by one of the desks.

The zombie backed Steve against the wall, right next to the key cabinet. With his eyes glued to the zombie's face, which seemed extremely animated, almost as if it really knew what was going on, Steve reached around on top of the key cabinet, trying to find some weapon. He almost wept with joy as he felt some tools in the cabinet and came up with a hammer. The zombie was just about to reach him when he pulled the hammer out and upset the cabinet. The zombie fumbled with the cabinet at its feet, but it did not fall.

With a sudden burst of energy, Steve raised the hammer in order to smash the creature's head, but he missed and the zombie grabbed at his arm, trying to bite it with its gaping hole of a mouth.

Steve was able to wrench free, and the force of his movement caused the two bodies to fall to the floor. Now the creature was clutching at the man's legs, its teeth bared like an animal's. Steve kicked desperately and managed to land a blow squarely in the creature's face. The zombie came on after him again, and from his crawling position, Steve was able to bring up the hammer against the creature's jaw. The creature fell back enough for Steve to crawl across the floor away from it. But, the ghoul followed persistently. Steve reached the desk, where he grabbed up his rifle. Rolling on the floor, he fired several shots into the creature. A gushing red hole appeared on its forehead and between the eyes. Finally, it rolled to the floor, writhing in agony, destroyed.

With a rumble, the second-floor gate rolled up and Peter ran out of the store with his cart full of merchandise.

The action caught the attention of several of the creatures that were still wandering around the balcony. They turned slowly in the direction of the disturbance.

Just as he rounded the corner, Peter almost collided with one creature. The momentum of the run across the floor almost caused the cart to fall over. Luckily, Peter managed to right it and get past, running as fast as he could toward the opening of the administrative corridor.

Roger did not let the gate roll up too high this time. He stabilized the metal grid well within reach; then he stood his post with Peter's rifle. Several creatures approached from the opposite direction. Roger fired at the closest one. It fell with a thud. He raised the rifle to fire at the others, but they were too far away for him to be accurate and he didn't want to waste any bullets. Even with all the supplies they had garnered, he knew that all the bullets would be needed sooner or later.

Concurrently, Stephen stepped over the corpses in the office and grabbed up the maintenance manual again. He rushed into the corridor, hoping that he wouldn't meet any more unwelcome guests. To his utter dismay, three more creatures moved toward him up the hallway. At first he froze, then he started backing toward the fire stair, his rifle poised.

Peter was charging along, with the supplies shaking on top of the cart like jelly. Just as he was about to reach the mouth of the corridor, a zombie stepped out of the hallway right in his path. Peter slammed the cart squarely into the creature's legs. The zombie fell into the cart, on top of the supplies. The big man slammed the load against a wall at the mouth of the corridor. Before the zombie was able to get its balance, the big trooper reached down and grabbed the creature by its jacket lapels. It was almost comical—a big bouncer ejecting the unruly patron from a bar. With all his might, Peter flung the dead thing out against the balcony railing. The creature flipped over the rail at its waist but did not fall off the balcony. Its arms and legs were flailing as Peter came up quickly behind it and flipped it over the rail. It plummeted to the ground silently, and made a loud thud when it landed.

At the second-level store entrance, Roger fired again at a zombie that was drawing dangerously near. Other creatures throughout the area were again attracted to the entrance and converged as if it were a giveaway being conducted during the normal working hours.

As Peter wheeled the cart into the mouth of the corridor, he saw Steve at the other end of the hall being boxed in by the three converging zombies.

"Hold it, Flyboy!" he screamed.

Steve froze at the sound, which seemed familiar. He could barely see Peter, since his line of vision was blocked by the advancing ghouls, who were barely thirty feet away from him now and steadily closing in.

"Don't go in the stairway!" Peter instructed, a note of panic in his voice.

Stephen was confused. The creatures were advancing, and Peter was giving him conflicting advice.

"Don't open that door, baby. You'll lead them right up with you."

Steve was on the verge of panic. The zombies were merely ten feet away. He was trapped!

"Run for it!" came Peter's strident command. "Run this way!"

The zombies drew closer and closer. Steve could feel the heat of their foul breath.

"Come on, man," Peter coached. "Run this way. You can run right through 'em. We gotta lead 'em away from here!"

With one deep breath, Steve sized up the corridor. It would be a squeeze, but there was room to run past the creatures.

"Come on, Flyboy. You can make it. Come on!" Peter cried.

With a sudden jerky move, Steve broke into a run. He passed the first zombie easily. The second made a grab as he passed but Steve kept his footing even though he slammed against the wall of the corridor, practically crushing his shoulder. A sharp pain shot through his right side. He kept moving forward. He knew to stop would mean certain death.

The third zombie loomed in his path. Like a charging bull, Steve lowered his head and slammed into the ghoul's chest. The creature fell back, flying against the wall. Steve fell as well, and tumbled toward the mouth of the passageway. He regained his footing as the creatures, now standing once again, turned to pursue him.

"Now . . . hit for the department store . . . go!" Peter told him as he ran to the end of the hall where the big trooper waited.

In unison, the two men ran across the balcony. They slammed into two other zombies, which clutched and grabbed at them without success.

Steve followed Peter to where Roger was firing at still another creature that was getting too close. It fell right under the balcony entrance arch of the big store.

Other zombies approached, but Steve and Peter dove into the arch in time, and the three men managed to lower the gate without a problem.

The zombies converged on the area as they had before, still clawing, clutching and shoving the metal cage, but they were unable to enter. It held them out securely.

The three men moved away, each giving silent thanks for their close escape. As they backed away, the only sound was of their heavy exhausted breathing.

"Downstairs again," Peter said after a moment's rest. "Same trick."

They moved through the aisles of the store and crashed down the escalator.

"What do we do?" Steve sputtered when they reached the first floor and ran toward the lower gate, wheezing with exhaustion.

"Let 'em know we're here," Roger said. He started to shout: "Whooooo hooooooo ... over here ... Yeeee ahhhhhhhhhhh!"

Steve started to laugh, out of relief and also at the ludicrousness of the situation. Peter smiled at him for the first time.

"You did all right this time, Flyboy. How 'bout it?" he said with genuine feeling.

Steve laughed some more. It was nervous at first, but soon it built into a real wholehearted belly laugh.

"Whoooooooooooooooooopeeeeeeee..." he let out long and loudly.

The new kid on the block had been accepted, and he felt just like a child again. They all hugged each other with the joy of their victory. And a temporary victory was better than none at all.

7

After a few minutes of whooping it up with the other men, the reality of the situation hit Stephen squarely in the jaw. His body wavered for a second and he felt sick and weak in the knees. But it was also a good feeling, a feeling that he could do anything he wanted to, as long as he put his mind to it. His family had always been a cerebral one, and he had never been taught the pure joy that comes from physical accomplishment. Now, as he stood sweating and panting with the two troopers, a strange calmness overcame him.

But the pleasant feeling was short-lived. The three men continued to shout at the creatures through the cage, and the repulsive beasts were already gathering at the gate. The zombies had lost all of the individuality they had when they were human, but Steve noticed that they were of many shapes, sizes and ages, some with the horrible wounds that had caused their deaths.

There was a middle-aged gray-haired man in a business suit; a housewife, possibly in her forties, in an apron; a well-dressed young woman, once attractive with long blond hair, in a skirt and sweater, probably an office worker. There were some children, about ten to thirteen, who looked like they'd just come home from school; a construction worker with a beard; a young black man with an Afro and wire-rimmed glasses; and a grandmother-type with a gray bun at the back of her neck. A few more men in nondescript work clothes hung around the gate, but it didn't much matter what any of them had been in their former lives, they were all horrible and partially decomposed now, and their strength had nothing to do with their appearance. The youngest were most repulsive, as many had died of violent causes and not of old age.

Peter had warned Steve not to soften when a child or older woman approached him. They were all deadly.

Out on the concourse, a few zombies wandered aimlessly, but most of them turned toward the direction of the first-floor department store arch, where the men were doing their best to stir up a racket.

On the upstairs balcony, the creatures that had collected there were again moving toward the stationary steps and the escalators.

The three creatures that Steve had battled with in the administrative corridor moved toward the open mall. Two walked out on the balcony, but the third turned into an open office. They seemed as stiff-legged and awkward as wind-up dolls. The last one staggered back out, spun around and headed down the hall toward the fire stair.

Fran, who had been waiting nearly an hour for Steve's return, heard the faint whooping of the men as she moved toward the stairway door, which was still open. She couldn't imagine what the sound was for. It seemed like a celebration of some sort, and then the horrid thought crossed her mind, What if they had cracked under the pressure? Or what if Steve were dead and Peter and Roger were happy? She stopped herself from those silly thoughts. Sitting up here alone was making her crazy. She was starting to imagine the wildest things. She wished Steve would hurry back.

She stepped out into the landing and looked down into the vast murkiness of the fire stair. Suddenly the shouting stopped. The silence was worse, and she felt desperate with fear. The trembling began, and she moved back into the storage room, and then back onto the landing. She didn't know where to turn. Where the hell were Steve, Roger and Peter? Who did they think she was, leaving her here all alone? She wasn't a child, she could be of some use, but all they wanted to do was play soldier and leave her up in this godforsaken room with a bunch of cartons.

"Shit," she screamed out to the empty landing, her fear turning to anger. She took a few steps down the stairway. She thought she saw something moving in the dark. Frozen with fear, she stopped on the third stair from the top, turned around and ran back up.

"God dammit!" The screaming seemed to help. At least she heard the sound of a human voice, even though it was only her own.

Once more she started down the steps. She wanted to see what was happening, but she really should have been armed. Steve had taken the only other rifle.

In the corridor below, the creature wandered into another office and then spun around and walked out again, as if it were playing some insane game with itself.

"We just gotta wait longer before we move," Roger told Steve and Peter as they crouched in the shadows of the aisles. The zombies crashed against the first-floor gate like a huge wave. The gate held fast.

"No. There's always a chance of some of them stayin' up on the balcony," Peter replied.

"Yeah, but we can handle that," Roger said, shifting position but staying down low. "We can break through."

"If any of them see us or hear us, they'll just follow us on up. It's no good."

"We can sure as hell outrun 'em ... load up what we can and get outa here."

The big man thought for a second. Then he said, seriously, "I'm thinkin' maybe we got a good thing goin' here. Maybe we shouldn't be in such a hurry to leave ..."

"Oh, man ..." Roger looked disappointed. He pounded his right fist into his other hand and wouldn't face Peter.

"If we could get back up there without them catchin' on, we could hole up for a while. At least long enough to catch a breath. Check out the radio. See what's happenin' ..."

"Man, I don't know ..."

Steve sat up and then crawled over to the troopers.

"There's some kind of passageway over the top of the stores."

The troopers looked at the young pilot, almost surprised to hear him speak. They had expected that he'd be too shell-shocked from his experience to utter a sound.

"I don't know if it's just heating ducts or it's some kind of access. I saw it on a map."

"Upstairs," Peter gave the command. "Let's go."

The three moved off down the aisles, then ducked out of sight around the corner. As if they were imprisoned against their will, the zombies clutched and grabbed at the metal gate, moaning and rattling the grid loudly.

In the maintenance hallway, the lumbering zombie tripped over the thick manual lying on the floor. Then it wandered blindly into another office, ignoring the book as well as the corpses that littered the corridor.

Fran had made it to the middle landing of the fire stair. Suddenly, she was overcome by a wave of nausea. She held her stomach, retching. Beads of sweat broke out on her forehead, and she felt dizzy. She practically fell to the landing, and sat there, letting her head flop against the wall. She could taste the salt of her tears.

She had never been so miserable in her life. And, what a life it was too. She didn't know what would happen in the next few minutes, let alone the next few years. And what would happen to the life within her? What future was there for the child that she carried inside?

"Watch it...don't let 'em see you," Peter told the men as the upstairs doors of the department store elevator opened and they trotted out. As they cleared the wall, they could see the entrance arch. There were no zombies at the gate, but two were seen drifting along the balcony outside.

The men moved stealthily along the aisles. Above

them in the ceiling was a series of large grillwork panels. Peter shone his flashlight beam into one.

"Looks big enough to crawl through," Roger said, as they observed the ceiling, which was about twelve feet high. The light beam penetrated the grille to reveal a fairly large space above.

"They're locked," Peter told him.

"Damn, that's those other lock numbers we saw on the chart."

"Why the hell would they be locked?" Steve asked.

"Jackpot, Flyboy," Peter said, patting Steve on the back. "You're all right."

"What?" Roger spun around, confused.

"They're locked because you can get through 'em easy from the other part of the building," Peter explained to his two comrades.

"Over here," Steve called to them. He had noticed that one of the ceiling grids was very close to the elevators. Peter looked at the grid and then down at the double doors.

"The elevator shaft!" It was as if a light bulb had gone on in his head.

He ran over and hit the button. The doors flew open.

"Hold 'em," Peter instructed Roger.

Roger stood against the rubber safety bumper, holding the car doors open wide. Peter stepped up on the hand railing that ran around the car, and he reached up for the escape hatch, which was held in place by four nub-headed bolts. He removed the bolts quickly and was able to dislodge the hatch cover and pass it down to Steve. Then, he stuck his head up through the opening.

"It's here." His voice sounded muffled. He shone his flashlight back and forth in the darkness. He could see another grid in the wall of the shaft. "Get a screwdriver and somethin' to stand on for in here."

"I know where the tools are," Roger volunteered. "Get one of those tables," he told Steve.

As Roger ducked off down an aisle, Steve moved to the nearby furniture department, where he grabbed a lightweight lamp table. The elevator doors closed like the jaws of a shark. He had to hit the button again and wait for the doors to reopen. Peter had already hoisted himself up and was climbing out of the car and up into the shaft. Steve used the first table to hold the door open, and he went to get another. This time he came back with a large coffee table. He set it under the opening in the car and placed the smaller table on top of it. It looked like a two-tiered cake. Then he climbed up, sticking his head up into the shaft. The doors closed again, leaving him in the small compartment in relative darkness.

"It's all right," Peter said as he examined the wall grid with his flashlight. It was filled with cables and elevator mechanisms and covered by a greasy black film.

"You found it, Flyboy." He spoke softly, but his voice had an eerie, echoing sound in the narrow shaft.

The car door opened again and Steve ducked down to see Roger, who bore a screwdriver and pliers along with some other tools in a shopping bag.

"One-stop shopping," he said cheerfully. "Anything you need right at your fingertips."

Steve relayed the tools up to Peter, who immediately began to work on the screws that mounted the grid into the wall frame. He passed the flashlight to Steve, who held the beam steady on the work area. The men worked in silence, each instinctively knowing his task and performing it with speed and precision.

Fran sat in the stairwell. The nausea had subsided, but she was afraid to move. She bit into the hand that she held across her mouth to keep from crying. She could feel all the pulse points in her body—at her throat, her heart, her wrist—beating furiously.

In the silence, she heard a faint click, and she felt a wave of relief flood her as she thought it might be Stephen. She stared at the bottom landing, hoping to see Steve's familiar shape in the shadows. Then there was a thump, as if something had fallen against the door, and Fran knew that her hopes would not be fulfilled yet. Those weren't the quick steps of Steve or the other two outside, those were the lumbering clumsy actions of one of the living dead!

Slowly, Fran stood, a scream of fright rising in her throat, her eyes transfixed on the door below.

"Stephen!" she emitted.

The door slowly opened. The crack of light grew larger and larger. The plodding, sluggish figure of the zombie moved into the fire stair. The light from the corridor illuminated the figure and made it seem tremendous. Its gigantic shadow appeared on the wall. Choking back a scream, Fran turned and ran up the stairs. She could hear the creature's steady, heavy footsteps following her up. Occasionally it would bump into the wall or trip, unsure in the dim light.

Panting and gasping for air, Fran made it to the top and into the storage area and slammed the door. For a moment, she just backed away in terror, her mind a blank. Then, she snapped back to consciousness and started to drag the good cartons over to use as a barricade. But the cartons were extremely bulky and heavy, and she struggled with one that was so large that she couldn't get a good grip. The smooth cardboard slipped out of her hands.

She could hear the zombie's footsteps on the middle landing, and anxiety gripped her.

With one great heave, she managed to shove the carton over against the door and moved to haul another. She felt weak and dizzy, and the thought passed through her mind that she might give herself a miscarriage, but it only stunned her for a moment that she would think that and then she went on.

She could now hear the zombie at the top landing and sensed that it was trying to open the door.

Before she was able to bring another carton over, the door moved slightly. She threw herself against it, all 110 pounds, but she knew that it wouldn't do any good. She had to lean over the carton against the door and couldn't get a proper footing on the slippery floor. As if in slow motion, the door moved a fraction of an inch at a time. Then, the creature's wounded and bloody hand appeared at the edge of the door. Its mutilated fingers clutched the edge, smearing blood all over it.

Fran backed away in terror and ran toward the escape pyramid. Then she turned suddenly and faced the door.

The creature was straining against the weight of the carton. Now, both its hands clutched the edge of the door. The carton moved another inch and then another. The creature's head could now be seen as it strained to get through the widening space. Fran's eyes were wide with fright, mesmerized by the approaching ghoul. She looked around for something to use as a weapon, but the room was almost bare except for the cartons and the water drums. In a split-second decision, she thought to run for the skylight; the creature would never be agile enough to follow her up there. Just as she was about to mount the pyramid, she caught sight of Roger's knapsack in the shadows. She ran for it as the creature finally broke into the room, shoving aside the heavy carton.

Fran's hands began to tremble as she rummaged through the cloth bag. To her dismay, nothing seemed appropriate. She dumped the contents out on the floor: ammunition, mace cans, batteries, flares...Her heart leaped when she saw the cylindrical containers and she nervously grabbed one up, her shaking hands trying to deal with the paper wrapping.

The zombie moaned as it drew nearer. It was approaching the pyramid of cartons.

Fran managed to free the wrapping, and she snapped the cylinder in two at the mark.

As she turned, she realized that the zombie was now between her and the pyramid, cutting off her immediate escape route. Its lumbering steps were bringing it nearer and nearer. Fran backed away a few steps as she tried to strike the head of the flare on the small striker at the tip of the cylinder cap. It wouldn't fire...she tried again...and again. Now, the zombie had reached the knapsack. It staggered over the spilled contents, knocking the other flares rolling about the floor.

Finally, Fran was able to get her flare to light, and it caught with a great blast of air. The bright whooshing flame startled the woman as well as the creature. Its eyes went wide, and it brought its arms up so as to cover its eyes. The intense white flame cast an eerie light over the creature and threw the zombie's enormous shadow against the cartons and the wall. The creature backed away from the flame a few steps, almost tripping over the articles on the floor.

All fear was gone from Fran now. She had an objective, and as long as she didn't think about what was happening, about what she was battling, then she was fine. She managed to advance close enough to snatch up two extra cylinders. Then she skirted around the zombie in a wide arc. The creature swatted at the air with its arms, keeping its distance, but still threatening.

Fran considered making a run for the door to the fire stair, but then she thought that she might run into others, and she didn't want to leave this hiding place open to more invaders. Finally, she decided to climb the pyramid, and try to escape onto the roof. She circled around to a point where she could climb up from behind the moaning zombie. She rushed for the cartons and started to climb, but she lost her footing, trying to hold the flares in both hands, and she crashed into the topmost carton. In a second's time, the momentum caused the carton to slide off, and Fran was unable to prevent it. The heavy case tumbled to the floor, almost crashing into the zombie. The creature started to clutch and grab at the cardboard pyramid.

Since the stack of cartons was now one too short, Fran was only able to reach the mouth of the skylight with her hands, but didn't have the strength in her arms to pull herself up. Accidentally, she dropped two of the flares, including the lit one. With a sinking feeling, Fran realized that the flare had not only tumbled to the floor but landed behind the pyramid, where it no longer offended the ghoul's eyes. Now the thing tried to mount the cartons.

Fran stuck the last flare in her mouth and reached up with both hands for the edge of the skylight. She lifted with all her might, her feet coming off the carton tops, but she still couldn't pull herself up. The muscles in her arms strained, but they didn't have the necessary power. Now, she tried to lower her feet back on the cartons, but the zombie's movement caused the pyramid to shake and wobble. The creature, unbelievably, was making progress, and it could almost touch Fran's foot.

During Fran's ordeal, the three men were making their way through the crawlspace in the ceiling. It was an area of large ductwork that seemed to run the length of the mall. Roger looked down through a grid. He could see the interior of a sporting goods store.

"Sweet Jesus!" he exclaimed when he saw that along

one wall was displayed an arsenal with the latest in weaponry for the sportsman.

"I seen it," Peter concurred. "Come on!"

They moved as quietly as they could. Several side tunnels branched off in both directions from the one that they were in.

Steve passed another ceiling grid, and he could see a fully equipped radio and electronics shop.

"I hope you know where you're going," Roger said to Peter, who was leading them in the dark tunnel.

"This is it. Come on." He dropped out of the ceiling grid, landing in a plush office. It had the same color scheme as the executive offices, but everything was of a much more expensive quality. Roger's legs appeared through the open grid, and then he too swung down, holding on as long as he could with his hands so as to soften his landing.

Suddenly, the two troopers felt the presence of another person in the room. Roger turned and was shocked to see a slumped figure in a large chair at the desk. Startled, Roger grabbed for his gun. Peter just stood there, openmouthed and staring at the dead man in the chair.

They were obviously in Porter's office. Plaques and diplomas, photographs of Porter with presidents and high government officials, dotted the walls. Some days earlier, when the reports of widespread looting and rampaging armies of zombies had come into Porter's office through his personal teletype machine, he had taken his own life. It just wasn't worth fighting to save what he had spent his whole life building up from a horde of mindless creatures. That explained why the door had been locked when Roger and Peter had explored the executive corridor earlier.

"Come on..." Peter said, stirring out of his stupor first.

Steve's legs wiggled above.

"Just drop, I got you," Peter told the neophyte.

"I can't...I..." came the muffled reply.

"The desk," Peter said to Roger. "Gimme a hand."

The two troopers took hold of the big desk and slid it away from the president's corpse. The action made the body's chair spin slightly, and its wide, terrified eyes seemed to watch the action.

With the desk in place, Steve's toes were able to reach the surface. He lost his balance and pulled back up. Then he kicked the picture frame off the desk and it fell to the floor, shattering the glass over the photos of the president's wife and children.

"Come on," Peter urged again.

Steve finally managed to get his footing on the desktop, and he lowered himself into the room. He stared at the corpse in the big chair, a totally unexpected sight that startled him more than the zombies, whom he was used to by now.

Peter had already moved to the door and was unlocking it so that they could enter the corridor. He opened it a crack and peered out. The corridor was empty except for the dead zombies. At the end, which opened onto the mall, he could see the cartful of supplies.

As the other men came up behind him, Peter opened the door gently and slipped into the hall. He started to walk as quietly as he could toward the cart. The other men, according to the plan, moved backward up the corridor toward the fire stair. Roger kicked the corpses to one side, making a path for the cart.

Peter grabbed the handles of the cart and started to pull it down the corridor, walking backward so that he was always facing the mall opening, on the lookout for possible intruders.

In the corridor, Stephen snatched up the maintenance manual that had been trampled on by the zombie upstairs.

Peter backed slowly up the hall. The wheels of the cart squeaked, and Peter bit his lip with the anxious thought that the sound might attract the attention of an aimlessly wandering creature.

Roger kicked the last corpse close to the corridor wall. Suddenly, Steve noticed that the door to the fire stair was wide open!

"Jesus Christ," he shrieked, bounding toward the door. Roger spun around, surprised by Steve's violent outburst. Peter turned around too, and saw what upset Steve. He quickened his pace, pulling the cart with him.

"Come on . . . you got it," Roger encouraged Peter.

Steve trotted off up the steps. After Peter had pulled the cart to safety inside the stairway, Roger ran up the stairs, too.

Steve broke into the storage area, dropping the manual.

"Frannie!"

Fran turned in Steve's direction, not believing her ears. The zombie, who had been steadily gaining on Fran, continued to swat at the flare that Fran had managed to light, and sent it flying out of her hand. She was startled, and the cartons felt as if they were going to topple, too. She tried to hold herself steady with both hands. The creature grabbed at her kicking legs.

Steve raised his rifle and moved in for a closer shot.

Roger came charging through the door.

"Don't shoot . . . they'll hear ya . . ." He ran to the pyramid with Steve.

The creature was still clutching at Fran. She kicked violently just as Roger pulled the back of the zombie's clothing. The combined force caused the creature to hit the floor. Just as it was about to kneel and stand up,

Steve brought his rifle around like a baseball bat, smashing the butt into the thing's head. Then, for good measure, Roger delivered a blow with his gun, straight down, like a battering ram.

Steve dropped his rifle and rushed to Fran. As if all the strength had been drained from her, she fell off the cartons into his arms, sobbing and choking.

"Frannie," Steve asked, his voice cracking. "Are you all right? You OK, Frannie? Hey ..." There was true concern in his voice.

But the woman was incoherent. She babbled between tears and sobs, clutching her stomach.

Peter appeared in the doorway carrying the TV and several other items. He dumped them on the floor. He glanced at Fran briefly, but didn't offer any assistance or sympathy for her terrible experience.

"Let's get this stuff up, come on," he said to Roger gruffly.

Roger dragged the dead zombie toward the door. Peter walked over to help. At that moment, Fran started to retch. Frazzled, Steve tried to calm her. He ran over to the water can and brought her some water in an empty Spam can.

"Frannie ... it's OK ... Come on, it's OK. Are you hurt, hon? Did ya hurt yourself? Frannie ..."

She looked up at him, tears streaming down her face. She seemed as if she wanted to stop, but the sobbing was too intense and she couldn't control it. All the fears and terror that she had been holding in burst like floodgates.

Meanwhile, Peter was downstairs at the door to the corridor. He peeked out and could see into the mall at the far end. The coast was clear, and he and Roger hurriedly carried the corpse into the hall and rolled it onto the floor. Then they retreated back into the fire stair. Peter held the door open slightly and watched the corridor for a moment.

"I think we're OK, brother," he said to Roger, convinced that they hadn't been seen. He closed the door quietly.

Grabbing more supplies from the cart, they started upstairs.

"We're OK ... we're all OK," Steve was telling Fran, trying to comfort her. "We got a lot of stuff ... all kinds of stuff."

In the background, the two troopers brought their load of supplies into the big room and deposited them near the TV. Mechanically, as soon as they dropped off one load, they went down for another.

"This is a terrific place, Frannie," Steve was saying, wiping the perspiration-drenched hair from her eyes. She was still sobbing and retching. "This place is perfect. We got it made in here ... Frannie."

Once more, the enormous barricade of food cartons was stacked against the door. A calm pervaded the little fortress, the silence broken only by the noise of rustling paper and chewing as the survivors ate. A faint electronic whistle threaded through the background. The refugees were sitting near the pyramid on the floor. Peter seemed to be sleeping sitting up against the structure. Roger was nibbling at the delicacies from Porter's gourmet department, known all over the East coast for its fine food. Around them, as if they were children after Christmas, lay their loot. Roger leafed through the maintenance binder as he ate, as casually as if it were the Sunday paper. In reality, they didn't know what day it was and weren't even sure of the time. No one had bothered to rewind watches or mark the passing days in a calendar. All normal functions, except for the very basic ones, had ceased.

Around them lay a stack of tools, some still in wrappings; electric razors, still boxed; some clothing articles, including the leather jacket that Roger had admired; the radio that could also play small cassettes of audio tape. In addition there were soaps, toiletries, pens, pencils and notebooks, flashlights, cigarettes and several decks of playing cards with a canister of chips. The quantity of necessary items was in inverse proportion to the quality of leisure items that could have been found in a family room or den.

The three figures were bathed in the blue glow from the television screen, which Steve tried to tune in. Its power cable was spliced into the leads of a bare light fixture overhead. Fran slept behind some cartons; her sobbing had finally subsided and left her weak and tired.

"What the hell time is it, anyway?" Roger asked, annoyed that there was nothing on the tube.

"Only about nine," Steve surmised.

Roger nodded his head toward the portable set. "And nothing?"

The only thing coming from the set was the high-pitched whine that the civil defense sent out, and only the C.D. logo appeared on the screen.

"As long as we're getting the pattern, that means they're sending," Steve said matter-of-factly.

Roger snapped on the large, battery-powered radio. He rolled the dial around, but all he got was static. Finally, he heard a signal, and he tuned it in. A badly modulated voice droned through the interference. It sounded as if it were a war correspondent sending a signal from very far away.

Steve clicked off the TV set so that they would better be able to hear the announcer:

"...Reports that communications with Detroit have been knocked out along with Atlanta, Boston and certain sections of Philadelphia and New York City..."

"Philly..." Roger said almost to himself.

"I know WGON is out by now," Steve said with animation. "It was a madhouse back there...people are crazy...if they'd just organize. It's total confusion. I don't believe it's gotten this bad. I don't believe they can't handle it." He looked around the room proudly. "Look at us. Look at what we were able to do today."

A few feet away, still in a slumped position by the pyramid of cartons, Peter's eyes blinked open. He had been listening to what he wanted to hear, and now this statement by the kid really made him take notice. His eyes moved slightly to the side so that he could watch Stephen. The young man was gesturing wildly with his hands, going on and on about their exploits as a team. The other two didn't realize Peter was awake. Roger nodded his head, but it didn't seem as if he were really listening to Steve's ramblings.

"We knocked the shit out of 'em, and they never touched us," Steve exclaimed. "Not really," he said in a quieter tone.

The rumbling voice erupted from the other side of the room.

"They touched us good, Flyboy. We're *lucky* to get out with our asses. You don't forget that!"

The two men looked at Peter. Steve's face colored at being caught mouthing off about something he really hadn't contributed to. The droning of the radio, announcing more disaster reports, was a counterpoint to Peter's speech.

"You get overconfident . . . underestimate those suckers. And you get eaten! How'd you like that?"

He spoke in a low, unemotional tone, barely turning his head so that Steve could see his expression. Peter hadn't moved a muscle except for his eyes and his mouth. Steve was transfixed.

"They got a big advantage over us, brother," Peter went on. "They don't think. They just blind-ass do what they got to do. No emotions. And that bunch out there? That's just a handful, and every day there'll be more. A couple hundred thousand people die each day from natural causes. That'll prob'ly triple or better with folks knockin' each other off the way it's goin'.

"Now say each one of them comes back and kills two, and each one of them two more . . . you know about the emperor's reward?"

As if they were children at story hours, the two grown men shook their heads.

Peter went on, "Emperor tells this dude, 'I'll give you anything I got, name it' . . . dude puts out a chessboard . . . says gimme one grain of rice on the first square, two on the second, four on the third, eight . . . double for each square on the board. Dude got all the rice in the kingdom, baby. Wiped the emperor out!"

"Yeah," Steve interrupted. "But these things can be stopped so easily...if people would just listen...do what has to be done—"

Peter swiveled his upper torso and faced Steve.

"How about it, Flyboy? Let's say the lady gets killed. You be able to chop off her head?"

Steve was stopped midsentence by the last comment. It was meant to sting and it did. He stared at the big man, his mouth open. He was just about to answer yes when he stopped himself again. All he could do in response was stare.

Fran, who was trying to get some rest on the other side, opened her eyes wide as the conversation drifted by her. When Steve didn't answer, she sat up, thinking that he had lowered his voice. Sitting in the shadows behind a wall of cartons, she listened; but there was silence except for the drone of the radio. Upset, she reached for her pack of cigarettes, part of the loot, and lit one.

She was awfully disappointed in Steve. He let the bigger man bully him. He had always been so confident and so reliable. That was what had attracted her to him at the station. Her ex-husband had been afraid of his own shadow, but in his home he tried to be the boss. Steve had always stood up to authority figures and spoken his mind. But Peter could silence him with one look—it was frightening.

The faint strains of the radio broadcast wafted through

the room. The announcer sounded unprofessional; he didn't have the clipped, midwestern accent of most newscasters. His voice was tired and he stumbled on some words, taking long pauses between paragraphs.

"...gasses or certain toxins that might affect the creatures. Experiments with hallucinogens have begun at Haverford, in the hopes of producing an agent that will cloud the brain and prevent the effective motor coordination of the body. However, scientists fear that the creatures function on a subconscious, instinctive level and that such drugs will have little or no effect. In Nevada, chemicals sprayed from crop-dusting airplanes have had more of an ill effect on the human population than on the walking corpses..."

Peter turned his attention from the broadcast.

"She all right?" he asked Steve, referring to Fran. "She looked blown."

"What did ya expect?" Roger asked, annoyed that Peter was being so hard on his friend. Steve wasn't a professional fighter like Peter and himself, but Roger still thought he had done damn good under pressure.

"No, I mean she really looked sick...physically."

Steve looked at him long and hard. He was a difficult man to figure. He was one way one minute and a different person the next.

"She's pregnant," he said softly.

There was a long, heavy silence. The radio droned

on. Finally, Peter heaved a sigh and closed his eyes again as though instantly falling asleep.

"How far along?" asked Roger, a concerned look on his face.

"Three and a half . . . four months . . ."

"Jesus, Steve," he said, rubbing his head. "Maybe we *should* try to get movin' . . ."

Without opening his eyes, Peter spoke:

"We can deal with it."

"Yeah, but maybe she needs a doctor or—"

Peter cut Roger off. "We can deal with it! It doesn't change a thing."

Now he opened his eyes again and looked hard at Steve.

"You wanna get rid of it?"

"Huh?" Steve was shocked at the coldhearted attitude. It wasn't even his decision to make.

Peter ignored his shocked look. He seemed to enjoy making people squirm.

"Do you want to abort it?" he repeated tensely. "It's not too late. I know how."

Tears streaked Fran's face. She strained her ears for Steve's retort. He should smash the bastard across the face, she thought. How dare he make that suggestion. And how dare Stephen not speak up and say it's not his decision to make. Her heart pounded as she waited for the reply. The only sound was the droning radio.

After a time, Fran heard Steve's footsteps rounding the corner to her sleeping area. He seemed surprised to see her sitting up. She was on one of the new blankets from the store. Another was rolled up as a pillow where her head had lain. She wiped away her tears, a lit cigarette still in her hand.

"Hey," Steve said, kneeling next to her. "You OK?"

"All your decisions made?"

He looked at her for a moment, speechless.

"Do you want to...abort it?" she asked pointedly.

"Do you?"

She met his question with silence. Looking away, she took another drag on the cigarette, which was burning down so low it practically seared her fingers. Stephen sat next to her and put his hands on her shoulders.

She looked into his eyes.

"So I guess we forget about Canada, right?"

"Jesus, Frannie," he said, taking her in his arms. "This setup is sensational. We got everything we need. We seal off that stairway...nobody'll ever know we're up here. We'd never find anything like this..."

He seemed as though his mind was made up. The decision had been made by the troika, the triumvirate, and the opinion of one Frannie Parker was of no regard.

"I guess nobody cares about my vote, huh?" She pouted.

"Come on, Frannie. I thought you were sleeping."

She pulled away from him, the end of the cigarette growing smaller and smaller. "What happened to growing vegetables and fishing? What happened to the idea about the wilderness...hundreds of miles from anything and anybody?...Steve, I'm afraid. You're hypnotized by this place. All of you. It's all so bright and neatly wrapped that you don't see...you don't see..."

She leaned toward him, making a final plea. "Stephen, let's just take what we need and keep going."

"We can't hardly carry anything in that little bird," he rationalized.

"What do you want?" she said, her voice rising in anger. "A new set of furniture, a freezer, a console TV and stereo? We can take what we need. What we *need* to survive!"

Peter's eyes popped open, and he leaped up. "Shut that thing off!" He had the hearing of a trained dog. And it seemed as if he never slept, just closed his eyes.

Roger clicked off the radio, and they listened. Slight sounds were coming from the fire stair. The TV had been turned on again with the sound low, and the blue glow made the barricade of cartons look surreal.

Roger crawled over and clicked the TV set off again. The electronic C.D. whistle died, and there was silence.

Steve had heard Peter's outburst, and he stepped tentatively from behind the wall of cartons. Crawling on her hands and knees, Fran peered around the corner to look.

There was another noise, sounding too familiar, just like the faint squeaking of the door at the bottom of the steps. Then footsteps on the metal stairs. Slow, deliberate, heavy footsteps...

The faces of all the refugees tightened. Peter and Roger pulled out their rifles, and Roger readied his.

They all tried to hold their breath, to make as little noise as possible, so that the intruder wouldn't know they were there.

More thumping in the hall and Fran grabbed Steve's hand. He squatted down and held her. The sounds seemed to be getting closer and closer. The door behind the cartons clicked, but didn't move. Then there came an insistent pounding, slowly at first, then stronger. It kept up for a few minutes; yet it seemed an eternity for the occupants. And then there was silence.

Peter gave everyone a look that meant, Don't relax, the worst is not over.

After a time, the footsteps receded down the stairs.

"Somebody better sit watch all the time," Peter pronounced, and the others shook their heads in agreement.

"They'll never get through there," Roger said, hoping that he was right.

"Enough of 'em will," Peter replied seriously. "And

it ain't just them things we got to worry about. That chopper up there could give us away if somebody come messin' around."

"What are they gonna do?" Roger insisted. "Land another pilot to fly it out. They're not gonna mess with a little bird like that. They got enough on their hands. You know, back in Philly we found a boat in the middle of Independence Square. Somebody tryin' to carry it to the river, I guess. Didn't make it. Damn thing sat there for eight days."

"Somebody finally got it, though. It come down to how much it's worth." Peter laid his rifle against the side of the carton and lit a cigarette.

Fran ducked around and lay back down on her blanket. She lit another cigarette from the first and then ground the first one out on the cement. She was becoming a chain smoker from this experience. And to think that she was planning to give it up because of the baby. What did it matter now? Who knew if she would even get out alive!

"Frannie..." Steve came around and sat next to her again.

She took a deep drag on the cigarette.

"Dammit, Fran," he looked at her earnestly. His brown hair was all matted, and there were smudges of grease in his hair from the trek through the ceiling ducts. He looked almost comical. "You know how many times we'd have to land for fuel tryin' to make it up north? Those things are out there everywhere. And the authorities would give us just as hard a time... maybe worse. We're in good shape here, Frannie. We got everything we need right here!"

Steve curled up with his head on the rolled blanket. He held out his arms to her.

"Come on ... get some sleep."

She still didn't respond or move toward him.

"Frannie. Come on."

Grinding her second cigarette out on the floor, she stretched out next to Steve. Tentatively, he put his arm around her. When she didn't push it off, he tightened his hold, and then began rubbing his hand up and down her body as he curled next to her. Staring into her eyes, that seemed to be focused elsewhere, he opened her blouse and reached inside. He closed his eyes and seemed to relax in the comfort of her softness. His hand moved under her clothing. Fran still hadn't spoken, and her face was set in a grim, thoughtful expression. At first she didn't respond physically at all, but then at Steve's insistence, she relaxed her body, and she brought one of her arms up around his head.

"I'm not just being stubborn," he told her softly as his hands explored her hardening nipples under her clothing. "I really think this is better. Hell, you're the one's been wantin' to set up house."

She continued to stare off across the barren room impassively.

In the administration corridor, all was quiet. A few stray zombies wandered among the corpses on the floor. One large and severely wounded creature came out of the fire stair, probably the one that had been pounding on the door upstairs.

A female zombie, dressed in jeans and a sweater, in her early twenties, squatted near one of the corpses in the hall. She lifted its arm and moved it to her mouth, but she dropped it quickly, repelled by its coldness. Then she leaned over and picked at another corpse, just like someone at a smorgasbord. This one was cold, too. Discouraged, the zombie stood and drifted toward the mall.

Slowly the creatures left the corridor and moved out onto the second-floor balcony. The central mall was strewn with the bodies of their not-so-lucky comrades. Here and there a few zombies squatted and finished off their dinner.

Meanwhile, the radio in the upper room droned on and lulled the inhabitants to a fitful sleep:

"...not actually cannibalism...Cannibalism in the true sense of the word, implies an intraspecific activity... These creatures cannot be considered human. They prey on humans... They do not prey on each other..."

On the mall balcony, zombies wandered past the stores, as if out for a Sunday stroll. Some moved down the stationary stairs onto the main concourse below. More and more zombies had been filing in from the surrounding communities, as if their normal lives continued; schools, offices and shopping malls continued to attract the walking dead.

The huddled bodies of Steve and Fran were intertwined behind the cartons. Roger was stretched out in a sleeping bag that he had found in the camping department. Only Peter slept sitting up, at his post near the fire door, his rifle slung across his lap.

The radio continued:

"They attack and... and feed... only on warm human flesh... Intelligence? Seemingly little or no reasoning power. What basic skills remain are more remembered behaviors from... from normal life.

"There are reports of the creatures holding tools, but even these actions are the most primitive... the use of external articles as bludgeons, et cetera. Even animals will adopt the basic use of the tools in this manner."

At the mall entrance, some of the creatures drifted out into the night, while others entered the enormous building. Although there were not as many as there had been in the afternoon, the number was enough to be reckoned with. Several creatures continued to claw at the roll gate to Porter's. In a strange and eerie montage, the staring, painted eyes of the mannequins inside seemed to watch the zombies on the outside. The rattle of the gate mingled with the droning, fading sound of the Muzak.

8

"These creatures are nothing but pure, motorized instinct..." a gravelly voice was saying to her. She shook her head, looking about for the person who belonged to the disembodied voice, and realized that she had been sleeping and the voice that had wakened her was only the television.

Her body was stiff from lying on the thin blanket on the cold cement floor. Couldn't those wise guys have thought to steal a mattress, she thought, as she tried to rub the stiffness out of her back. The morning sunlight spilled through the skylights above. Sitting up, Fran peered into the next area of the room. The television was playing to no one. The men were gone. On the tube a disheveled man sitting in an emergency newsroom read the report:

"Their only drive is for the food that sustains them. We must not be lulled by the concept that these are our family members or our friends. They will not respond to such emotions. They must be destroyed on sight..."

Fran quickly glanced to make sure that the barricade was in place at the fire stair door. At least they weren't stupid enough to go on another search-and-destroy mission this morning, she thought.

Looking up, she realized that the men must have gone up on the roof through the open skylight.

At the edge of the roof, Peter looked through binoculars. To the untrained eye, it would have looked like a lovely countryside, the mist rising as the sun climbed higher in the sky. But Peter knew better. About a quarter of a mile away, he saw the large warehouse of a food-processing chain. Probably owned by old man Porter, he thought to himself. And considering the state he's in now, he certainly wouldn't mind lending the survivors a hand.

In the yard and in the large open garages of the building, Peter noticed a fleet of enormous trailer trucks that were parked in rows. A plan was forming in his mind. He had explained the germ of it to Steve and Roger over their breakfast of lukewarm instant coffee and Spam.

"You sure we can start 'em," Steve had asked.

"You haven't spent enough time on the street," Roger chimed in. Starting cars, especially these big semis, was Roger's specialty. He had practically learned it at his daddy's knee. When his daddy was home from the road, that is.

"Well, let's get it up," Peter barked. He was never one for idle chatter, and for all the time they had been together, Steve and Roger still felt that Peter was a stranger. He hadn't opened up once or said anything personal except for the few short minutes of conversation in the chopper.

"There's not too many of 'em around yet this morning," Peter continued, looking at the parking lot below.

The parking lot was dotted with the lumbering figures. There were fewer than there had been the day before and they wandered aimlessly, spread out rather than in clusters.

The men walked toward the skylight. In the storage area below, Fran examined the maps in the manual. The TV droned on. It was a familiar sound now, almost like white noise. They didn't hear it when it was on, but if it were off, they'd notice it.

"Hey, Fran..." Roger called in a friendly tone as the men made their way down into the room.

"I would have made coffee and breakfast, but I don't have my pots and pans," she said bitterly.

Roger laughed, thinking it a joke, but Steve could sense the tension in Fran's face and waited for her to explode. Peter seemed preoccupied with his equipment and hadn't even acknowledged Fran's presence.

"Can I say something?" she asked.

"Sure. What do you mean?" Steve said gently, hoping to forestall any argument.

She looked at the three men, who had stopped their fiddling around and stood waiting for her to go on. "I'm sorry you found out that I'm pregnant, because I don't want any of you to treat me any differently than you'd treat another guy."

Steve blushed and looked around at the other men.

"Hey, Frannie, come on . . ."

"And," she went on, shooting Steve a deadly look, "I'm not gonna be a den mother for you guys."

They all looked at her now, even Peter, giving her their undivided attention.

"And I want to know what's going on. And I want something to say about the plans. There's four of us, OK?"

"Jesus, Fran . . ." Steve bellowed, putting his hand to his head. She was really blowing it now. They probably thought she was a hysterical female, Steve decided.

"Fair enough!" Peter chimed in, a smile on his face.

For the life of him, Steve couldn't figure that one out.

"Now," Fran went on, picking up confidence. "What's goin' on?"

"We're goin' out," Peter said, but this time he wasn't smiling.

Fran started to say something, but at this point he cut her off.

"...and you're not coming with us!"

Fran started to turn red and protest. Peter had made believe that he agreed with her, and now he was back to being his same overbearing male chauvinist pig self.

"You will not come with us until you can handle yourself," he said slowly and deliberately, as if he were speaking to a child. "That means you learn to shoot and learn to fight."

He turned, not even waiting for her reply, and started back up the pyramid. Roger followed, his head down. He couldn't look Fran in the eye.

"Something else." She said it with determination. She wasn't going to let Peter step all over her as he did to Roger and Steve.

They all turned to look at her again. This time she faced Roger and Peter directly, without giving a second glance to Stephen.

"I don't know about you two, but I wanna learn how to fly that helicopter."

Stephen's mouth fell open, and he looked at Fran in disbelief. She glared at him and then lowered her eyes.

"If anything happens...we've gotta be able to get out of here."

Stephen was speechless. Not only was Fran humiliating him in front of the two troopers, but she was implying that he was dispensable. He looked at her and then at the others. He could feel a flush spreading up from his neck.

"She's right, Flyboy," Peter chimed in. "Come on, let's go."

"And you're not leaving me without a gun again."

Stephen started to protest, but then he changed his mind.

Dejected, he set his rifle down on the cartons and fished in his pocket for a fistful of shells, dumping them next to the gun. He stared at Fran, as if he were a beaten dog, both angry and hurt.

"I just might be able to figure out how to use it," she said as she picked up the weapon and shot a glance up at Peter.

The two troopers disappeared through the skylight. Stephen seemed frozen to the spot, focusing on a speck of dirt on the floor.

"I'm sorry, Stephen," Fran said, moving close to his side. But it wasn't an apology.

"I know...I know...it's all right." He started up to the skylight.

"Stephen," she said soothingly.

"Yeah?"

He stopped and turned to look at her. She seemed to be crying out for understanding, but he was incapable of running to her. She had damaged him in front of Peter and Roger, and he had tried so hard to gain their respect. Now, by standing up to him, defying him, and showing the troopers that she wanted to be on her own, they probably thought less of him.

But Fran's intention wasn't to hurt his masculine image, and this was something Steve couldn't fathom. Fran could see in his eyes that he didn't understand the necessity of her actions. She shrugged off whatever she was going to say and sighed with exasperation.

"Be careful," she said tonelessly, as if by rote.

"Yeah, we'll be all right." He disappeared through the skylight. Fran stared down at the weapon in her hand and then stepped over and clicked off the television set.

It was ironic, but this situation was teaching her more about Stephen than she could ever have imagined. It was sad, too, that with their lives on the line they had to deal with such pettiness. The experience was also teaching Fran a lot about herself that she hadn't realized before. It was teaching her that she had a lot more strength than she had ever thought and that she didn't always need a man to lean on.

Stephen entered the pilot's seat of the chopper. He was really upset by Frannie's actions. He started the controls, and the sudden loud noise of the chopper engine made him jump. Roger and Peter ran over, ducked under the whirling blades, and got in. Slowly, the bird lifted off the rooftop. The plan was for Steve to fly the chopper over to the tractor-trailer parking field and let the troopers off. Once in the big trucks, Roger would hot wire the motors and they would drive the trucks over to the various entrances to the shopping mall and park them flush against the doors, preventing the outside zombies from entering, and the inside zombies from leaving—alive.

As Steve hovered above, Roger worked on the wiring beneath the dashboard of one of the big trailer trucks. His fingers moved nimbly, as skilled and trained as a surgeon's.

Peter was in the cab of another rig already started by Roger. He tried the complicated shift mechanisms and fidgeted with the other controls. Then he pulled the big semi out of its parking space and stopped his cab just abreast of the cab Roger was working in.

"How about it?" he called over the roar of the engine.

"Gettin' it," Roger called back.

Peter looked around the mall parking lot and out to the mall in the distance. On the ground there were a few zombies scattered about in little clusters, but none of them seemed to present any imminent danger. So far, they hadn't noticed the activity going on over by the garage.

Roger sat up and the truck vibrated steadily.

"I'll just ride pickup," Peter shouted across the gap between the two trucks. "I'm not too sure of this thing..."

"I grew up in one of these," Roger returned, his eyes lighting up like a child's. "Let's go!"

The huge vehicles pulled away from the warehouse. They rode across the little loading lot and down a ramp toward the roadway. Stephen hovered overhead in the chopper, following the trucks as closely as he could. It was difficult, since they had to ride a while before the trucks could gather any speed up a slight incline. But once the giant trucks picked up speed, there was no stopping them. Fran was up on the roof of the mall, clutching the rifle to her chest. She could make out the big trailers in the distance and watched them roar over the hill, the helicopter wavering above them. It was a strange-looking convoy speeding toward the shopping center.

Along the road, several zombies tried to stagger after the trucks, but they were left in the dust of the barreling vehicles. As the wind whipped by them, they wavered slightly but continued their sluggish, creeping pace.

The vehicles pulled into the long grade that loaded into the mall's parking lot. With a gigantic roar, they drove straight toward the building.

At one of the building entrances, a gathering of zombies was moving in and out of the main doors like robots. Some wandered nearby in the parking lot. The area seemed to be filling up as the morning progressed. Some of the creatures were attracted by the sounds of the engines, and they turned and faced the trucks.

As Peter pulled his vehicle in a wide arc, Roger drove his right up to the side of the building and roared toward the entrance doors. Then he skipped his right wheels up onto the curb, and with a great, scraping crunch, the big truck pulled directly abreast of the building, flush with the entrance. The tremendous truck crushed several of the helpless creatures and knocked them against the wall as if they were flies being squashed on a windshield.

The trailer of the truck had effectively blocked off the mall entrance. Several zombies trapped inside tried to push the glass door open. The doors moved slightly but did not allow any room for the creatures to escape.

The few creatures immediately around the truck began to clamor at its sides. Roger shut off the engine and grabbed his gun. Other zombies began clutching at the windows of the cab.

Roger watched their ghoulish faces flush against the cab windows. Their nails made screeching sounds on the glass as they tried to gain entrance. Some of them pushed their faces up against the windows, making them look even more fiendish.

Overhead, the chopper hovered like a bird in flight. With a rumble, Peter pulled up his big truck alongside so that his passenger door was directly abreast of the free door on Roger's cab.

Peter's truck also crushed one or two of the creatures, but there were still several in the immediate vicinity of the cabs. They made a slight thud as they hit the wheels.

As Roger opened his door and scrambled into the other truck, one of the zombies grabbed hold of his leg. Roger managed to kick the creature off just as the big truck pulled out and roared across the lot.

The helicopter flew straight up and directly over the roof of the big shopping center, where Fran had been watching the action. She had been fascinated and repulsed at the clockwork precision with which Roger and Peter worked. As she ran to the other side of the roof, the wind from the chopper whipped her hair.

The chopper turned and waited for the big truck to move up under it, then it escorted the trailer back to the warehouse down the road.

In the cab that Peter was driving, Roger was jumping up and down in the seat, whooping it up like a cowboy. They pulled alongside another of the parked trucks.

"Come on, come on," Peter tried to calm him down. "Three more, baby."

"Like a charm, huh?" Roger was yelling for joy. "Like a fucking charm!" He grabbed his knapsack and climbed into the new cab. Immediately, all frivolity was forgotten, and he went to work on jumping the engine cables of the second rig.

From the helicopter overhead, Steve spotted something moving around the warehouse. He jockeyed the chopper slightly for a better look and saw a small group of zombies wandering out of the big garage directly toward Roger's truck. It looked like a group of farmers. They were all wearing jeans and work boots. They also seemed to be moving more quickly than the lumbering ones in the parking lot.

In the meantime, Peter's truck pulled away from the cab Roger was in. The big vehicle rolled into the large paved area behind the warehouse, where Peter was able to turn it around easily.

Stephen swooped down with the copter, buzzing as close as he could to Roger's truck, trying desperately to signal the man.

But Roger was still immersed in his work on the cables. Every once in a while he would remember their success and whoop like a child. The zombie group drew closer. They had just about reached the cab. Steve swooped low again and buzzed once more. Roger still didn't notice.

Peter had now backed up into a position that enabled him to pull out. He looked up to see the helicopter heading straight for him.

Is this guy losing his marbles, Peter thought, but then he saw the big chopper buzz right over his cab and spin around, heading back for Roger.

It seemed to be some sort of signal. Peter looked toward the other truck. He was now able to see the lumbering creatures. Frantic, he tried to slam the truck into gear, but the complicated shift mechanism fought him.

One of the approaching zombies reached Roger's truck and slammed its hands against the driver's side window. The man was startled and tried to untangle himself from his cramped position under the big steering wheel. For a terrible moment he was stuck. Other creatures appeared at the passenger side of the cab, where the door was open. One of the zombies grabbed at Roger's leg. He kicked violently but couldn't seem to get a good position. He fell lower onto the floor of the cab, his body almost knotted among the controls and the shift sticks.

With a lurch, Peter's truck started to roll, accelerating slowly. From above, Steve tried to buzz the clutching ghouls, but they didn't even look up or flinch as the wind generated by the blades whipped through their hair and clothes violently. They were a frightening sight as they clawed and banged at Roger. The trooper's eyes were wide with fear and revulsion at being at the creatures' mercy. He kicked and twisted his body to push them away, but he was unable to deliver a solid blow from his pinned position. Blindly, he groped for his rifle on the seat of the truck. Inadvertently, his finger hit the trigger and a shell blasted through the chest of the lead creature. But the ghouls didn't react and kept clawing and grabbing as if nothing had happened.

Finally, Peter was able to get his truck in the proper gear, and it started to roll a little faster. Desperately, he headed for Roger's cab. In the chopper, Steve realized that he could be of no assistance and hovered closer to get a better look at the action. He could see that Roger now had a good grip on his gun but was unable to clear the weapon from around the gear sticks. To Steve's horror, he saw that the zombie who was now in the lead was actually scrambling into the cab with Roger, and was all but on top of the struggling trapped trooper.

Just as a second creature was about to claw his way in, Peter, now moving with a good amount of speed, swung his truck up and crushed it against the side of the cab. Blood splattered all over the truck and trickled to the ground.

Meanwhile, Roger was frantically trying to keep the first zombie's mouth away. Its gaping hole was filled with rotted and blackened teeth. The two bodies entwined in a wrestler's hold. Even though the zombie was the weaker of the two, Roger was hampered by the position he was in. He had to channel all his force in an upward direction, thus losing most of its effectiveness.

Peter, who had pulled his truck too far past Roger's, now slammed his rig into reverse and backed up. This time he managed to get his window in a direct line with the open door on Roger's cab. He raised his rifle and aimed, but he could not get a clear shot. The zombie had managed to pin Roger against the steering wheel and the blond trooper's head was directly in Peter's line of sight. The zombie's head was positioned behind Roger's.

"Get its head up...get its head up," Peter shouted, trying to overcome the noise of the truck engine and the hovering helicopter.

Hearing the sound of a human voice, Roger realized that Peter was outside. He struggled with the creature, in the process dropping his rifle on the floor of the cab. It clanged against his tools. Finally, he managed to get a stranglehold on the creature's neck. He pushed up with all his might, but he couldn't budge the ghoul. The zombie's hands clutched at his face, its fingers pushing on Roger's eyes, and the pain was unbearable.

In a split second, Peter saw the opportunity to fire at the zombie while it held Roger at arm's length. The gun gave out a deafening roar. The zombie's head flew apart. Remnants of blood and brain tissue splattered the inside of the cab and the driver's window. The gummy stuff flew into Roger's face, blinding him momentarily. He wiped away the wet matter, cringing when he realized what it was. The zombie fell limp, its dead weight crushing Roger against the controls of the cab. Desperate, blood running all over him, Roger frantically tried to free himself. With a great heave of his body, he pushed the leaden creature out of the cab. His eyes stared in terror and revulsion. Instantly, he brought his sleeve up to wipe the stains from his face, feeling the bits of flesh and blood caked to his skin and even on his lips. His body shook and quivered in disgust.

A sudden crash brought Roger to his senses, and he spun around. One of the zombies had actually recalled the instinct to smash through the driver's side window with a tire chain. Roger was stunned for a minute that the creature could have managed such a feat. Still shaking, he dove to the floor for his weapon.

"Get down, stay down," Peter called, trying to level off a shot. "I got it!" he screamed, but once again he was unable to get off a shot because Roger was in the way.

Roger, his adrenaline pumping overtime, sat up with his gun and leveled off at the creature himself. The shell crashed through the already shattered glass and squarely into the creature's head.

Roger's body shuddered as the bullet hit. "You bastards...you bastards..." he started mumbling incoherently, his voice quivering and a glazed look coming into his eyes.

Suddenly, he gave a war whoop and looked at Peter, semi-deliriously shouting, "We got 'em, buddy...we got 'em, didn't we?"

"Cool it, man," Peter hissed at him over the noise of the big engine. "Get your head."

Peter had seen this reaction many times during combat. A soldier would do something that he found utterly repugnant but necessary, and if he couldn't accept what he'd done, his mind just snapped. He had seen it happen in Nam and on the streets of Philly. And, sometimes, the experience was so totally devastating that the trooper or cop or soldier never recovered.

"We got this by the ass...got this by the ass!" Roger leaped around in the cab, his face a fiery red, sweat pouring down his neck and collecting in a pool by his collarbone. He dove down again, and started to work on jumping the truck.

"Hey, Rog," Peter said more gently. "Get your head, man. Come on...we got a lot to do. Roger?"

There was a rustle of movement and then nothing from the floor of the cab. Peter looked about himself cautiously and then started to open his door and step out, when suddenly Roger popped up again. The engine of the truck roared and Roger just smiled calmly at Peter, sending a steady gaze across the space between the two cabs.

"Let's go, baby," he said, as if nothing out of the ordinary had happened. "Number two—"

"You all right?"

"Perfect, baby...perfect!" he said, gunning the engine happily and pulling the big vehicle out of the area. Peter followed, a look of confusion and concern on his face.

As the two semis rumbled out of the warehouse lot and started down the grade toward the road, the helicopter followed suit. Stephen had craned his neck to watch the action, and his eyes had been wide with fascination as he observed the struggle below. He believed that Roger and Peter had more guts than anyone he'd ever known. He didn't think he could have lasted one minute in that cab with those creatures without puking his brains out!

The trucks moved along at a fast pace. Suddenly, a few zombies loomed up before them as they ascended a grade. The creatures were walking slowly up the road. Roger's eyes widened with anger, and he steered his rig right for the creatures. The front of the cab smashed into two of them. One was crushed under the wheels, and the other flew back from the impact.

Fran, too, had been watching with horror, although from her vantage point she could barely make out a thing. She had wished those jerks had thought to rip off some binoculars, but that was too easy. She should have made them a shopping list. At least they would have accepted that as part of her function.

But now, anxiety was choking her. She could see the two trucks pull up over the rise. The helicopter buzzed along with them. Then the trucks roared around the entrance ramps into the parking lot, and again the chopper zoomed right over the roof.

Fran trotted across the roof to see the action in the lot. The trucks rumbled toward the second set of entrance doors. Roger steered the huge trailer truck directly broadside with the doors. In the process, the vehicle knocked over several creatures and scraped against the building as the big trailer blocked off the entrance. This time there were more creatures still alive in the immediate area. They clutched at the cab and leaped at the doors.

Watching from above, Fran decided to take action. She seemed to become inspired from the real bravery that Roger and Peter had shown that morning. As the creatures converged on the truck, she aimed her rifle down at them. Before she fired, Peter's rig slid in very close to Roger's, the cabs abreast.

Peter's truck knocked over several of the clutching creatures. One of the zombies, which was caught directly under the front wheels, was still moving and clawing at the air. Several creatures jumped at the driver's side window of Peter's cab.

Roger grabbed his gun and moved to level his cab on Peter's side, but the rigs were too close and he couldn't open the door. Rolling down the window, he shouted, "The windows...open your windows...your window," to Peter.

Peter noticed that the door wouldn't open, too, and he fumbled with the gear shift in order to pull away, but noticed Roger gesturing.

Then he dove across the cab and rolled down the passenger's side window. Roger leaned out of his open passenger window and tried to get his weapon into a firing position. One or two zombies squeezed through the narrow space between the trucks. They were just about to reach Roger when he managed to fire. His bullet killed the lead ghoul. Other zombies moved around the front of Roger's cab and they reached him in a moment.

The steady buzz from the helicopter sounded overhead. Steve was getting more and more frustrated as he watched his companions. He wanted to land the helicopter and help, but he had given Fran his gun and was sure that if he disobeyed Peter's orders, he'd have hell to pay later on.

Fran was perched on the edge of the roof, watching in desperation. She tried to aim her rifle at the creatures, but her hair kept blowing in her eyes from the pass of the chopper. She brushed it away with irritation.

"Roger, in front," she shouted over the engine noises. "Roger, in front, Roger," she screamed, very excited and agitated.

Roger fired again and again down the narrow space between the vans. Another zombie fell. The dead bodies littered the parking area like so many pieces of paper. Roger was not in direct danger any more, but he seemed to be getting sadistic pleasure out of his target practice.

"For Chrissakes, come on!" Peter yelled out angrily.

But Roger was like a crazy man. He leaned out of his window in a very vulnerable position, whooping like a child as he tried to level off another shot.

Suddenly, a zombie grabbed him from behind, and he almost fell out of the window. He struggled to hold himself and keep a grip on his gun. Peter leaned over and tried to get a shot at the creature, but he couldn't get a clean sight. Roger grabbed frantically at the window frame on Peter's door and tried to pull himself up. A second creature grabbed him from behind as well.

"Monsters, monsters," Fran uttered emotionally. She fired her gun. The bullet slammed into the pavement, kicking up a cloud of smoke. It narrowly missed one of the creatures. She fired again, and this time her shot tore into the shoulder of the zombie, but it didn't stop him.

The chopper zoomed in very close. Dust and debris flew up in the trooper's face in its wake. Peter was still unable to get off a shot, and the added particles frustrated him. He shot a look of disgust up at Steve.

Roger, using both hands, swung his gun butt in an uppercut. It slammed against one of the creatures that was grabbing him, and it drove the ghouls back with a staggering motion. Then, in a desperate heaving of strength, Roger climbed through the window into Peter's cab.

Peter pulled the big rig away even while Roger's legs were still hanging out the window, bouncing around from the movement. The zombies grabbed at Roger's ankles, and one managed to hold on as the truck picked up speed.

Like a madwoman, Fran fired again and again. One shot ripped into the zombie that held onto Roger's legs. It let go and fell, rolling across the pavement. She fired again and this bullet hit the pavement. The creature managed to struggle to its knees, raising its head and looking about wildly for its unseen opponent. Once more, Fran brought the rifle up, sighted it and fired. This time the shot hit the creature's neck. Once again, she fired. Now it was the zombie's shoulder. She was really cooking now. Confidently, she aimed for the head, and the bullet hit its mark. The creature sprawled on the cement. Fran leaped for joy and aimed at another creature and began to shoot.

The helicopter passed overhead. Steve had watched, fascinated, as Fran picked off one zombie after another.

The woman was really remarkable—once she set her mind to something.

"Jesus," Roger suddenly exclaimed.

"What?" Peter asked, just as his truck was about to roll out of the lot.

"My goddam bag," he suddenly realized. "I left my goddam bag in the other truck!"

Peter brought the vehicle to a screeching halt.

"All right, now, you son of a bitch," he fumed in anger. "You better screw your fuckin' head on, baby!"

"Yeah, yeah," Roger assured him. "I'm OK. Let's go."

Suddenly, Peter grabbed the other man by his lapels and slammed his back against the door of the cab.

"I mean it! Now you're not just playin' with your life, you're playin' with *mine*!"

The two men stared at each other for a moment. Roger was startled somewhat out of his emotional exhilaration. He stared at Peter, a confused, hurt look on his face. He thought they were buddies in combat, through thick and thin.

"All right," Peter softened. "Now are you straight?"

"Yeah," he sulked.

Peter released him and returned to the wheel. He gunned the engine, and the monstrous rig roared into a big arcing turn in the parking lot.

Through her gun sights, Fran could see the truck returning. The helicopter had already flown over the roof, and Steve was wondering why the truck hadn't appeared on the road. Fran turned and tried to signal Stephen with the tip of her rifle extended.

Finally, he saw her and flew closer. The woman waved a high sign, and the chopper buzzed back over the lot.

With her hair whipping around her face, Fran took up her position again, her rifle at the ready. She thought for a moment and then began to reload the weapon, pulling the shells from the breast pocket of her shirt.

Peter's truck zoomed back into position, again colliding with some of the zombies in the area.

As soon as the truck pulled to a stop, Roger leaped out and climbed in through the window of the other cab. He snatched up his knapsack and several tools that were strewn over the seat and floor. The wires where he had jumped the engine were all entangled in colors of blue and red and yellow. Bits of glass and blood had splattered the seat covers.

As soon as the activity started again, more zombies were attracted to the vicinity. They converged on the cab area. Two more came up between the trucks, and several came around the front of the cab.

Meanwhile, Fran struggled to load the gun quickly. She had taught herself to shoot it in a matter of minutes, just applying some simple logic.

Again, the helicopter buzzed overhead.

As Roger climbed through the window to enter Peter's cab, his pack accidentally fell to the ground. With a reflex action, he dropped between the two cabs, landing on his feet. Panicking, he realized that he was facing the two creatures, who were approaching quickly. He reached up and with one hand on each of the open window frames, swung his legs up hard. His kick sent the creatures sprawling. Then, he bent to collect his pack. Once again, he was grabbed from behind.

And once again, Peter tried to level off his gun but was unable to get a shot. At this point, he almost felt like shooting Roger. The guy was going off half-cocked. He wasn't all there. His actions and his decisions were not the reactions of a well-trained soldier, and if there was one thing that Peter couldn't abide, it was sloppy maneuvers.

Fran tried to get a shot, but she didn't have the confidence in her accuracy with Roger in the way.

Surprisingly, Roger kept his cool this time, and his first thought was for the pack of tools. He reached out and tossed the sack into the cab of Peter's truck as though he were making a hook shot with a basketball.

Peter caught the pack as several of the tools clattered out and onto the floor of the cab.

The creature that was holding on to Roger gained an advantage from Roger's imbalance when he threw the pack, and now it bit at the man's arm. Roger tore away as soon as he felt the bite, but blood appeared at the wound. Then Roger squared off a solid punch right to the zombie's jaw. The creature flew back and, in a domino effect, almost knocked over the others behind it.

Roger jumped, making a grab for the window of Peter's cab. Meanwhile, the zombies that Roger had pushed over had struggled to their feet and were regrouping. They advanced and grabbed at the squirming trooper. He tried to get a hold on the side of the door by pushing with the soles of his feet, but the surface of the door was too slippery.

Peter dropped his rifle and moved to help Roger by grabbing his hand, but Roger fell from the high window back to the pavement. Peter drew his handgun, sitting up in his seat to see where Roger had fallen.

Once again Roger leaped, his hands catching the window frame. The zombies clutched at him viciously. He swung up his legs and kicked the creatures off balance. This time he managed to get his feet locked against the door, and Peter grabbed the trooper's arm with his free hand, but another zombie was pulling at his shirt and still another made a grab for his legs.

Peter took careful, deliberate aim with his pistol and fired point blank at one of the clawing ghouls. The impact caused it to fly back, and it freed Roger so that he was able to pull himself higher. His face was straining from the agony of exertion. Just as his torso was through the window, another creature grabbed him.

Peter could no longer get a shot as Roger filled the window, so the big trooper dropped his pistol and pulled Roger's arms, struggling to haul him through the opening.

For the second time that day, Roger dangled from the window, his legs kicking. Peter started the truck, and as it began to roll away, one of the clutching zombies was able to get a solid hold on Roger's leg. The creature opened its cavernous mouth and bit into the calf. Blood gushed out through the material, and the creature bit again, relishing the flavor and coming away with bits of flesh tangled in a bloodstained strip from Roger's trouser leg.

A shriek of incredible agony came from Roger, and he whipped his legs around violently. The truck accelerated with a lurch and sped away, the final zombie thrown to the ground from the momentum.

The creature rolled a little way on the pavement before stopping. Then it sat on the ground, hunched over like a gorilla, the bloody mass of flesh and material still dangling from its mouth. It tried to separate the cloth from the more appetizing morsels.

A bullet whizzed by, disturbing the thing's tasty treat, but it continued chomping on its morsels. Another bullet tore through its shoulder, but it was still only concerned with its prize.

The bullets were coming from Fran's rifle, and as she fired, she swore through her teeth. The gun roared, and clouds of dust flew up around her. Finally, she hit the seated creature cleanly through the head with her third bullet. She could see it fall, unnoticed by the others that walked by it.

Up in the sky, the helicopter escorted the big truck back to the warehouse for the third time.

The truck rumbled along, jostling the two passengers as Roger struggled to tie a tourniquet around his bleeding leg. He used his belt and pulled it tightly.

"That's it," Peter stated as he heard Roger suck air in through his teeth in agony.

"Bullshit," Roger said, teeth clenched in pain.

"We gotta deal with that leg!"

"I'm dealin' with it . . . I'm dealin' with it fine! I won't be able to walk on this at all if we wait."

"Can you walk on it *now*?" Peter shot back, anger rising in him at Roger's stubbornness.

"You're damn right I can . . . damn right I can!" he shot back just as arrogantly.

He struggled to wrap the bloody part of his leg with the torn piece of trouser.

"I stop movin' this leg . . ." Roger said sharply, with great deep breaths between his words. He could hardly keep from screaming out, the pain was so intense and the gash so deep. "May not ever get it goin' again ... there's a lot to get done before ... before you can afford to lose ... me ... "

Peter turned and stared at his friend for a second, not believing that Roger could think him so callous. But then he guessed he never really told Roger about his feelings one way or the other. Dismissing it as an emotional outburst, he drove on to the warehouse, escorted by Steve's chopper.

9

An eerie stillness had come over the parking lot. A huge trailer truck now stood in front of each of the four entranceways to the mall. The trucks were remarkably close to the doors, if not completely flush. Some of the glass portals could be opened slightly, but not enough for the zombies inside to pass through.

After a while, the stillness was shattered by the collecting mob of zombies who were trying to get into the building. They swarmed around the trucks, frustrated and confused. They clawed at the enormous vehicles but to no avail. Some tried to climb up onto the cabs, while others tried to claw at the loading doors on the trailers.

Some of the creatures had even managed to crawl under the rigs and were pawing at the underside of the trucks. Then they would squirm their way toward the doors but couldn't stand because there was no room. Creatures inside pushed the doors out so that the zombies under the trucks couldn't push them in. They were all working at cross-purposes, and so none of them would be successful.

One creature, who had crawled under a trailer, managed to push open a mall door. It crawled into the building through the milling legs of the other ghouls who were trying to exit. They all buzzed around like a swarm of insects.

Still, the revolving door offered the best access for the creatures. Although it was complicated and baffling to their empty brains, two creatures did manage to crawl under a truck that blocked one of the doors, and one of the ghouls was able to negotiate the rotating action and enter the concourse.

"It all depends on how many of them are still inside," Peter was telling Steve as they huddled over maps of the building. They were safely back up in the crawlspace, the cartons still piled up against the fire stair entrance. "That's a long haul between those entrances."

"Well," Steve replied. "If we can get some more flares ... or maybe some of those propane jobs."

"The guns are first. Guns and ammunition," Peter stated bluntly.

Nearby, Roger moaned with pain. Fran was applying a dressing to his leg. The wound was wrapped with several layers of cloth that Fran had cut in strips from one of the blankets. She had used the disinfectants from the open first aid kit.

"You sure you're gonna make it, buddy?" Peter asked, crouching near his friend. He gestured to Fran and took over the wrapping of the wound, tying more strips around it tightly and around the upper thigh.

"Just hurry up with that!" Roger exploded irritably. He didn't like to show any weakness around Peter. His wound was really bothering him, and he secretly wished that he could let loose and bawl his eyes out. They didn't have the proper pain killer. Morphine would have been the most effective. Guess he would just have to "bite the bullet" and carry on. He cringed as another wave of pain shot through him.

He watched Peter motion Steve over to a corner. The serious expression on Peter's face showed that they were probably talking about another supply raid. And the fear on Steve's face showed that Peter was sparing no one. He would go on as before, experienced partner or not.

Steve scurried over to Fran and tried to talk to her quietly. What do they think, I'm a baby? thought Roger, annoyed at their patronizing attitude toward him.

Suddenly, Fran exploded.

"Where do you think you're going?" she screamed at Steve. She seemed shaken from the day's exploits. They all were; but she seemed especially changed.

Steve tried to quiet her, but she merely turned on her heel, and if there had been a room with a door to slam, she would have slammed it. Since they were still in the big, practically empty room, she sulked to a corner.

A ceiling grid opened, and a tall figure dropped out of it. He landed on the floor of the sporting goods store. It was Peter, with a rifle slung on his shoulder and an empty pack on his back. Several of the maintenance room key rings were strapped into his belt.

Attracted to the movement, a zombie suddenly charged from across the room. The gate to the mall balcony was open in this particular store. Another creature also tuned in to the noise, joined the first, and they started through the open entrance.

A few seconds later, Stephen descended into the darkened store. His equipment was also strapped onto his body. Instantly, he noticed the moving creature. Peter was trying to unsling his rifle and was unaware of the danger. In a split second, Steve conquered his fear of heights and let himself fall to the floor. He landed in a heap, rolled into a store exhibit and sent the displayed items flying.

Peter looked up and quickly untangled his gun and managed to level off a shot at the charging creature. Meanwhile, Steve regained his footing, brushing himself off from the fall. The second creature rushed steadily up the aisle. With quick reflexes, Steve grabbed a powerful crossbow and arrow from a nearby exhibit. He cocked the simple mechanism and fired it. It gave off a strumming sound. The small shaft ripped cleanly through the creature's skull and embedded itself in a wall beyond. The zombie staggered forward a few steps before it fell. Steve stared at it in openmouthed astonishment.

Peter hit him on the shoulder, rousing him from his dazed position. Then they ran toward the entrance arch. Peter jumped up on an adjacent countertop and managed to reach the lip of the roll gate and swing it down fast. Then Stephen caught the cage below and slammed it into place just as another ghoul fell against it moaning and clawing.

Stephen unslung his gun and was about to level it off on the creatures outside when Peter jumped down from the counter.

"Don't try to shoot through those gates," he commanded. "Openings are too small. Bullet'll wind up chasin' us around in here."

A zombie crashed against the gate with all his might, startling the already nervous Steve.

"He can't get through," Peter assured him. "Come on."

The men crashed back through the store and Peter moved right to the racks of weapons. He pulled down a gorgeous high-powered rifle that was equipped with a sophisticated scope for sighting.

"Ain't it a crime!" he ejaculated.

"What?" Steve asked, confused by the man's sudden outburst.

"The only person who could ever miss with this gun," Peter said, looking through the telescope, "is the sucker with bread enough to buy it."

His line of sight was on the cross hairs of the telescope that zeroed in on the enlarged forehead of the same zombie who was thrashing against the roll gate. Peter could sense the superweapon's lethal accuracy with one glance through the viewer.

Stephen was busily diving into the ammunition, and he moved behind the counter, where he pulled out boxes of shiny new handguns.

Peter, meanwhile, found elaborate holsters and ammunition belts. He pulled several other rifles from the rack. The firepower that Steve and Peter were collecting for their own private arsenal was mind-boggling.

"You just wait out there," Peter called to the creatures gathering at the gate, trying to break in. "We're comin'... and we are *ready*!"

By the time Peter and Steve had returned to the crawlspace hideout, Fran had informed Roger of the plans, which she thought were ludicrous. But Roger was already excited and raring to go. They all dressed with double holsters containing handguns. Each had a rifle strapped over his or her shoulder and another in hand. Ammo belts were slung around their hips, and they carried packs with other supplies. Ceremoniously, they dumped Roger into the big gardening cart that Peter had used to carry the initial supply load out of the store. The wounded trooper looked pretty comical perched in the cart.

Peter urged the group on, pushing Roger in the cart before him. When they reached the balcony, they noticed that there were only a few creatures about. The living dead turned in confusion at the sound of the attacking commandoes. Roger, his hands free to shoot, fired his weapon several times at some of the closest creatures.

The creatures from the main concourse below began to move up the stationary staircase and struggled with the escalators. The rotting, bleeding corpses of the creatures slain in the earlier battles were still cluttering the area.

Fran and Steve were the first to reach the entrance to Porter's department store. Immediately, Steve started to work on the gate locks. Peter pulled up, the small rubber wheels of the cart leaving marks on the linoleum floor. He turned the cart a full 180 degrees so that the blond trooper was facing out toward the mall.

As Steve fumbled with the second lock, Peter faced the few zombies that were converging along the balcony. He lifted his new superweapon and stared through the scope. The gun went off with a stupendous growl, the sound of its power reverberating through the mall. The single shot ripped cleanly through the center forehead of one of the creatures.

A pleased smirk on his face, Peter took aim again and made another perfect kill. Then a third time— whammo—and another zombie bit the dust. All the while, Roger fired several times, some of his shots going wild, others making the target.

As Fran stood ready at the roll gate, Steve finished with the final lock. Then she pushed against the cage, and it started up. Now, Steve stood and the two rolled the cage into the ceiling, but Steve was particularly careful not to let the gate roll out of his hands. They had been instructed very carefully by Peter, and they both wanted to make a good impression. This is like the first day of school, Fran thought cynically. They were both afraid to do anything wrong and have Peter's wrath brought down upon them.

Fran moved into the store followed by Peter, who pulled the cart behind him. Then, Steve, Peter and Fran pulled the gate shut long before any of the advancing creatures could reach them.

Once again, the zombies pounded on the locked gates, but the humans were already running through the aisles of the big store, and the pounding was very distant to them.

"How's the ride?" Peter asked as he wheeled Roger into the elevator and hit the button for the first floor. The doors closed and the car started down.

"Kinda bumpy," Roger said, trying for humor, but Peter could sense that he was in extreme pain. In a movement that was out of character for the stern trooper, Peter put his hand on Roger's shoulder.

"Look here..." he started, his voice cracking a bit.

Roger was immediately embarrassed, for himself as well as Peter.

"I know, I know...Shut up," he said affectionately.

They had both been through a lot together, and it was something not easily put into words. It was an unspoken truce on the battlefield, something that men in combat would carry about with them forever.

The elevator doors glided open, and Peter pushed the cart out into the first floor of Porter's. His expression did not show any of the softness that the conversation with Roger, seconds before, had exhibited. He was ready for action.

Fran and Steve charged down the store escalator, moving faster than the steps. They ran through the hardware department, where Steve snatched up several propane torches. Fran stuffed a few extra bottles of gas into her backpack.

Then, as Fran held two torches, Steve lit them. A great hiss exploded, and one of the propane nozzles spat out a white hot flame as it was ignited by one of the new disposable lighters that the foursome had "liberated."

Peter wheeled the cart up to the first-floor entrance gate. Several creatures outside the cage flew into a sudden frenzy at seeing the humans, as if they were animals in a zoo. They slammed against the grid but it only swayed, holding up against their weight as usual.

"Unlock the middle one last," Peter instructed.

Steve fell on the right-hand lock with his keys. He could feel Peter's eyes boring into the back of his head and wanted to do the job properly. His hands shook as he tried the keys in the lock. As he crouched by the gate, the zombies converged, pushing and shoving. He could smell their hot sour breath and feel their insistent pressure against the cage. Fran held one of the lit torches very close to the gate, and the creatures backed away, cringing and shielding their eyes. Finally, Steve found the correct key, and the lock gave way with a solid click.

Once more Steve crouched. This time he bent over the lock to the extreme left. As if they were trained seals, the zombies followed. Fran stood at attention with the flaming torch. No longer did she shrink away when the creatures approached. She had become almost inured to them.

"All right," Peter said to Steve's back. "The toughest part'll be gettin' by these right here . . ."

The second lock clicked open. The zombies continued to push, and the gate was more pliant with only the middle lock securing it now.

"It's a long haul down to the entrance," Steve replied, moving to the middle and final lock.

Peter craned his neck to see past the zombies and down the concourse. Attracted to the noise and commotion, several other zombies started toward Porter's entrance.

"We'll be all right," Peter told him, looking off toward one of the main entrances, where a truck trailer blocked off the entrance from the outside.

"It's too far!" Fran cried out, panic rising in her voice.

"There's no backin' out now," Peter insisted. "We gotta lock those doors!"

"We'll never make all four," Fran countered, her fear in control and the power of reasoning replacing it. "It's too risky."

"You just stay here and be ready to open up for us," Steve told her from his crouching position.

Suddenly her eyes lit up.

"The car!"

"What?" a startled Peter asked.

"The car!"

She pointed to the slowly spinning exhibit that displayed the new automobile. It was a sleek, sporty Mustang that looked fast and maneuverable.

Peter immediately grasped the plan forming in Fran's mind. He looked trepidatiously at Roger, who had been uncharacteristically quiet during the last few hours.

"You OK to start it?" he asked the other trooper, who cringed with pain but nodded his head affirmatively.

Despite Roger's discomfort, he moved quickly and efficiently, reaching for his supply pack.

The zombies continued to clutch at the gate with renewed strength. At the unlocked ends, the grid gave a little but still managed to hold the ghouls out. Fran approached the gate and waved the torch menacingly. The creatures moaned and moved back. With a flick of the wrist, Steve unlocked the middle and final lock.

"It's goin' up," he warned.

With a thunderous roar, the gate swung out of Steve's fingertips. The zombies charged, but Fran's torches made them hold back slightly. Steve grabbed one of the propane canisters with one hand and drew a pistol with the other. Fran drew a handgun from her holster too, and they both fired into the pack of zombies. A few fell by the entranceway, knocking over a small perfume display. Others tried to approach but were frightened away by the bright flames.

With remarkable agility, one male ghoul started toward Steve, but the pilot managed to blast his torch directly into the monster's face. The black matted hair caught fire, and the creature threw itself wildly about, scattering other zombies around him.

During the altercation, Peter saw his chance to break away with the cart and charged through the opening.

Wincing in agony, Roger gripped the sides of the cart until his knuckles turned white. Peter maneuvered him through the throng of zombies, and they crashed through, scattering the creatures about like so many bowling pins. They headed straight for the car exhibit, successfully dodging the few zombies on the concourse in the cart's path.

"Close the gate . . . close the gate . . ." Peter shouted over his shoulder as he made his way toward the spinning vehicle.

Steve grabbed the lip of the roll cage, and it started down. Fran stood by, still inside the store, with one of the torches held high as if she were the Statue of Liberty safeguarding New York harbor.

"The keys, Stephen," she realized as the gate rolled down steadily. "The *keys*!"

Steve dove toward the gate and tried to impede its downward progress, but it slammed shut with a metallic crash.

"Jesus Christ!" Fran swore in desperation at Steve's clumsiness.

Peter stopped in his tracks when he heard Fran's outburst. He looked back but several creatures had followed him and they advanced slowly, blocking his view.

Other creatures had stayed with Steve, and they approached him as he tried to pass the keys back through the small opening in the gate. The big ring was too big.

"You mother!" Steve cried out to no one in particular.

"Keep 'em...just keep 'em," Fran shouted frantically. "Look out!"

The zombies approached Steve from the back now and they were very close. He lunged at them with his torch. They backed off slightly.

"Come on, man! Get outa there!" Peter cried out as the creatures on the concourse continued to draw closer to him and Roger.

Still in agony, Roger managed to level off several shots, but he was very shaky from his extreme discomfort. With much skill and a little luck, he was able to down one of the zombies.

"Stephen," Fran shrieked. "For God's sake..." she held up her torch so that the bright flame faced the converging ghouls.

Stephen crouched and put the key in the right-hand lock, which was also approachable from the outside. The zombies continued their slow relentless crawl toward him.

Peter was also in a terrible predicament as another group of the creatures drew nearer. He started to push the cart again, and managed to dodge around two little clusters of the walking dead.

Just as the lock clicked, one of the bolder creatures grabbed Stephen from behind. A quick-thinking Fran managed to aim her torch closer, and it disarmed the zombie for a moment. Stephen was able to thrash his body back and knock the ghouls off balance. Then he deftly lifted the gate just high enough to slide the keys underneath it with just one lock undone.

The creatures swarmed around him now, closing in. One of them grabbed Steve from behind, knocking his torch flying. It rolled away with agonizing slowness, but Steve was blocked from retrieving it. Desperately, Fran tried to aim her pistol, but she couldn't shoot through the grille. Instead, she held the torch higher. She was horrified as Steve kicked and scrambled, rolling on the floor. The zombies smothered him as if they were flies attracted to a discarded sandwich. He managed to roll onto his back and kick his legs high, knocking one or two of them to the floor. Then he pulled himself up to one elbow and fired with his pistol, killing another. He crawled to the torch and grabbed it, the clutching creatures tugging at his pants and shirt, all the while.

They didn't have any particular system, but merely seemed to reach out and grasp whatever was close by. Their movements were wild and random, but there were so many of them that they managed to throw Steve off guard, and he had to struggle to regain his balance.

He was able to bring the flame up and flashed it at the zombies. They backed away enough for him to crawl to an open space. Once there, he was able to scramble to his feet, and he charged down the concourse toward the car.

Once at the exhibit, Peter stopped the cart, even though two lumbering creatures were practically breathing down his neck. He raised his rifle and fired at the oncoming ghouls. Roger, mustering all the strength he could and grimacing with the agonizing pain of his wounds, managed to pull himself up out of the cart. He limped to the exhibit as Peter's supergun scored two perfect hits.

The platform was spinning slowly, but the wounded trooper lost his balance as he mounted it and fell, rolling against the car. The turntable carried him around toward another creature. Helpless, struggling in pain toward the driver's door of the vehicle, he didn't even have enough strength to call out.

"Watch it, Roger," Steve, who was approaching, cried. "*Roger!*"

Roger turned his head and saw the ghoul just before the creature grabbed him. The thing's hands randomly clutched at Roger's dripping bandage, and its hands were covered with the trooper's blood. Roger shrieked in pain.

Peter jumped onto the spinning turntable and leaned across the hood of the car. Without pausing, he fired point-blank into the creature's skull, and his supergun drilled a hole the size of a half-dollar through the creature's head. The momentum of the spinning turntable caused the thing to fall off the exhibit stand.

Peter rushed to Roger's side. Excruciating pain shot through him as he tried desperately to open the driver's-side door.

Peter tried to help Roger, and as they managed to open the door, which was unlocked, he eased his friend onto the seat. Immediately, almost numb, Roger went to work under the dash.

"Get in!" Peter shouted to Steve as he saw the zombies advancing now. As if a battle cry had gone out, they arrived from all points of the concourse. Steve rushed up to the platform, and he and the big trooper scrambled into opposite sides of the back seat. Simultaneously, they slammed the doors, making sure both the front and back locks were secured. Roger still worked as quickly as he could. The sweat drenched his face and neck, and his face twitched uncontrollably.

The leaders of the separate bands of creatures converged on the turntable. Some fell as they tried to step onto the moving disc, but others were successful and struggled over to the car. They smashed at the windows of the car with their hands, trying to find a way inside. From Fran's point of view, it was a nightmarish scene: the men huddled in the shiny new, slowly rotating car, surrounded by the living dead, pounding and scratching the car.

She now relocked the gate mechanism that Steve had previously opened. She stood again, and tried to see over the zombie crowd, but it blocked her line of vision to the car. She could only hear the moaning of the creatures and their insistent pounding. With a sigh of despair and frustration, she turned the valve on her propane nozzle, extinguishing the flame.

"I'll drive it ..." Steve called out as the car's engine roared to life. Roger gave a weak smile at his victory.

"I got it," the wounded trooper insisted.

His face contorted in agony as he moved into position behind the wheel. Although he was shaking, he bit his lip and slammed the car into gear. As if they were cockroaches, at least eight creatures crawled over the car, and more threatened to approach. Roger waited patiently as the platform spun to a more desirable position. As soon as the nose of the car aimed directly down the concourse, he stepped on the gas and the car pulled out quickly. The men in the back watched in horror as zombies still pounded at the windows, their distorted faces pressed very close against the safety glass. As the car roared away, the creatures fell off into a heap, one on top of the other.

The front wheels moved off the platform easily and bounced onto the floor of the concourse, but the frame scraped the top of the disc and it was stuck for a moment. The disc continued to spin, carrying the rear of the car with it. But Roger only gave it more gas, and the rear wheels spun, finally catching.

The car shot out onto the mall floor. Some of the zombies clung for a moment, but they all fell away quickly, scrambling to regain their footing; then they followed, the exhaust fumes billowing up in their faces.

The car skidded and swerved on the shiny mall floor. For a second it seemed that the pain was too much for Roger and that the car was out of control, heading directly for a marble column in the concourse. But Roger managed to pull the car out of the skid and maneuvered it toward the exit with tremendous energy.

One of the laggers of the zombies' group tried to intercept the speeding auto by stretching out its arms, but the car crushed it unmercifully, splattering blood all over the floor.

Now Fran was able to see the car as it rounded the corner and headed directly for the main entrance, which she could see from her position.

The zombies at the entrance had already started back into the mall, attracted by the commotion. As the car zoomed down the concourse, it easily broke their ranks, scattering and splattering bodies everywhere.

Roger, his body drenched with sweat, his jaw set and teeth clenched, threw the car into a screeching tailspin, stopping with almost perfect precision at the doors.

The big trailer blocked the entrance effectively, but some creatures had managed to get inside the door. Under the big van, several zombies were struggling with the doors. One just pushed in, and it seemed that it would be able to enter.

Peter and Steve slammed against the door. Steve aimed his torch directly at the clawing creatures. The one in front withdrew its arm. But the grotesque things continued to writhe and kick under the truck. An image flashed in Steve's mind—it was just like one of those medieval paintings of the gates of hell. And for one slight second, he began to question what he was doing. But then he put the thought out of his mind.

Peter returned to the car and searched around for the set of master keys. Slamming the door, he fell upon the lock mechanisms with the coded keys. Finding the proper one, he locked the swinging doors.

"That's not one hundred per cent," he told Roger, "but I don't think they'll get through."

"Can't they smash the glass?"

"Safety stuff . . . pretty indestructible . . . They got no leverage under the truck." He turned to survey the situation. "Gimme the alarms."

Steve rummaged in his backpack and produced two portable battery-operated burglar alarms. Peter activated the units and stood them against the base of the now locked doors. As he crouched near the glass, the creatures outside went into a frenzy, clawing at the glass doors. They were unable to get in.

"I'm hoping they'll go away after they find they can't get in," he said to Steve as they watched the other creatures slowly moving down the concourse, approaching the action at the locked door.

The men jumped back into the car with not a moment to spare, and Roger put the vehicle into motion with a deafening blast.

Once again the sleek auto ripped through the ranks of advancing zombies. Like cardboard figures, they fell and were crushed under the powerful wheels.

Although Fran was practically paralyzed with fear, she felt helpless as she watched the car speed down the concourse. It was almost as if she were watching a terrifying, large-as-life movie. She stood by the department store gate as a muffled voice came over the walkie-talkie.

"We're OK," Steve's voice crackled. "We got it made . . . it's gonna work."

She stared out through the roll gate. The surviving zombies in the concourse staggered weakly after the car. Almost a hundred bodies littered the concourse; some were beginning to move again, their blood mingling with the grease and debris kicked up by the speeding vehicle.

Once again, the shiny auto, with snazzy racing stripes, pulled up to the second door, sliding into a tailspin. The men scrambled out and again the zombies outside tried to crawl under the second trailer. But the men were able to shut them out easily, locking the door and planting the alarms. They worked as a team, silent this time, absorbed in their work.

When they had finished, they stood to look down the concourse. The creatures seemed to be more spread out now, but their numbers seemed to have multiplied.

"How many do you figure are already in?" Steve asked.

"Dunno," Peter said, shaking his head, and stretching his arms outward. "Not too many. We'll get 'em easy. We get it all locked off and we're goin' on a hunt!" he said with a malicious gleam in his eye.

It gave Steve a chill as he watched the big trooper raise his supergun and sight through the telescope.

Peering through the cross hair on the scope, Peter settled on the forehead of one of the creatures that was lumbering down the hall. The face appeared magnified and distorted, by the telescope. Peter applied pressure to the trigger, and the gun roared. After the impact, he still kept his eye on the scope and watched with pleasure as the sight filled with red. Without taking his eye away he knew that his bullet had hit the mark. He had the utmost confidence in the supremacy of his weapon.

10

The day had been overcast and chilly. Now nightfall descended on the lonely countryside. The zombies in the parking lot gathered around the semis that blocked the entrance to their sanctuary. In the moonlight, the creatures' eerie moaning was like dogs baying at the moon.

Some creatures crawled under the trucks but could not enter the mall building. They pounded and scratched at the doors, but to no avail. In their nonthinking brains some instinct had triggered the impulse to smash against the glass doors, and they tried frantically to get inside.

The banging of the mob was muffled from the inside. Even though the revolving doors were locked, they seemed most vulnerable, but the crawling creatures could not quite get the leverage they needed to smash at the glass panels.

On the other side of the revolving door, the automobile offered added protection. And, as an early warning device, several of the alarm units sat atop the car, guarding against any penetration.

Like in a battlefield after a hand-to-hand-combat war, the zombies' corpses were strewn all over the concourse. The only difference was that the bodies were from one side only. There was no mingling here of East against West, North against South, rich against poor, one culture or religion against another. Either the four humans were the victors or they were the victims. And once one of them was destroyed, it wouldn't be long before they all fell prey to the living dead.

It was an eerie juxtaposition—the bleeding, putrid corpses superimposed against the now darkened and ransacked mall. The slumped and crushed shadows lay where happy, hard-working families had come to purchase the new and intriguing products that the great wheels of industry churned out for the unsuspecting, naive consumer. Now their haven had become a bizarre graveyard.

The band of humans appeared on the second-story balcony. Moving to the railing, they looked down into the expanse of the building. They looked like guerilla fighters, struggling in a foreign land, their weapons strapped to their backs, their faces creased with sweat and dirt, their eyes blank with fatigue and the abominable horror that they had witnessed.

They had taken the temple, and they surveyed their spoils. Even Roger seemed triumphant in his anguish as he limped to the railing, supporting himself by leaning against it.

Fran had mixed emotions as she viewed the spectacular expanse of dead bodies. She didn't think of them in human terms, although many of them, only days before, had led their lives of quiet desperation. But it was a terrifying way to die, and she hoped that when the end came for her, she would go peacefully.

"We put the wall up here," Peter told Steve after they had returned to the storage area. His pencil pointed to a map of the maintenance corridor. He drew a line just past the washrooms at the end of the hall near the fire stair. "There's no door from the last office into the washroom, so nobody'll get nosy...and this way we can still get to the plumbing..."

"Why can't we just board up the stairway?" Steve asked. "Hell, they can't even get through a stack of cartons."

"I'm not worrying about them," Peter told him somberly. He looked the younger man in the eyes. They had been through a lot in the past few days and all of them felt a bond of friendship. Both Steve and Fran felt they had proved that they were just as capable and necessary as Peter and Roger. They functioned as a team. No longer were they four separate individuals battling for survival.

Peter continued. "Sooner or later there might be a patrol through here . . . or even looters maybe. I don't want anybody to ever know that stairway exists."

They all looked back down at the map. On one side were the offices, with the washrooms to the right. The ducts and grille were above these. The maintenance corridor led along the rooms to the fire stair, directly across from the washrooms. It was at the point where the wall of the washrooms joined the maintenance hall that Peter wanted to build their fake wall. This way, from the outside it would look as if the hallway ended, but they would get the benefit of running water and flushing toilets as well as entrance, by way of the fire stair, to their hideout.

"The ductwork runs all the way into the washrooms," Peter further explained. "We'll have to get in and out that way. We'll bring up any big stuff we want before we put up the wall."

The two men huddled around the map. Surrounding them in the large storage area were mounds of supplies brought up from the small stores, but they were all in disarray.

Fran had been sitting and watching Roger and was quite concerned at his feverish condition. The trooper's clothes were soaked through with sweat. His hair was plastered to his forehead, and underneath the closed eyelids, his eyes seemed to roll around. She figured he must be delirious, since his skin practically burned to the touch. She had been trying to soothe him with a wet cloth on his forehead, and tried to make him comfortable behind his barricade of cartons. Gently she wiped his face and his neck and then realized that he was shivering. Wrapping the blanket around him tightly, she gave him a reassuring pat. Then she moved toward Stephen and Peter.

"He seems to be sleeping," she said with a nod in Roger's direction.

"Good," Peter said softly. He was torn between running over to Roger and remaining aloof. It was a tendency of his that had developed during his youth. When things got too heavy, too emotional for him, he tried to stay as far away as possible. That way things couldn't hurt him. He had done that when his grandmother was dying. He couldn't stand to see her frail body becoming a parcel of bones. He couldn't stand to see her watery eyes watching him mournfully. So he chose to ignore it. Three days before she died, he enlisted in the Marine Corps.

Fran moved to where she had stored her medical supplies atop one of the cartons. She had assembled bottles of various medicines, vials of pills, and diabetic hypodermic syringes, as well as bandages and dressings from the pharmacy in the mall.

"I don't know what else to do . . ." she mumbled to herself glancing furtively at Roger.

Steve stood up, brushed the dust off his pants leg and walked over to her. "You're doin' fine," he reassured her, placing his arm around her shoulder.

Fran looked up at him with her tearstained face. She looked devastated by the recent events. Her hair hung in limp strings across her face, her complexion was sallow, and there were dark circles under her eyes. Steve knew he didn't look any better. They weren't living any more— they were barely existing. He longed for the familiar tedium of his past life. Anything but this nightmare!

"His leg is awful," Fran said somberly. "The infection is spreading fast. Can't we fly him out of here? . . . try to find a med unit?"

Steve looked at her sympathetically for a second and then turned to Peter.

"I've seen half a dozen guys get bitten by those things," Peter told them quietly. "None of 'em lasted more than thirty-six hours."

The finality and seemingly coldhearted manner with which Peter spoke stunned Fran. She had thought the two of them were friends—true friends. But then she realized that it was only Peter's way of preparing himself for the inevitable.

"Peter . . . Peter . . . where are you?" Roger screamed from behind the cartons.

Peter gave the couple a quick, knowing glance and answered kindly, "Right here, buddy."

Some inner resource had allowed Roger to sit up. He was now sweating even more profusely than before, and his eyes looked very dark and sunken.

"Yeah, yeah," he called softly. He licked his cracked and swollen lips and looked around the vast, barren room, trying to get his bearings and clear his eyesight.

Fran could no longer take it. She moved to the far corner of the room and sat down on some cartons, her head in her hands. Occasionally, Roger would call out, his voice sounding pathetic as it echoed through the big storage area.

"We did it, huh, buddy? We whipped 'em."

"That's right, Rog," Peter's soothing voice answered him.

"Didn't we?" he asked, his voice empty and strained.

Peter's methodical, patient voice answered him again. "We sure did, buddy."

"We whipped 'em and got it all!" Roger screamed out frantically. "We got it *all*!"

Fran, Steve and Peter had been working on the fake wall for over two hours. They had created a great network of two-by-fours, which they had braced up at the rear of the corridor. More lumber was wedged against the walls, making a frame. Stephen slammed large nails into the framework for reinforcement. They had already nailed a Masonite panel into place on one side.

In the corridor, Peter carefully nailed in a molding, which made the new partition look like a finished wall.

"This must have been for a touch-up," Fran said as she carried an old can of paint out from one of the washrooms. In her excitement, she nearly tripped over the vast array of hardware and power tools that were scattered around the gardening cart.

She held the can up to the hallway wall, matching up the paint spilled along the sides. "It looks perfect."

Peter grabbed the can and pried its lid open quickly with a screwdriver. Then he dipped his finger into the liquid and smeared some onto the new wall where it butted against the corridor. He smiled and nodded affirmatively toward Fran.

"Anything else you want before we close it off?" Steve asked her.

"No." She stared down the corridor toward the mall proper thinking about Roger. He had acted like a child in a candy store in the mall, frolicking around, yelping like a puppy. And now he was upstairs dying a terrible death. Fran swore to herself that she wouldn't go that way.

She could see the corpses that had littered the hallway piled together at the mouth of the corridor on the balcony.

"No," she repeated, turning away from the grisly sight.

She stepped back through the unfinished partition and leaned against the framework. Suddenly, her hand flew to her mouth to stifle a gag. Steve sensed her discomfort and ran up behind her, but she felt another wave of nausea and darted for the washroom. Concerned, Steve set down his hammer and quickly followed. She had been really marvelous through all of this, never once complaining. She hadn't mentioned the child inside of her since the time of her outburst. He had often wondered what she was thinking and how she felt about it. But he was afraid to question her. It was her private terrain, and he feared to tread upon it.

When he reached her, she was kneeling on the floor, propped up by her hands on the seat of the toilet, vomiting. He approached her quietly, his hands falling on her back.

"Leave me alone," she said without raising her head to look at him. "It's all right . . . It's my problem."

"Frannie—"

"Just get outa here, Stephen. I don't want you here."

She made the statement so simply and yet so determinedly that Steve was stunned for a moment. He let the words sink in, not wanting to believe them, not understanding them.

Fran saw the confusion in his eyes and reached up and took his hand. She clutched it tightly, trying to show him that she wasn't angry, but just wanted to be alone.

"I don't want you to see me this way—" She had barely got the words out of her mouth when she retched again.

Leaning over the toilet bowl she told him, "Please go ... I'm all right. Please ..."

He stood up reluctantly and then drifted out of the room.

Fran clutched the side of the toilet bowl, waiting for the next wave. Then she retched again but she was dry. She tried to swallow and take a deep breath. Then she rolled over and leaned against the wall separating the two stalls and held her stomach. She fumbled with the flush handle and depressed it, the rushing water making a gurgling, ugly sound.

She stood and looked down at her stomach, which was beginning to show. She wondered what effect all this horror was having on her unborn fetus. She had read that the child could pick up vibrations from the mother even while it was in the womb. Many times she had thought of trying to abort. If they ever got out of this alive, children would be the only salvation for earth. Maybe with this child, and others, a new generation could start, one that would not know the despair of its parents.

Stephen walked slowly out of the washroom and toward the unfinished framework.

"This place is gonna be rotten," Peter said as he

walked by. The trooper was gazing down the corridor at the pile of corpses. "We gotta clean up, brother."

Peter walked past the staring faces of the dead creatures on the balcony to the enormous safe in the president's office. He put his hands on the large round hatch wheel.

"They're usually on a timer," he told Steve. "Opened at nine, locked at four. Keeps the bankers honest."

He spun the wheel, and the giant door creaked open.

Inside was the huge safety deposit vault of the bank. They stood in the glittery room in awe for a moment, stupefied by the clean metal walls that were lined with drawers and doors where depositors had stored their valuables. At one end of the room there were stacks and stacks of paper bills. The men approached the piles of money and stooped down.

They both had never seen so much money in one place at one time. It was ironic now, because it was really only worthless paper. They flipped through the stacks of tens, twenties, hundreds, all crisp and new.

"You never know," Peter said with a smirk and started to stuff several packets into his knapsack.

Steve looked at him quizzically and then realized that the trooper was being optimistic. But he didn't want to miss out if there was even a glimmer of hope. He too took several stacks and stuffed them into his kit as well. "Don't ya wonder what the archaeologists are gonna think," he said thoughtfully, looking around the enormous vault. "Guys in the future...diggin' this place up. Imagine all the stuff's in these boxes...jewelry, cash people stash to avoid paying taxes. Maybe they'll figure it's all some kind of offering to the Gods...like in the pyramids...a burial chamber."

"That's exactly what it is now," Peter said and turned to the decomposing pile of bodies awaiting them.

They braced themselves and started to shovel the corpses into the cart. They each used big snow shovels and lifted one corpse from opposite sides and threw it into the cart. They wore elbow-length industrial gloves and had tied handkerchiefs around their noses and mouths, but the stench was still terrible.

They wheeled a cart filled high with bodies across the lobby to the bank. Then they guided it into the vault and unceremoniously dumped the bodies on several others that had already been deposited. The corpses lay askew, their arms and legs protruding as if it were a giant centipede that they had come to bury. Stacks of money were knocked off the shelves and mingled with the extended limbs. When the last body was disposed of, Peter and Steve shut the vault door and the automatic timer clicked on. Then the two of them silently and slowly walked back across the concourse to the maintenance corridor. Peter went over to the controls for the Muzak and reactivated the switch. Steve was grateful that they didn't speak. He was too choked up, and he knew that if he opened his mouth, it would only be to wail.

While Roger slept fitfully, Fran, Steve and Peter ambled through the barricaded building, drifting in and out of the stores and dropping various items into their shopping carts. Understandably, the novelty of having anything they wanted just for the taking had worn off. Like sleepwalkers, they moved through the aisles. Fran rummaged idly through the cosmetics department. Peter looked through a bookstore, picking up paperbacks and hardly noticing the titles. Stephen played the pinball machines in a huge games room, but his heart wasn't in it.

Soon, Fran motioned Steve over to another corner of the store toward a big mechanical barber chair. She trimmed his hair in silence, both of them avoiding each other's eyes in the mirror.

Then Fran brushed the hairs off Steve's shoulders, and he got out of the barber chair. She put the scissors away and wandered over to the pet store to play with the kittens and puppies. She changed the soiled newspaper and kitty litter, filled the water bowls and gave them all fresh food. She watched with a wan smile on her face as the little animals lapped up their food joyfully, oblivious to the desecration around them. Then she ambled over to the tall cage in the concourse and threw bird seed to the tropical birds that fluttered and flapped about, screeching loudly.

A half an hour later, the team regrouped on the upper balcony. They still had their weapons and survival kits, but Peter was wearing a wide-brimmed hat and Fran sported a new mink coat. They looked wearily down the main concourse to the deserted and ransacked stores. It was empty of corpses, but they could still hear the moaning and pounding at the main entrances. It was extremely dark outside, and so the group could not see the creatures there. But their persistent sound was evidence enough of their presence.

"They're still here," Fran said wearily, scanning their realm.

"They're after us," Steve replied. "They know we're in here."

Peter fiddled with the brim of his hat. It looked outlandish with his trooper's uniform.

"They're after the place." He turned to Steve and Fran. "They don't know why ... they just remember ... remember that they wanna be in here!"

"What the hell are they?" Fran's eyes darted nervously. The noises at the entrance seemed to rise to an eerie crescendo pitch.

"They're us, that's all," Peter droned on, his voice barely above a whisper. "There's no more room in hell." His face was set in a grim expression, his eyes downcast.

"What?" Steve spun around, not believing what he had just heard uttered.

Peter took the wide-brimmed hat off his head and wiped his forearm across his sweating brow. He leaned against the railing and gazed long and hard at the couple.

"Somethin' my grandaddy used to tell us. You know Macumba? Voodoo? Grandaddy was a priest in Trinidad. Used to tell us, 'When there's no more room in hell, the dead will walk the earth!' "

The room spun around Roger. He reached his arms out for some stability, but they only thrashed about in the air—there was nothing to hold onto. He felt as if he were in a madly tilting Ferris wheel. His mouth opened and he emitted an urgent scream, which came from deep within him and seemed to echo long after his mouth clamped shut. He felt clammy and wet, as if he had been immersed into a pot of cold water and left to dry in a draft. His face, which was ashen, contorted in pain as the needlelike stings traveled up his black and swollen leg. His arm, which was wrapped but oozing, was all but numb.

A distant voice reverberated through his pounding head.

"Get more morphine in him," Steve determined as Fran fumbled with one of the hypodermics. In her haste, she dropped the vial of serum, and it shattered on the floor. The sound was like thunder to Roger's ears.

"Get another one..." Steve urged, struggling to hold the wildly thrashing Roger in place. "Come on..."

Fran rushed into the other room to the medical supply area, which had been organized with little cabinets and a small refrigerator. She took a new vial of serum from the refrigerator.

After the crew had built the fake wall in the maintenance corridor, they had decided to give each other more privacy and built separate rooms.

The huge storage area was now arranged so that there was a central living room in the middle, with three bedrooms and a general room, which contained the medical supplies and a workbench with tools, surrounding it like the spokes of a wheel. They had managed to drag up fairly large pieces of furniture, including mattresses, tables and chairs, lamps, and a few sectional pieces that formed a couch in the living room area. This was in addition to the television, the microwave oven, and other large electronic pieces that they had brought up earlier. Although there were still many cartons scattered about, it was beginning to look more like a home—or at least a college dormitory—than a storage area.

Downstairs, Peter was intent on checking the covering at the floor base of the fake wall when he heard the violent screaming emanating from above.

He ran into the far office and climbed up a rope ladder that dangled from the ceiling. Scrambling through the grille-work in the ceiling, he entered the duct. Then he pulled up the ladder and closed the grille. Wriggling through the tight space for a few feet, he came to another opening and dropped through that grille into the washroom. Then he moved around the back of the finished partition, and through the wooden framework, into the fire stair. It was a circuitous path, but one that would not be detected by unwanted intruders.

As he rushed up the stairs, several steps at a time, Roger's screams became more and more agonized. As Peter charged into Roger's makeshift bedroom, he could see Fran withdrawing a hypodermic from Roger's good arm. The man kicked his legs and whipped his arms around with abandon, striking anything or anybody within reach. Steve tried to wrestle the man still, but even in his sickness, Roger was exceptionally strong. Peter ran over and clamped his big hands onto the other trooper's shoulders. Whether it was his powerful arms pressing down, or simply his presence, Roger miraculously relaxed. Fran watched for a moment with tears in her eyes and then drifted out of the room.

"Go on," Peter said to Steve after Roger had settled down enough to allow the drug to take effect. "I'll stay with him."

Steve gave him a long, hard look, as if to say, "I know what you're going through," and left the room.

In the living area, Fran was sitting in an inflatable chair, which was molded to her body. She felt safe in that chair, as if she were in a womb, and often found refuge in it when things got rough. Steve came up to her and put his arms around her neck from behind. She cupped his hands with hers and held them tightly. He rocked her gently back and forth as she sat staring off across the room.

In Roger's room, a heaviness fell over the air. He caught his breath and looked up at Peter.

"You . . . you'll take care of me, right, Peter?" he asked, feeble and childlike. He licked his lips and tried to speak coherently. "You'll take care of me . . . when I go?"

Peter stared directly ahead, his eyes focused on a nail in the temporary wall. "I will."

"I don't wanna be walkin' around like that, Peter . . . not after I go . . ." Roger tried to sit up to better make his point, but Peter merely applied slight pressure and the blond trooper lay down again. "I don't wanna be walkin' around like that . . ."

Roger's eyes were terrified. Like a frightened deer, he looked this way and that at the walls, the ceiling, at Peter—but he couldn't focus. The spinning started again and he felt nauseated.

"Peter? *Peter?*"

"I'm here, trooper," Peter said, almost mechanically. The man's face was impassive. He was prepared.

"You'll take care of me...I know you will..." Roger pleaded.

"I will."

"Peter?"

"Yeah, brother?" his voice softened. His eyes glistened and the lines around his mouth tightened.

"Peter, don't do it...till you're sure...sure I'm comin' back. Don't do it till you're sure...I might not come back, Peter." Roger's voice weakened, and a shudder passed through his body. "I'm gonna try not to...I'm gonna try...not to come back..."

His body gave a final heave, and his eyelids fluttered but remained opened. Peter reached across the still chest and closed the lids. Then he sat very still, the tears streaking his dust-covered face.

Moonlight filtered down through the skylight in the living area, a pathway to heaven. The path to freedom through the skylight was now a sturdy wooden ladder, that had replaced the pyramid of cartons. Someone had superstitiously left a derringer pistol on the top step.

Stephen was huddled over the huge twenty-one-inch color console television that they had lugged up to replace the first one. He had wired the set to a makeshift antenna that stretched up through the sky-light. Now he fiddled with it, but only a faint signal came in. Nearby, a table lamp sat on a small end-table, shedding some light on the darkened room. Its cable was patched into a network of wiring that stretched about the room.

Fran unpacked in the dining alcove. She had chosen a pale wood butcher-block with four rush-seated chairs. Nearby was a matching breakfront, which she had filled with dishes and silverware. It was something she had always wanted, and she felt foolishly like a newlywed. She was trying very hard not to think about what was going on in the other room. For quite some time now, Roger had been silent, but neither she nor Steve had the nerve to investigate. At every sound, she turned to see if Peter was coming out of the room.

Steve was intent on the television. At first he had turned it on to get his mind off Roger, but now he was seriously listening to the two men who were talking. One was a commentator, the other a government offi-cial. It amazed him to see others who were still alive. He felt so isolated here. It had only been about three or four days, but since their total existence had been dis-rupted, all time had lost its meaning.

"I've got to...be careful with words here..." the scientist was saying. He was dressed in a suit, but his tie was rumpled and his shirt open at the collar. His face was unshaven and his eyes drawn, with dark circles under them. "We haven't been able to study their habits. We've repeatedly asked for a live capture so we can have controlled studies..." he seemed to stutter on the last word and his cheek twitched nervously. "We need s-s-supply-and-demand ratios."

The commentator was also dressed in a rumpled suit, but he wore no tie. He, too, looked as though he hadn't slept in days.

"You mean," he questioned, "their need versus—"

The scientist cut him off. "Versus the amount of food available. Let's be blunt." He pulled his folding chair closer to the camera. There was a commotion in the TV studio. The noises and shouting reminded Steve of the confusion at WGON before they had escaped.

"Jesus Christ," he mumbled, thinking how far away they were now from that scene, and how much they had gone through to be here now.

He squatted near the set, his eyes transfixed. Fran came up to the screen from behind him.

The scientist continued, his eyes growing wider and darting nervously.

"Project their rate of growth. There's a critical balance. And it's the waste that kills us, literally. They use...they use maybe five per cent of the food available on the human body. And then the body is usually intact enough to be mobile when it revives. There's an ecological imbalance, and they're incapable of understanding." He finished his sentence, and wiped his forehead with the sleeve of his jacket. The stains on his sleeve were noticeable over the air.

"What are you proposing?" The commentator had gray hair and an unshaven face as well. He wore rimless glasses, which kept slipping off his nose. The hot lights from the studio caused him to perspire.

"We have to be unemotional," the scientist replied. "We have to provide countermeasures or we're all . . . they can't control the rate of growth and consumption. We have to control it for them."

"You're suggesting that we help them?" the commentator asked, horror-stricken.

"By helping them in this case we save ourselves." The scientist looked around at the studio audience, hoping to get some support for his radical idea.

A great outcry greeted his words. The image on the set bobbled around as if the camera were being jostled by an irate crowd. The speaker fumbled for the right words to describe the situation.

Steve watched with fright in his eyes. "Good God," he uttered.

The scientist's whining words reached Peter in the

other room. His face was impassive and expressionless. His eyes, however, were pinpointed on something straight ahead of him.

"I'm proposing that certain...necessary measures be put into effect at once," the scientist continued. "Measures applying to all official search-and-destroy units, while they're still operative...Hospitals...rescue stations...and any...private citizens..."

Peter's eyes fluttered and he looked down at the rifle stretched across his lap. The TV droned on from the living room:

"In cooperation with the mobile units of the O.E.P., the corpses of the recently dead should be delivered over to the authorities for collection in refrigerated vans... they should be decapitated to prevent revival..." The words rushed out of the scientist's mouth, as if they were distasteful.

When he had finished, he took a deep breath, as if anticipating the outburst that followed.

Peter's eyes went from the rifle on his lap to the floor, where twenty feet away lay Roger's corpse. His face was covered with a blanket. A slight breeze from the fan in the living room wafted over the inert form, lifting the corners of the blanket.

"This collection...this collection," the scientist shouted over the voices clamoring in the studio. The staff was now on stage, protesting vigorously. Emotional and foul language was being thrown around with no concern for the FCC regulations.

"This collection could be . . . stored . . . rationed . . . for distribution among the infected society . . ." He could barely be heard over the angry shouts. "In an attempt, in an attempt to curb the senseless slaughter . . . the senseless slaughter of our *own* society . . ."

Peter blinked his eyes. He wanted to make sure of what he saw. He wanted to be certain that it wasn't his imagination playing tricks on him. But now he knew it to be true—Roger's foot had definitely moved under the blanket. He tightened his hands on his weapon.

He tried to shut off his mind from the scientist's insistent, rasping, high-pitched voice.

"The dissection . . . the dissection of the corpses can be carried out . . . carried out with respect for the dignity of the human body . . ."

Roger's arms seemed to move and were now twitching slightly. The blanket started to slide down his face.

"The heads . . . the heads and the . . . skeletons . . . whenever possible . . . could be identified and . . . buried in consecrated grounds . . ."

All hell broke loose in the studio. Chairs were thrown on the stage and the picture wavered.

Peter stared with fascination mixed with disbelief as the blanket continued to creep down Roger's face. Soon, his vacantly staring eyes were visible . . . the drooling mouth . . . the pasty, green-tinted face. A putrid stench filled the air. Peter couldn't believe the transformation. He almost expected Roger to jump up as if it were a joke.

Suddenly, the figure tried to sit up. Peter snapped back to reality and clicked a shell into his supergun.

Then, the corpse sat all the way up. It stared blankly at Peter, then with recognition. It struggled to its feet. Peter calmly sighted the center of its forehead through his rifle. He, too, rose.

"We've got to remain unemotional . . . unemotional . . . rational . . . logical . . . tactical . . . tactical!" the scientist pleaded above the raging commotion in the studio. Nervously, he once again wiped his brow with his sleeve.

"They're crazy," Steve muttered, staring at the tube, disbelief written all over his face. "They're crazy."

"It's really . . . all over, isn't it?" Fran asked, mournfully.

From the other side of the room, a sudden blast roared through the wall. Fran jumped and fell into Stephen's arms, shaking and hysterically crying.

Steve closed his eyes tightly and started to tremble uncontrollably. A few seconds later, the TV was clicked off. Steve opened his eyes and saw Peter standing by the set, the rifle still in his hand. The man's eyes were blindly staring at the blank screen.

Without speaking, Steve untangled Fran's arms from

around his neck, rose, and walked over to Peter. Gently, he took the rifle from the immobile man.

A little while later the two of them dumped Roger's corpse on top of the stack of bodies in the bank vault. The whole time, neither man had uttered one word, nor exchanged one sentiment, but went about their work purposefully. The dead man's eyes stared at them with a puzzled expression as they placed him in the huddle of arms and legs. Blood oozed from the familiar gun-shot wound in the center of Roger's forehead.

As the heavy door of the vault closed with a metal-lic slam, Peter thought the whole image was one of hell itself.

As the clanging sound resounded throughout the mall, Peter uttered a long-forgotten prayer of salvation for Roger's soul, just in case.

They had missed Roger's presence painfully at first. His hearty laugh, his lively personality. He had really been a uniting force for the little band of survivors. They had expected him to come charging around corners, dashing through the room, always full of life and vitality.

After three months, things returned to relative normalcy. Now Fran chased a little puppy across the room. It had just left a puddle under the dining room table.

"Adam, no, no!" she called out as it scuttled through the room, sliding across the scatter rug.

She grabbed the little spaniel by the fur on its neck and dropped it on some papers that were layered in a corner of the general room.

As she straightened up, she was aware of her protruding belly, her pregnant condition very noticeable now. She wiped her brow as if she were an exhausted housewife and shuffled back into the bedroom that she and Steve shared. She picked up the sheet and continued to make up the double mattress. One thing she enjoyed was that instead of doing the laundry she just discarded the dirty sheets and towels and unwrapped new ones.

On an end-table near the bed there was a reading lamp. Piled up around the table were all the best-sellers in hard and soft covers from four months ago, piles of out-of-date magazines, and half-empty cups of instant coffee.

She and Steve had done their best to make the living room liveable. There was a large sectional couch in brown velvet, small end-tables with lamps and ashtrays and knick-knacks. The huge TV set was near some large potted plants, which got sunlight from the skylight overhead. The hard cement floor was covered with the finest oriental rugs from the department store. A few leather easy chairs completed the room, each with a footstool. On the wall were posters and paintings. They had even managed to carry up a fake fireplace before they closed the fake wall, with an artificial log and an electric flame. The whole place had a very homey atmosphere.

In the dining area, there was a microwave oven, a refrigerator and more cabinets with dishes and silverware.

While Fran straightened up, Steve wandered about the department store. He fiddled with a new supersonic calculator and looked at adult games. In this isolated environment, he had become obsessed with the gadgets and other items in the department store. It was his habit to explore each day and try everything in sight. He had become very possessive, hiding things from Peter and Fran.

On the roof, in the bright sunlight of early morning, Peter played tennis against a wall of one of the utility sheds. He wore a new sweat suit and brightly colored sneakers. His sleek new silver racket slammed phosphorescent orange balls against the wall with lightning speed. He attacked each shot with determination and strength, his face set in anger. It was his only release. For in three months, the image of Roger's puzzled expression had never left his mind.

Peter hit one ball too high and it flew over the shed, bouncing on the other side and banking off the lip of the roof. Then it flew over the edge and landed in the parking lot below, hitting the pavement. It bounced several times before rolling off among the feet of the army of zombies that was still wandering this way and that through the area. The number had never really diminished, for as others were killed, fresh, new ones rose from the corpses of the recently dead to take their place.

The creatures mobbed around the trucks at the main entrances. They moaned and gurgled as they clawed at the building. There were hundreds of the living dead—

all different ages, sexes and shapes. Some were clothed, as if they had just stepped out of their homes that morning, on their way to work; others were naked, their large wounds gaping and oozing.

Fran waddled around the kitchen area, preparing dinner for the two men. They played cards on a table in the living room. In the middle of the table were hundred-dollar bills.

"Dinner," Fran called half-heartedly, and the men pushed their chairs back from the bridge table and crossed to the dining room table. It was set with the best linen, silver, china and crystal that Porter's had to offer, directly from the bridal department.

After a dinner of warmed-up canned beef stew, canned vegetables and stale cake from the bakery downstairs, Fran served coffee.

"There hasn't been a broadcast for three days," she said to Steve, indicating the television set, which was on. Only grayish snow filled the screen, and the speaker hissed as it received no transmission signal. "Why don't you give it up?"

"They might come back on," Steve said morosely, staring into his coffee cup. Peter sat silently at the table, his food practically untouched.

Suddenly, Fran felt a rage. She slammed down her apron angrily and stomped over to the TV. She clicked it off, and the blue glow disappeared, the drone stopped.

She returned to the table. Steve stood up, and moved to the set. Without looking at either Fran or Peter, he clicked it back on. Peter watched the two sheepishly. It was a familiar domestic scene to him. They played it out every night from boredom and frustration. He glanced over the food-laden dishes, across to the suburban-looking living room, and then off into the distance.

"What have we done to ourselves?" Fran asked plaintively. Steve huddled over the set, trying to focus it. Fran moved to the table and started to clear it. When she reached for Peter's plate, he put out his hand and touched her gently. When she looked at him, his eyes were filled with tears.

The next morning, Fran awoke with a start. She had determined that this day would not be the same as the others of the past three months. She shook Steve awake roughly.

"Get up, now. You promised."

He opened one eye and rolled over.

She shoved him again.

"After breakfast?"

"OK, but get moving." She struggled up from the mattress on the floor. It was getting more and more difficult to maneuver herself with her growing belly.

After breakfast, the couple climbed the ladder and emerged on the roof in the bright sunlight. They entered the helicopter, this time with Fran at the controls. Steve leaned over her and indicated some levers and buttons. Soon the thunderous roar of the engine disturbed the quiet morning air. The helicopter rose and hovered over the roof of the mall.

"OK, easy now...easy...bring 'er down..." Steve instructed Fran after she had completed a successful take-off.

In the cockpit, Fran was flustered, but she managed to handle the controls. She was intent on learning to fly the damn machine. She had thought they were all becoming too morose, too limited, and that it was time for them to stop feeling sorry for themselves and make the best of it. Who knew, maybe they would get word over the tube or the radio that the disaster was over. Then they could return to civilization. She wanted to be ready. She had learned a lot about herself over the past few months. And one of the things she knew was that in order to survive, one had to be self-sufficient. In fact, she had been reading up on home birth methods, and if necessary, she was confident that she could deliver her own child. The American Indian women had done it, and so could she.

"Easy...stabilize it," Steve told her. He had remained relatively calm and responsive, she thought. She guessed he was getting bored with all his gadgets. "That's it."

She reacted efficiently, handling the controls better now as the chopper's runners just touched the roof's surface.

"That's it...that's it...You got it!" Steve said excitedly.

The runners hit the roof's surface, and the chopper settled.

With joy, Fran impulsively threw her arms around Steve's neck. It was the first time she had touched him in two weeks.

"You did it, you did it," he said with sincerity. "Hon, you did it."

She excitedly hugged and kissed him with the happiness of a ten-year-old learning to ride a two-wheeler. She practically bubbled over. It was the greatest release for the two of them since they had been holed up in the mall.

As seen from a great distance, the helicopter on top of the mall roof looked very small, the whine of its dying engine barely audible.

But two beady eyes, nonetheless, had seen the action. The figure to whom they belonged pulled the binoculars away and turned to his companion.

The first man was named Thor. He wore a Viking-like outfit, complete with a fur tunic, sandals laced up his calves, two swords with gilded hilts secured to a six-inch-wide leather belt and long, straggly hair, pulled back with a leather thong. His companion was known as Hatchet, for his fascination with sledgehammers, hatchets and machetes. He wore skin-tight faded jeans, and a short denim jacket open over his bare chest. His chest was tattooed with a snake sliding its way up the leg of a woman. The woman was nude; her decapitated head lay at her feet.

One of Hatchet's eyes was covered with a patch. His head was completely bald, and one of his ears was missing. In the other was a gold hoop earring.

The third person who stood with them stared off in the other direction. He was an older man with a pure white beard, dressed in red and white. He looked familiar enough, like Jolly Old Saint Nick. In fact, that's what he was called.

"They must get in through the roof," Thor said, putting the binoculars up to his eyes again. He could see that the chopper blades were stationary now.

"Son of a bitch!" Hatchet declared, rubbing the tattoo on his chest absently.

"There's trucks blockin' all the entrances."

"No sweat!"

"What do ya think?" Thor put down the binoculars and turned to the others. "Hit 'em now or wait for tonight?"

"Tonight!" Hatchet and Old Nick said in unison.

After dinner Fran, Steve and Peter were seated in the

living room reading when the voice came over the speaker of the shortwave radio that had been installed near the television.

"We know you're in there," it rattled over the unit. "Seen the whirlybird on the roof."

Fran stepped closer, attracted by the signal. Peter moved over and sat by the radio, not knowing whether or not to send the signal back. Steve got up from one of the leather armchairs and walked over to listen.

"Hey, er . . ." the voice cackled. "Could ya use some company in there?"

Steve opened his mouth to reply, but Peter put out his arm to stop him.

"We're just ridin' by . . . We could sure use some supplies . . . What's the chance us gettin' in there to stock up?"

Peter strained to hear, listening intently, and trying to read into the voice's inflections.

To his trained ear, there was something mildly curious about the voice. It hadn't identified itself with any code and sounded too self-confident and cocky to be anyone in distress.

"How many of you in there, anyway?" the voice probed. "There's three of us. Couldn't ya use three more guns?"

"Raiders," Peter surmised. No one would be dumb enough to disclose their number unless it was a tactic to get Peter to discuss theirs. The cockiness of the leader implied they were quite adept at scavenging. They must have spotted them when the helicopter took off. Peter knew that they had chanced it but hadn't wanted to spoil Fran's enthusiasm for learning to fly.

"Well, they know we're here, maybe we should," Fran started, but Peter cut her off abruptly.

"No chance."

The little puppy scrambled up to Fran's feet, his tiny tail wagging furiously. Fran picked it up in her arms and cradled it to quiet its excited whimpering.

"Well, if there's only three of them—"

"Who says?" Peter quizzed her grimly. He seemed to revert to his old self—serious and cold as it was. But at least he was taking charge again. For the past few weeks he had become melancholy and morose. It was ironic that a situation that put them in direct danger would bring him back to life.

There was a long silence. Then the radio sputtered with static. Voices were muffled, as if someone had put a hand over the microphone to hide their conversation. Steve started to speak.

"Shhhh! Quiet!" Peter reacted, cutting him off.

He strained to hear the disguised conversation.

"I think we should," Fran insisted.

Peter turned on her with fire in his eyes.

"Jesus Christ, shut up and listen!"

His outburst was greeted by more static and then slight laughter could be heard. Steve looked into Peter's face, but the big trooper just stared at the speaker impassively.

"Hey, you in the mall," came the voice over the speaker again. It sounded malicious and arrogant. "You just fucked up real bad! We don't like people who don't share."

Instantly, as if he recognized the voice, Peter reacted. Slipping out of his jogging suit, he put on his army fatigues. He removed his Adidas sneakers and put on his combat boots. Then he grabbed his weapons and strapped on his holsters. He looked down at his hands and made a ritual of removing the thousand-dollar electronic watch, the gold bracelets at his wrist and the jeweled rings on his fingers.

"Come on, man," he said to Stephen, coldly. "Get it up."

Steve jumped at the command and ran to strap on his weaponry.

Fran stood by frantically, holding her stomach as if it hurt, her eyes wildly scanning the room as the men darted back and forth energetically.

The little puppy clamored for her attention, but she was too absorbed by the action around her to notice.

The band of raiders traveled together like a rat pack. In fact, most of them were survivors of the big cities, street rats who had managed to survive in the sewers and tunnels and subways that crisscrossed the metropolises. They were a straggly bunch, with loyalties to no one, not even each other. They roamed the countryside like scavengers, looting, burning, stealing and raping. The women who didn't protest much were taken along. All children were left behind to fend for themselves. There were others besides Thor, Hatchet and Old Nick. There was one who looked like a Mexican bandito, replete with a large sombrero and leather holsters filled with bullets crisscrossing his chest.

Several men and a few women were huddled inside a van. Thor stored a microphone on a portable radio unit and chuckled to himself. The van was cluttered with junk: empty food tins, an arsenal of weapons, including every kind of gun imaginable, hatchets, knives and explosives.

The majority of the men and one or two of the women had roamed with motorcycle gangs. They were all outfitted with sleek, powerful motorcycles that had custom gas tanks and lots of chrome. They mounted the big bikes now, turning the controls with their hands and stomping down on the accelerators with their heavy, steel-tipped boots. Even Thor had changed out of his beloved sandals for this escapade.

The bikes roared into action, creating a thunderous din that could be heard by Peter and Stephen, who ran across the roof, fully armed. Clouds of dust and fumes rose into the air as the few remaining men and women stood by the vans and waved the marauders on.

The two men reached the edge of the roof and Peter peered off at the horizon. Nothing could be seen, but the ground seemed to vibrate from the approaching bikes. Peter brought the binoculars up to his eyes. Through the lenses he could make out the vague shapes in the darkness. As the sound swelled, he could see the raiders charging toward them. He counted them as they came up the rise. First two powerful bikes . . . then three more . . . three more . . . at least fifteen bikes in all. They were accompanied by two vans, which skidded and almost collided in their attempt to keep up with the thundering bikes.

"Just three, huh?" Peter commented over the deafening sound.

Steve could hardly believe his eyes. "Holy shit!"

"They'll get in. They'll move the trucks," Peter said matter-of-factly. He seemed to display no emotion, but his heart was pounding. He knew he could have handled the raiders with Roger's help, but now all he had was a pregnant woman and a weak-kneed boy.

"There's hundreds of those creatures down there," Steve said, but he couldn't even reassure himself of that fact.

"Come on, man," said Peter, losing patience. "This is a professional army. Looks like they've been survivin' on the road all through this thing . . . Damn! How many of those stores are open?"

Steve looked frightened. "I dunno . . . several of 'em . . ."

"Well," said Peter with uncharacteristic animation, "let's not make it easy for 'em . . . Come on!"

The two men charged across the roof and back down the ladder that led from the skylight. The rumble of the convoy now filled the living space.

Fran was desperate with fear and worry as she watched Steve and Peter rush by her. They didn't even stop to look at her, but she accosted Steve as Peter continued to crash on ahead through the door and onto the fire stairs.

She grabbed onto Steve's arm.

"What's happening?"

"There's fifteen or twenty of 'em," Steve said, panting from exertion and also terror of the raiders. For some reason he could deal with the mindless zombies better than with these thinking, yet lawless, barbarians. "We're gonna shut off the gates."

"Stephen!" She felt panic overtaking her, and in her more delicate condition, she wasn't as confident of defending herself as she had been the last time.

"We're just gonna shut the gates," he assured her. "They'll never find us up here."

He disappeared through the door to the stairway. Fran dropped the puppy, which she had been cradling the whole time, and it skittered across the floor and went running after Steve, its ears flopping and tail wagging in its innocence.

Fran started to chase after the dog, but instead she moved to the storage area and snatched up her own weapons. Determination on her face, she started to load her rifle.

Outside, the motorcycle convoy made a pass at one of the trucks. In the darkness, the zombies clutched at the swiftly moving bikes. Whooping their war cries, the raiders fired their guns, dropping several of the creatures along their path.

A mob of creatures gathered at the commotion. They formed an impenetrable wall. Thor raised one of his swords as a signal and the raiders regrouped, dropping back across the parking lot. Some of the riders lost their balance as the zombies clawed at them, but they generally managed to stay on their bikes. A couple weren't so lucky.

Thor pulled up to the other side of the lot and told his lieutenants, Nick and Hatchet, "They'll spread out comin' after us ... then we go in with the van ..."

The other bikers gathered around their leaders. A psychedelic painted van pulled up, and two bikers scrambled aboard the side doors.

Thor's woman, Chickie, whom he had picked up in a raid outside of Pittsburgh, jumped into the driver's seat of the van, revving up the engine.

The zombies, attracted to the sound, started to move out after the convoy. The migration thinned out the mob at the mall entrance.

In the mall, Peter dropped out of the grille into one of the offices. He immediately charged out of the room and into the maintenance corridor, where he broke at a dead run for the mall proper.

"Downstairs first," Peter shouted back to Steve, who followed close at his heels.

"OK," Steve panted, trying hard to keep pace with the big trooper.

"Got your talk box?" Peter asked over his shoulder.

"Yeah."

"Keep it handy," he cautioned.

Outside, the psychedelic van with huge wheels and a special souped-up engine roared toward the mall entrance. The bikers waited on the other side of the lot, their engines idling. They continued to whoop and holler like the savage band of renegades they were.

The van, with Chickie at the wheel, crashed through the ranks of advancing zombies. Chickie's blonde hair was wild and matted. She was dressed in black leather from head to toe and toted a switch-blade six inches long. On many occasions, she used it well. She pulled the little vehicle up alongside the truck cab. Three men piled out and scrambled into the big trailer. The zombies in the immediate area clutched at the men, and the raiders had to fight their way clear. Chickie revved the engine again, and with the zombies clawing menacingly at her windows, she pulled out and went squealing back toward the main group of bikers.

The zombies continued to advance upon the regrouping ranks of motorcycles in the parking lot, but they were still pretty far away. The raiders didn't worry. They opened fire with guns of all sorts and sizes and the barrage was deafening, as well as effective.

Several creatures fell in the hail of bullets. Some of the zombies that were only wounded struggled to get up only to be cut down again.

The van pulled up behind the bikes. The men still whooped and shouted, picking off the zombies as if they were ducks in a row at a carnival.

On the first floor of the mall, Peter and Steve dashed about, slamming down the roll gates on the still-open stores. In the background, the din of the shooting and screaming was clearly audible. They left the entranceway to Porter's open until last so that they could get upstairs within the store if necessary.

At the trailer cab, one of the bikers stood guard, picking off zombies, which clawed at the passenger side window, at point-blank range. Another biker, this one clad in army-green fatigues, looked to jump start the engine, but to his surprise the engine started with a burst.

"Shit," the raider said, sitting up at the wheel, revving the big engine, "it's still taped up. It's all ready for us."

The ghouls still jumped and scratched at the windows as the truck pulled away.

Inside the mall, Steve looked up as the familiar sound of the cab's engine filled the air. His heart skipped a beat, and he went to find Peter, slamming down the gate of the pharmacy before he took off. Peter was already running into Porter's. He crashed up the escalator and into the second-floor aisles. Stephen broke for the hardware store, which was also open.

Meanwhile, the huge trailer rolled away from the mall entrance. A shout of victory went up from the raiders all over the parking lot. The zombies at the doors didn't even try to enter the now unprotected doors since their attention was focused on the raiders. From all the other mall entrances, creatures began to converge on the parking lot.

On the other side of the lot, the bikers revved their engines loudly, as if giving one unified bellow. They prepared to make a run on the building. The three raiders from the truck hopped out of the cab and ran toward the doors. As they moved, they shot any zombies that got in their way. Some of the creatures fell, others clawed as the men ran swiftly by. The raider in the army fatigues was pounced upon by a huge redneck zombie who had been wounded in the shoulder by a bullet. The creature brought the running man down and started gouging at him. Still, the biker's comrades did not lose one step or look to see if he were alive. They kept running toward their destination.

One of the raiders reached the mall door and slammed into it. To his surprise it was locked, so he just hauled off with his machine gun and blasted his way through. With a barrage of shells, the mechanism ripped open. The men pushed in through the doors. The little alarm units were knocked flying and sent out an incredibly high-pitched signal. The raiders' heavy boots stomped on them, crushing them into wire and metal, as they charged by.

Peter was just slamming down the gates on the balcony when he heard the high-pitched alarms sound. He dove across the balcony. One of the raiders heard the rumbling gates and looked up to see Peter dive along the railing upstairs. He opened fire with his machine gun. The bullets just missed Peter and he started to crawl around the balcony, just out of sight from below.

In the meantime, Steve had just slammed down the hardware store gate, and he made a mad dash for the department store. But the raiders spotted him too, and opened fire. Like a commando, Steve ran in a zigzag pattern and dove into the big store, where he ducked into the shadows, leaving the big gate wide open to the marauders.

Springing up from behind the balcony railing, Peter leveled off his supergun on the raiders. One of his shots hit its target, and a raider fell back with a giant gaping wound in his chest.

The last raider, Thor, sensing Peter's ability with his weapon, ducked out of sight, behind a column.

Steve now saw his chance to charge the roll gate. He jumped up and ran over, slamming it shut. Now he was securely inside the store.

The convoy roared toward the mall now, trampling zombies in their wake.

Just as the group reached the building, the remaining inside raider rushed to the doors. He held them open as the big fleet of rumbling cycles came screaming into the building. The tropical birds in the cages fluttered frantically. Some dropped dead from sheer fright.

Steve stood in awe, his fingers clutching the grid of the roll gate, as if he were a child watching a circus. The machines tore down the concourse, the sounds erupting as if from a giant earthquake. The zombies, many of them wounded and bleeding, lumbered after them. The raider at the door was grabbed by a zombie, then another. Peter, shooting from above, aimed first at the zombies, downing one of them, and then at the raider. His death by bullet was far more humane.

The main band of bikers, upon hearing the alien gunfire, pulled down a side concourse to regroup. As they turned very close to the department store, Steve had to run back into the shadows of the aisles in order not to be detected. He was sweating and trembling at the same time.

Peter moved to another spot on the balcony. The zombies wandered back into the building and onto the big concourse. Peter was indignant as he watched his once zombie-free building being invaded again by the despicable creatures.

Upstairs, Fran could hear the noise of the battle and was sick with anxiety. She was sure that the two men couldn't fight off both the zombies and the raiders. She stood at the top of the fire stair with a few handguns in her holster, which barely fit around her swollen belly, and a loaded rifle poised and ready to shoot. On the landing below, little Adam scampered and barked excitedly, thinking it all a big game. Fran called to him, but the little dog did not listen.

"All right," Thor told his followers as the bikes raced around, and several of them pulled directly in front of the department store. "Couple of guys hold off them zombies. Mad Charlie? Hit the gates . . . We gotta get that sniper."

Thor rolled his bike out and the others followed. Peter sighted their movement from below and opened fire on them again. Hatchet caught a bullet in the leg and fell, and his bike propelled through the crowd of approaching zombies. The zombies pounded on their helpless prey.

The action below was too fast and furious for Steve and Peter to focus on it all at once. Neither of them could see the whole layout of the concourse. Steve was able to see Thor pull off behind another set of columns out of range while several bikers dismounted and started up the stationary stairs.

"They're comin' up, Peter," Steve said into the walkie-talkie. "They're comin' up the stairs."

Peter moved to another spot on the balcony.

Suddenly, the raiders at Porter's door turned a machine gun on the roll gate locks. One flew open, then another.

Steve ran deeper into the store. His eye was caught by a glittering display of watches. On the other side of the counter were diamond rings. Another display case held pocket-sized calculators. He turned and couldn't see the raiders but could hear their approaching footsteps. Suddenly he was filled with rage that these scavengers would dare invade *his* store. Using the butt of his rifle, he cracked the glass display case that held the rings and gathered them up, shoving them into his pocket. The pounding of the bikers' boots grew louder. He could see some of the men rounding the corner. He started to charge up the escalator, but realized that he would be in the line of fire, so he ran into the elevator at the side. He hit the button, and the door closed, and the car started up for the second floor.

Peter continued to fire at the charging men on the balcony. He dropped one of them, and the others took cover. Just as Peter started to move further out on the balcony to get a better shot, the lights in the mall blinked out, the escalators stopped. They were in utter blackness, all power gone.

Upstairs, a frightened Fran was totally alone in the darkness. From below, she could hear the scared barks of the puppy. She carefully picked her way down the stairs toward the frantically yelping puppy.

"Peter, Peter," Steve said into his walkie-talkie. He groped around in the dark in the stuck elevator.

The big trooper charged through the darkness and found his way into the maintenance corridor. Leaning back against the wall, he listened. He ignored the insistent buzzing on his talk unit.

The raiders on the balcony approached quickly, flattening themselves against the walls for cover.

More and more of the bikers spilled into the department store. Like a plague of locusts, they descended on the goods, raiding the counters and ransacking the displays. They threw things indiscriminately into their backpacks. One burly guy took a pair of delicate ladies' panties, soiling them with his hairy paw as he threw them into his pack.

Other bikers moved to the various stores, breaking the roll gates easily by shooting off the locks. They raided the remaining arsenal in the sporting goods store with relish.

The main pack of bandits managed to hold off the wave of zombies for a while. But the creatures came at them with renewed vigor, and the raiders tired. The creatures pounced on them, and some of the bikers fell. The ghouls devoured them, ripping at their flesh with their teeth and hands. The men's anguished cries were drowned out by the luckier bikers' cycles as they roared into the now liberated shops.

Chickie pulled her van outside the door and two of the bikers rode out to it and started loading supplies in through the double doors. The zombies were everywhere, but many of the bikers had a cavalier attitude toward them, throwing pies from the bakery in their faces, showering them with shaving cream from the pharmacy and pelting them with BB guns from the toy department. The slow-moving and slow-thinking zombies were befuddled by the looters' antics. They seemed to be bothered more by the fooling around than by the sporadic gunfire.

Several creatures followed the raiders onto the balcony. One zombie pounced on the corpse of the raider that Peter had shot. It began to tear at the body, savoring the still warm flesh. Another zombie tried to muscle in on the catch, and the two of them began to wrestle over an arm that was almost severed from the body.

Other zombies continued to steadily move along the balcony. Some of the remaining raiders appeared at the mouth of the corridor, and Peter opened fire again. He killed one of them with a clean shot through the heart. The man flew back against the railing, his chain-wrapped body jingling and jangling. Then he toppled over, a resounding crash of metal heralding his fall. Several zombies attacked his body when it landed.

Peter dashed into the maintenance room. He rushed immediately to the power station and threw the emergency power switch. The portable emergency light units blinked on all over the mall.

Steve, who had managed to work his way to the top of the car by crawling through the hatch in the elevator ceiling, suddenly felt the car move. He tried to grab onto the cables but his hand slipped on the grease. Unfortunately, his rifle fell down between the wall of the shaft and the moving car, where it wedged itself.

Suddenly, the car stopped again, and Steve could see down through the escape hatch. Light spilled in as the main elevator doors opened. Just as he was about to jump to safety, he heard the voices of the raiders below. Two of the big bikers charged into the car. Whooping and shouting, they pointed to the open escape hatch.

Steve tried to blend into the wall as much as possible. The watches and rings in his pocket jingled against each other.

One of the raiders, with long greasy black hair, looked up.

"Come on, man," said the other, sporting a handle-bar mustache and a swastika emblazoned on the back of his jacket. "It's your nerves. Let's go ..."

But the other raider was persistent. He aimed his machine gun up through the hatch and whooped loudly as he fired off a barrage of bullets.

"That ought to finish off them bastards," he said as the shells banged and clattered around in the shaft. They ricocheted off the walls and pinged off the metal gears. One shell nicked Stephen on the arm. He cringed but did not cry out.

Finally, the raider had emptied his gun to his satisfaction, and they charged back into the store.

The remaining bikers continued to loot the store, stocking up on weapons, ammunition, tools, articles of clothing and food. Every once in a while, they would try a prank on the unsuspecting zombies, like locking them in the meat freezer or chopping their heads off with the meat cleaver. They seemed to have more fun torturing the creatures than collecting their loot.

Chickie pulled the van to the side doors where the men shoveled in the booty. Another woman had joined her in the front seat, and they guarded the material with giant pistols. Zombies tried to pound their way into the vehicle, but the women remained steadfast, plugging a few here and there through cracks in the window.

In the mall, another biker was brought down by a pack of lunatic zombies to the amusement of his friends. They simply laughed and pointed as the creatures devoured the still screaming man.

Several creatures now wandered through the department store, having entered through the open second-story gate. They moved through the aisles, knocking against the displays and sending items scattering all over the floor. One zombie grabbed a mannequin dressed in swimming apparel and was shocked to find that when it took a bite, its teeth cracked on the hard surface. It threw the doll aside roughly, tagging after the others.

Nick, up on the balcony, was approached by several zombies. He ran down the maintenance corridor and into the office. Peter, miraculously, was nowhere to be seen. The raider scurried out and broke into the various offices. They were deserted. He charged up to the fake wall and assumed it was a dead end. Then he was distracted by the faint barking of a puppy. He checked the panel again, this time suspicious. He ran his hands along the edge, feeling it give way.

Just as he was about to kick the wall in, he heard a sound in the corridor. He turned, and to his shock saw three ghouls approaching him. He raised his gun to fire and knocked off the lumbering creatures one at a time. Then, he rushed out onto the balcony. The full spectacle of what he saw took his breath away. Creatures wandered everywhere, bikers roared this way and that. Even to a hardened Hell's Angel like Nick, it looked like a ghastly war zone. He was just about to run downstairs when he was distracted by another noise, this time above him. He spun around and looked up. Just as he focused, a dark shadow passed over him. It was Peter, his big supergun aimed squarely at the raider's head from the ceiling grid just above. The gun roared and Nick flew back over the railing.

Below, the surviving handful of raiders started to regroup. Their bikes began to peel out of the mall entrance one at a time. Just as he was about to leave the mall, another raider was snatched off his bike by a clawing zombie.

Chickie readied the van to pull out as the last bit of booty was shoveled into the vehicle. As a parting gesture, the woman lowered her window and fired point blank at the heads of the clutching creatures that had been trying to get in through the glass.

The last wave of raiders tried to get out through the first-floor entrance to the department store. The zombies mobbed their bikes outside and the men had to struggle to get to their cycles, shooting and beating their way past. One man was brought down, but three others managed to mount their machines. With a final roar, the men pulled out, accelerating to catch the little van, which sped away in a cloud of dust.

Peter had crawled through the ductwork, and he could see the last bike roll across the concourse just as he opened one of the grids. He leveled off with his scope, shooting one raider out of the saddle. Two more rode out of range and drove through the main doors into the parking lot.

The band regrouped out in the lot around the van. Where there had been twenty, there were now only seven or eight, including the two women.

Thor, who had ducked out of sight when Peter opened fire, now revved up his engine and roared through the concourse. It was as if he were the general of the victorious army accepting the honors. He dodged several of the creatures on his powerful bike and headed for the entrance. Just as he was about to exit through the doors, he threw his head back and yelled triumphantly.

Peter leaned practically all the way out of the grid in the ceiling. The cross hairs on his scope settled on the back of Thor's head. As the biker pulled through the door and started to roar across the parking lot to his waiting band, Peter applied pressure to the trigger of the supergun, and the roar muffled that of the cycle. A second and a half later, Thor's body was blown ten feet into the air. When he came down, a pack of hungry zombies awaited him.

Unfortunately, for him, he was not dead. As he rolled over on the cement, he saw to his horror that a swarm of creatures was moving to tear him apart, limb from limb. He let out a bloodcurdling scream. Without so much as a backward look for their lost leader, the other bikers moved their convoy off into the night, and gradually the roar of the engines faded away.

The silence was overwhelming for Fran. Even Adam had stopped barking. She looked down into the darkness. Tensely, her fingers clutched at the rifle. She stood on the landing as the silence enveloped her.

In the parking lot and over the main concourse of the mall, the creatures wandered freely, as they had before the humans had arrived in what seemed like a lifetime ago. They fought over the remains of the bikers, eating ravenously, their slurping sounds the only noise in the cavernous mall now.

Peter continued to crawl through the ductwork. He peered down through the grids at the feasting below. Some of the bikers were now coming to as zombies themselves.

Suddenly, he heard the beeper on his talk unit. He hit the button.

"Peter!" came the frantic cry.

"Where the hell are you?" Peter grumbled.

"In the elevator!"

"Listen," Peter told him carefully. "Those things are all over the place. Climb up top ... I'll get you out the grid in the shaft. I'm comin'."

The big trooper squirmed his bulk through the ductwork once again.

In the elevator, Steve hit the button for the second floor and the car started to climb. He clambered up with his feet on the handrail of the car. His hands reached up and grabbed the mouth of the escape hatch, and he managed to get his head and shoulders out through the opening. Just as he kicked his legs to force himself up, the car stopped.

The doors opened to the second story of the department store as Steve gazed once more at the attractive displays. He yearned to gather up more things for his huge stockpile upstairs. That moment's hesitation was all the zombies needed. With startling abruptness, several of them darted into the elevator. They clawed at Steve's legs and pulled him down out of the hatch. Screaming, he thrashed violently, but the creatures held on with super strength.

In the ducts, Peter heard the bloodcurdling screams. He stopped short, listening intently. All was quiet. He had a sinking feeling in his stomach. Then he snapped to and backed away, heading for the maintenance corridor.

In the elevator car, Steve thrashed and kicked ferociously. The creatures had a hard time, but they finally managed to pull him out of the car. The elevator doors closed and opened, their safety bumpers slamming against the creatures that blocked it.

A zombie took a bite out of Steve's arm. Another took a large chunk out of his neck. He scrambled, trying to free his handgun from its holster. Punching and kicking, even though he was bleeding profusely, he managed to pull his weapon. He fired the big pistol once . . . twice . . .

Peter was just dropping out of the duct in the washroom when he heard the pistol shots. The thought struck him that he may have made a terrible mistake in thinking that Steve was dead. Unless it was a raider's gun, which he truly doubted, he had left his comrade to die!

He started to climb back into the grid, but he stopped himself. What good would he do now, those were the desperate shots of a dying man. Confused, angry with himself, utterly exhausted, he punched at the wall violently, shattering a bone in his hand.

Once more the big pistol sounded and its shell ripped through the head of one of the zombies. The zombie flew back out of the car, but the doors still slammed against one last creature. Others poured out from the store as Steve fired one last time. The zombie that had been wedged between the doors flew back, and the doors finally closed shut.

Outside, Steve could hear the remaining zombies pound against the door. They scratched and pawed, none of them with the intelligence to push the button, but narrowly missing it with their random banging.

Once the doors closed, Steve fell to the floor. The wound in his neck ran red, his eyes widened with terror, and he stared at the pistol in his hand. He was finding it increasingly harder to breathe.

Peter appeared alone at the bottom of the fire stair. First the yapping puppy, then Fran, ran to him.

Fran could tell by the way Peter hung his head.

"No...*no*!" she shrieked, feeling faint.

She threw herself down the remaining steps. Peter caught her before she managed to charge out into the hall.

He held her tightly in his arms.

"I heard his gun...maybe he's all right. We'll wait. We'll just wait a while..."

A slight blue haze appeared in the eastern sky. The mall stood silently in the impending dawn, mute to the disaster that had taken place within its walls that night.

Armies of zombies, reinforcements for the wounded and killed, moved in and out of the building unimpeded. They walked through the halls and lumbered through the aisles.

Several creatures pounded and scratched at the closed panels of the elevator doors in Porter's. As they pushed against one another, one of them inadvertently pressed on the elevator call button with its shoulder. The door glided open and in the open car, Stephen stood. The blood on his body was caked and dry, his eyes were vacant, drool filtered down from his mouth. He stepped forward. The other creatures drifted away, some bowing a welcome to a new member of the tribe. He was among them now, no longer prey—one of the living dead.

The doors slid closed and banged against Steve, but the bumpers reacted electronically and opened again. He lumbered into the store and started down the familiar aisle. Other creatures drifted by him in total acceptance.

Upstairs, a red-faced, tearful Fran packed supplies into a sack. She moved ponderously, as if each action was an effort.

Peter stood at the top of the stairs, his eyes focused on the landing.

With more and more determination, Fran planted the filled bags next to the base of the escape ladder that led to the roof. Her movements were deliberate. She had filled her head with the hope that Steve was alive, and that this packing was for them—and the baby. But now she realized it was not to be so.

A lumbering zombie walked almost purposefully up to the maintenance corridor entrance as if it knew the way. It did—it was Steve. Other zombies passed him, wandering aimlessly. He looked past them, seeing the fake partition wall. Something deep inside his dead brain triggered a reaction, and he lumbered forward.

"It's almost light," Fran said softly to Peter. He had not left the stairway since he had returned from the battle. "Let's go."

He looked at her silently, his face drawn and tired. She had never seen him looking so vulnerable.

"He doesn't answer the radio. It's been hours." She had prepared herself for the worst and some inner resource of strength that she didn't even know she had welled up inside, filling the void.

"For God's sake," she began to cry. "You better come on because if I get to thinkin' about this, I'll just go down there and let them...let them..."

The puppy began to growl and charged down the steps through Peter's feet.

In the hallway, Steve had reached the fake wall and was pounding on it. The other creatures moved up behind him and joined in.

Upstairs, Peter heard the pounding, but stood stoically, gazing down into the darkness. Adam continued to bark, as if in recognition, below.

"What is it?" Fran asked, fear rising in her throat.

"They're comin' up!" Peter cried out. "Maybe Stephen's with them!"

With a great crunching noise, the fake partition gave way. The army of creatures, led by Steve, staggered over the splintered lumber and the crushed plywood and moved up the stairs.

Peter slammed the door just as the puppy scurried by and leaped into Fran's arms.

"Go on," he spoke to her quietly. "You get out of here."

"Peter..."

"I said you get out of here." His face was set with grim determination, and Fran didn't dare question him any further.

Fran was in a panic. She didn't want to leave without Peter, but she could see his stubbornness setting in.

"Oh, Jesus, Peter . . . please . . ."

"I don't want to go," he said sadly. "I really don't . . . you know that? I really don't."

Suddenly, the door flew open and the advancing creatures lumbered in.

Fran started to scream. The puppy cowered in her arms. She practically crushed it.

"Stephen, Stephen . . ." she started for her lover, but Peter raised the supergun, a slight, enigmatic smile curling on his lips, and he shot the zombie clean through the head.

As Stephen fell, Fran startled to reality.

"Move, woman," Peter commanded, rushing her to the ladder. She grabbed the sacks, and with the puppy under her arm, she climbed the ladder to the roof. Peter picked up the derringer that he had hidden by the ladder and covered her as she made her escape.

The creatures advanced on Peter, and he managed to lead them away from the skylight, toward his room. They crashed through the carefully set up living room, upsetting the furniture, overturning lamps, crushing the knick-knacks.

On the roof, Fran ran toward the helicopter and threw the sacks in, securing the puppy in his cage, which she had installed in the back of the passenger section. She jumped in the pilot's seat and sat staring at the controls. Then she moved into action and started the copter up.

Peter backed into his room, the creatures gaining. He slammed the door in their faces. Just as he was about to raise the small handgun to his head, his mind flashed on Fran, sitting alone in the copter. He stared at the gun in his hand and then violently kicked the door open. Suicide would never be his cup of tea. The sudden movement scattered the zombies and allowed Peter a clear path to the ladder. He made his escape as if he were a quarterback running for the winning touchdown.

Fran had waited patiently at the controls, idling the engine. But so many minutes had elapsed that she was sure now that Peter was not coming and lifted the copter off the roof. The puppy yelped in the back, hating his confinement. A sudden movement below caused Fran to look down. She could hardly believe her eyes. Peter had rushed up onto the roof and had made a leap toward the landing apparatus of the copter. He had managed to grab a hold and was hanging on, his legs kicking and thrashing as he made his way to the passenger side door. Fran could hardly contain her joy as he squirmed his way up and into the passenger seat as she lifted off the roof.

The little vehicle jolted as he swung into place beside her.

"Do we have enough gas?" he asked, scanning the parking lot below as the zombies looked up in the sky at the disturbance.

"Very little," Fran said, as the little bird puttered away into the welcoming arms of dawn.

George A. Romero is an American film director, screenwriter and editor, best known for his gruesome and satirical horror films. Nicknamed the "Godfather of all Zombies," he directed the original zombie classics *Night of the Living Dead* (1968), *Dawn of the Dead* (1978) and *Day of the Dead* (1985).